Praise for Emma Gold and EASY

The meanest, rawest, funniest book about sex and relationships you'll ever read. Move over, fluffy heroines! Here's the woman with the guts to tell the truth!

"A wickedly funny exposè"
—*Cosmopolitan*

"The heroine of this thirty-something, man-quest novel is different from the rest of the breed: she's bawdy, lusty, talks dirty, and will do almost anything for a good shag . . . She's also rawly honest and amusingly self-deprecating. It has a loud-mouthed charm of its own."
—*The Big Issue*

"Written in the first person, this hilarious book is a laugh a minute . . . What I really liked about *Easy* is its honest and sometimes vicious portrayal of dating in a 21st century urban jungle."
—*Woman's Way*

Emma Gold is a unique new voice in fiction—fearless, honest and outrageous. She has had over 150 jobs from secretary to media lawyer, but has finally found career satisfaction as a therapist and writer. Emma Gold lives in London.

EASY

Emma Gold

KENSINGTON BOOKS
http://www.kensingtonbooks.com

KENSINGTON BOOKS are published by

Kensington Publishing Corp.
850 Third Avenue
New York, NY 10022

All Kensington titles, imprints and distributed lines are available at special quantity discounts for bulk purchases for sales promotion, premiums, fund-raising, educational or institutional use.

Special book excerpts or customized printings can also be created to fit specific needs. For details, write or phone the office of the Kensington Special Sales Manager: Kensington Publishing Corp., 850 Third Avenue, New York, NY 10022. Attn. Special Sales Department. Phone: 1-800-221-2647.

ISBN 0-7582-0388-8

First Kensington Trade Paperback Printing: April 2003
10 9 8 7 6 5 4 3 2 1

Printed in the United States of America

In memory of Sarah and Fanny Barteck

"I'm tired. Send one of them home."

—Mae West, on being told that ten men were waiting to meet her in her dressing room.

"A little coitus never hoitus."

—Anonymous

Prologue

"Who wants my number?" I yell menacingly at the end of the party. A paltry few hover around, but quickly disappear when they realize that I am the girl whose aggressive party interview technique had earlier reduced a doctor to tears. One brave soul approaches. I barely take notice of the man himself as he scribbles down my number with an eyeliner on an empty cigarette packet. This small detail is irrelevant. I have achieved my sole aim as a single girl on the North London Jewish party circuit – my number has been taken. This is far preferable to any more immediate results as this has promise; it is the ultimate going home present. It doesn't matter who takes my number, or the manner in which it is taken; someone out there has my number and the thrill of the call and the consequent pursuit of my charms are to be deliciously anticipated.

The call comes on the Tuesday with an invitation to dinner on Valentine's day. "No, sorry, not Valentine's day," I demur. I don't tell him I have other, somewhat alternative romantic plans for the night – drinks, some pot and a porn movie with the girls – I just sound aloof and mysterious.

He persists. "Another night perhaps?"

"Yes, that would be lovely."

A mutual consultation of diaries and a date is fixed.

I had hurled myself back on to the Jewish social scene at the grand old age of twenty-seven on my return from Italy where I had lived for the past few years. Finding a suitable life partner wasn't proving as easy as I had thought and seven months after my return to the scene, all I had accomplished was a few dates with exes. It was a depressing welcome back after the attentive Latin charms of the studs in Italy.

I had returned to London with the distinct feeling of having missed the boat to the magical fairyland of marriage. Panic set in. This was a time to be proactive which meant putting all pride aside on the quest for Mr. Right(berg). Sad and desperate you may be thinking, but hadn't it just been effective? I had a date, goddamit.

I am surprisingly nervous just before the date, especially when my friend Claudia hears who has actually taken my number and reacts with unconcealed horror: "Not that Jewish grandma!" I am slightly alarmed, then remind myself that we have completely different tastes in men – something that should never be underestimated in friendships between women, by the way. I try to put any doubts to the back of my mind as I apply another coat of lipstick. The doorbell rings at 8:30 pm on the dot. A good sign I always think. I open the door and in a microsecond make the following observations: not bad looking in a small, dark Jewish way, well dressed too. He has a relaxed, smiling face with only a hint of the Jewish grandmas about him. Oh yes, and I also clock the BMW parked outside, ready to whisk me away. I don't remember him from the party and can't work out whether this is a good thing or not. I immediately revert to my cool and sophisticated, slightly bored, but perfectly charming good-time girl persona.

We float up to Highgate in his chariot and I saunter to the bar waiting to be asked what I would like to drink. I used to be a high-minded feminist whose standard retort on being offered a drink was "I'm not a prostitute," but now I am older, wiser and poorer and have thrown enough good money after bad men. Principles no longer come into it. So we drink and drink. Or rather I drink and drink, and we laugh and chat and gossip about important things like whether our respective watches are real or fake and how long our journeys into work take – you know the sort of thing. The next thing I know, we are sitting in another pub around the corner and I have a fresh drink in my hand. I think this is my fifth glass of wine. Suddenly he looks gorgeous. Or rather, I see myself looking gorgeous through his eyes. Another victory, I think, as he flatters, flirts and flutters around me. I have to tell you, I am really enjoying myself. I float out of the pub and into his car. And that's when the problem starts.

Apparently the suspension on a BMW is excellent. But not, may I tell you, when you've drunk the equivalent of two bottles of vinegary wine on a nervous and unsettled stomach and you actually need a grounding experience rather than a deluxe floating one.

"Pull in," I groan. The charming, sophisticated good-time girl act is on its way out . . . through the window. I fall out of the car as quickly as I can, note with irony but no humor that we are in The Bishops Avenue, and throw up my dinner, a risotto as white and fluffy as the snow around me. He stays in the car for a decent amount of time – I appreciate that, as it allows me to cough and splutter and make all the necessary, disgusting noises that follow a hearty vomit. Eventually he approaches cautiously and with a look that I would describe as a mixture of alarm and concern. I am helped, or rather bundled, back into the car. All of a sudden, I am the Jewish grandma.

I must tell you, without pride, that he is forced to stop the car five times on the short journey home, each time with patience and concern, but I also detect an element of puzzlement. I can almost hear him thinking, "God, I really thought this gal could take care of herself . . ." but by the time this thought registers, I have passed out in the back of the BMW, dribbling on the cream-colored leather seat.

What an ignominious ending to such a promising date. I collapse into bed, fully clothed, and pass out until morning when I fall upon the phone, eager to confess my shameful story to anyone who will listen. Male friends laugh with glee at another man's misfortunate date from hell.

"You won't hear from him again," is the unanimous verdict.

Don't Blink

Well, he did call. And quite frankly, I wish he hadn't bothered. Saul was the worst premature ejaculator I have ever met. The first time we actually got around to having sex was, I am afraid to say, the second time we got around to seeing each other.

Much to everyone's surprise, he called me the day after our first date to find out how I was. Saul told me that he had been concerned that I might choke on my own vomit and that he would then have to face my father's wrath as to why he had taken me home in that state. I did not feel obliged to point out that, unfortunately, this was not the first time I had returned home in a semi-comatose, vomitous state. Instead I let him know that, contrary to appearances the night before, I was actually able to look after myself. He said he would call me in a few days' time to arrange another date, and this time he promised to look after me a bit better and I promised to lay off the risotto and wine combo.

A few days turned into a month, and when he finally did get round to calling, I told him that it was now too late. I explained that the two-week post-date calling period had elapsed and he no longer qualified for a second date. He made a very good case for himself (buying out his partner at work, late-night meetings with lawyers, stressful financial scenario, etc.) and I finally relented on the grounds that he had bothered to telephone me when all my male friends had advised me that after a date with a mad, drunken bitch like me, they would not have come back for more. I made it quite clear that as his record was, up to this point, otherwise unblemished, he would be granted the pleasure of a second date. He was chivalrous in his gratitude and arranged to pick me up after work in the week and take me out for dinner.

We had a very merry dinner date and, as we were bang smack in the middle of the spring mating season, I took him up on his offer to check out his flat. Once I had been given the grand tour, he immediately went into ardent mode. Unfortunately, it was the sweaty schoolboy kind of ardor which gave me the distinct impression that he was completely overwhelmed with excitement at grappling with some real live tits rather than a picture of the same in a magazine. In fact, I felt that I ceased to exist as a human being and became instead a physical manifestation of a female participant in a porn movie that he had been jerking off over earlier in the day.

Once he had manhandled my breasts in this rather unpolished manner, and after he had spent the minimum required time indulging in pre-shag making out, he suggested that we consummate our union (he didn't use those exact words). I already felt like a machine going through the motions of a supposed passionate encounter; if you had been in the room, say, sharing the sofa with us, you would have thought we were both crazy for it. In fact, I also felt a little like I was sitting on the sofa next to us, watching the scene but emotionally and sexually detached from the proceedings. But as it seemed like he was enjoying himself enormously, I felt I should be enjoying myself enormously too. Besides, I wanted him to like me and (wrongly, I now realize) I believed that if I was a willing and passionate participant in the sexual act, he would want to see me again.

I had to remove my own panties (always a bad sign) and once he had fetched some condoms from his condom drawer, he removed his pants. As I remember it, he was very hot, flushed, sweaty and excited at this stage.

As a student, one of my friends at the time was training to be a doctor and we spent more than one animated evening poring over the sexual dysfunction chapter in one of her medical textbooks. The only thing I remember of what I gleaned from this chapter is the technical definition of premature ejaculation (and the fact that it is possible to have at least two extra balls, as shown in memorable color photographs). Apparently, ten thrusts or under qualifies you as an official premature ejaculator. Ten thrusts or under! The textbook was obviously written by a man. I wouldn't bother taking my panties off for that. Twenty is disappointing and, in my book, still a little early.

Now, I wasn't counting thrusts on this particular occasion with Saul (although it did become a hobby of mine during future encounters with him), but let's just put it this way: it was definitely not worth removing my undies. Once he rolled off me and lit a cigarette, it seemed that the moment (and I mean "moment") of passion had passed. No mention was made of the brevity of penetration and it seemed mean to draw attention to it, especially after the lovely dinner to which I had been treated. Due to the earlier lack of buildup of passion, I had no real needs of my own, and once I joined him in the cigarette smoking stage of the evening, we started chatting about other things and the disappointment waned.

On the way home in the cab, I rationalized his premature

ejaculation. He was overexcited, it was the spring mating season, I was too sexy, it was our first shag and next time would be better. I reminded myself of his good points, which, to be perfectly honest, amounted to little more than a heartless checklist of marriage criteria: he had a great sense of humor, by which I mean he laughed at all my jokes; he was relatively handsome – his genes would not prevent me having beautiful children; he was Jewish, although his cultural connections only extended to the removal of his foreskin – in all other respects, he appeared to wish to pathologically deny his heritage; he was extremely comfortably off, which meant that I would not have to deal with my aversion to full-time employment; he was intelligent, although completely uneducated, having left school at sixteen to join the family's diamond business. What I am trying to tell you is that I felt Saul had *potential*, and I was therefore prepared to overlook the sexual disappointment at this early stage of the proceedings.

However, next time was no better. If anything it was worse. I blinked and it was all over. Still, I said nothing. I find that it is not until most women reach the age of thirty that they start to be able to insist on mutual sexual satisfaction and I was, at this time, three years off this enjoyable stage of gratification. So, for the next two or three dates, I prided myself on being sufficiently sexy to bring this man successfully to orgasm, whilst at the same time denying my growing frustration. You see, the thing was that, as with most premature ejaculators, he did not bother to stimulate me in other ways. There was no licky-licky and no clitoral dexterity. To be honest with you, I wouldn't be surprised if he did not know *how* to please a woman in these ways as he had clearly not inconvenienced himself finding out. Maybe because he was rich and good-looking he did not think he needed to be good in bed too.

Despite being sexually non-assertive, I was otherwise pretty mouthy, and on the third or fourth occasion of Saul shooting his load quicker than I could snarl the words "premature ejaculator," I decided to raise the issue. I was quite sensitive, although due to the buildup of frustration-induced fury, my comment was not tact-free. I said something like "That was quick," followed ominously by the word "again."

Not a flicker of response. It was like I hadn't spoken. "Would you like a drink?" he asked.

No, I'd like a decent fuck, is what I thought, but not, on this occasion, what I said. "Yeah, all right then," I replied instead.

It wasn't as if he was denying that he had a problem, and it wasn't as if he was acknowledging that he had a problem. He was actually denying that I had even raised the issue. It was bizarre. There was no apology and no promises to try harder, or should I say longer, in the future. I felt as though I had only imagined speaking. Maybe I hadn't said anything. So I tried another tactic. I would demand a rerun.

You see, that was another part of the problem. He was a once-a-night man. You could count to five and, literally, it was game over for the evening. It's often the way with premature ejaculators.

The thing is that I am not a hard liner on the subject in that I fully understand the basic principle of sex; that men are brought to the boil much quicker than women, who are slower to boil, but once there can simmer quite nicely for hours. Which is why I am perfectly prepared to accept the existence of a ten-second shag if it is followed by a ten-minute shag and then preferably a twenty-minute shag. I am not an unreasonable woman. But it never seems to happen that way. If the first shag lasts ten minutes, it is more likely to be followed by a twenty-minute shag, however if the first shag lasts ten seconds, it is likely to be followed by no fuck at all. It's all part of life's sick irony.

Look, I know it can be flattering to arouse a man to fevered heights and the consequent loss of control. However, constant repetition of the problem, with no subsequent satisfactory compensation, is intolerable. Delicious dinners at fabulous restaurants with an otherwise fairly adorable companion are no redress for the nagging dissatisfaction of a sexually inept partner. And let's face it, all a sexually inept partner really boils down to is a selfish bastard.

Saul and I therefore reached an amicable solution. We would just be friends. I would not have to tolerate his premature ejaculation problem and he could find a new partner who would put up and shut up. I would no longer torment him by raising the issue again (except in coded asides which he goodnaturedly chose to ignore).

Having discussed this story since with friends, I have come across some interesting theories on the subject. Claudia reckons that we should thank the good Lord for premature ejaculators on the basis that they enable you to (quickly) identify the commitment-phobes. Apparently, premature ejaculation is a classic sign of a man who doesn't want to hang around too long. A wham-bam man will be in and out of your life almost as quickly as he was in and out of you.

My friend Matt, meanwhile, reckons that the reason premature ejaculators can only come once a night is that they know they have a problem, so before you come around, they jerk off and hope against hope that this will mean that they will last the second time around when they have sex with you. This theory would certainly account for the

sweaty fetid smell emanating from Saul's pants when he
pulled down his trousers, as he was otherwise scrupulously
clean. And in fact, when you combine this theory with
Claudia's about it being a mental problem, it all starts to make
sense. It's no good them trying to jerk it out of their systems
beforehand as they really need to see a good therapist and
deal with their horror of becoming too intimate with a
woman.

I know women who have walked out on men in
anger at an untimely emission. It is the most distressing thing
in the whole world. It's a more intense form of all-dressed-up-
and-nowhere-to-go and can turn the most mild-mannered
ladies into sheet-clawing, leg-chewing, wall-climbing maniacs.
We don't talk about it in public. No one seems to mention
it. But in private some of us commiserate with each other.
My roommate Gabriela walked out on someone who wasted
her time in this way, whilst I once came close to knifing a
boyfriend who "disappointed" me, and for the purpose of this
story he understandably wishes to remain nameless.

This particular boyfriend (let's call him Lance, a suitably
preposterous name) and I had split up for a week after a
non-PE related argument. He came around to see me to talk
things through and after a week of abstinence in an otherwise
extremely sexually amorous relationship, debating our problems soon became a low priority on the afternoon's agenda.
As it was summer, we lay in the garden. It was a very warm
afternoon, what you might call sultry and sticky. Soft,
friendly, making-up kisses soon turned into fierce, hungry,
teeth-gnashing, deep-throat making out. As we were both
exhibitionists by nature (sexually speaking), the fact that the
garden was overlooked by other houses only increased the
urgency of our passion. Lance was soon grinding into me and
I could tell through his sweatpants that he had attained the

four necessary penile attributes of elongation, swelling, heat and hardness. As he continued to thrust against me, I nearly fainted from desire.

Although we were both exhibitionists, we were not immune to the restrictions of public decency and we ran up to the bedroom to consummate our fervent passion. Clothes melted away and he entered me. He came immediately.

To his credit he did apologize, and I accepted his apology on the basis that he stiffen up again soon and we continue. As Lance lay on his back recovering, I could see him formulating excuses for his future lack of erection.

"Look, I'm really sorry about coming so quickly, but I am absolutely wiped out after the most stressful week at work and to be perfectly honest with you, I was not expecting to see you today and I jerked off a couple of times this morning. I really don't know if I can get it up again," he whined.

Meanwhile, I was writhing about on the bed, *desperate* for more. I decided to be proactive and take destiny into my own mouth, and I gave him a deluxe, top-of-the-range blowjob. After approximately ninety seconds he quickly pulled his cock out of my mouth, apologized and then came into his hand. I couldn't believe it. By this stage, I don't mind telling you that I was furious. With barely concealed aggression, I told him straight. "I am not interested in any more excuses. You had better get it up again and soon. In fact, you have precisely fifteen minutes to restiffen and re-enter."

He looked really worried and was practically crying with fear and panic. I was not interested in his pitiable whimpering. I needed to have sexual intercourse (note: not *wanted*, but *needed*) and there would be hell to pay if I was not satisfied.

"Look, I am prepared to grant you a cigarette break but I am afraid that we need to get straight back to business the minute the cigarette is extinguished."

He smoked nervously, wearily and reluctantly stubbed the cigarette out, and we started kissing again. To his credit once again, he hardened up quite quickly and, once again, he entered me. It was delicious. DELICIOUS. I had been fantasizing about this event for the last week and the activities of the last hour had only served to intensify this longing a hundred-fold. I had been teased to insanity-inducing proportions and now he was moving inside me. I truly believed that I was in heaven. Suddenly, after the third thrust, he withdrew and clutched his penis, his face contorted in agony.

"What the fuck is wrong now?" I gasped.

He investigated the tip of his cock. "I am really sorry but I think I've got a blister on the end of my prick. It must have been caused by the friction from all that hard grinding in the garden." And, get this, "It is just too painful to continue," he whined.

"Did you kick him out?" my roommate Gabriela asked me later that evening when I told her what had happened.

"No," I said, "but I should have."

She nodded her head gravely in sympathy. "Yes, you should have."

I think that is the closest I have ever come to murder, or at least grievous bodily harm. And you know, if the judge had been a woman, I reckon I would have been let off. If premature ejaculation isn't included within the definition of mitigating circumstances for manslaughter, it bloody well should be.

Please God by Me . . .

Two and a half years have passed since my first date with Saul and I am still trawling the parties looking for someone prepared to marry me. Actually, that's not strictly true. I am trawling the parties trying to find someone that I would not mind spending the rest of my life with who is prepared to marry me. My assets are many (I'm attractive with a great figure and a lively and outgoing personality; I believe the virtue of modesty is seriously overrated as humble people also tend to be boring), so I can only conclude that I must have some major character failings that have prevented me from attracting a suitable life partner, or indeed, any partner at all. As a result of a fruitless search for a permanent boyfriend whom I like and who likes me too, whilst watching less attractive, fatter and less lively girlfriends settle down, I have spent countless hours in conversation with myself, with friends, counselors and psychotherapists, trying to figure out just what the hell it is about me that has left me as a statistic and the subject of articles, books and television documentaries on the phenomenon of the single woman.

I could tell you that I just haven't met the right man yet. Which is true. But I think there must be something more to it than that. I am quite fussy, so that obviously makes the task a little harder. Sometimes I torment myself by thinking that if I were boring and ugly, it would be easier to find someone to marry. My standards would be lower and there appears to be a higher proportion of boring, ugly single men than stimulating, handsome single men at this late stage of the game. And then I torment myself by thinking that if I were more attractive (with long blonde hair as opposed to short reddish hair), with a demure demeanor and a body that reflected membership and an ongoing commitment to a gym, I would have been snapped up by now. As you can see, it is very important for me to find a man.

You may find this rather pitiable and even annoying. Maybe you think that I should just get on with the rest of my life and stop obsessing about my single status. In which case, I would tell you that although it is very important for me to find a man, it is not *so* important. I mean, I could be with someone right now. I could be with someone who is healthy, wealthy and sexually repulsive to me. I could be unhappily married to someone who is kind, thoughtful and about as stimulating as your average tree stump. I could be with someone devastatingly witty, a high performer (sexually speaking), but who just smells all wrong. Please believe me when I say that I could find someone, *anyone*, if all I really wanted was a man to save me from spinster status. It's just that I want to find someone who I really like *and* who I really fancy. And while I am waiting to meet him, I'd rather be single and independent.

And anyway, I *am* getting on with the rest of my life, which is full to bursting with activity, people and, occasionally, meaning. Admittedly, my job could be more fulfilling. I am a lawyer and I am going to let you in on a secret that only lawyers know. The life of a lawyer is actually nothing like the exciting, vigorous and adrenaline-filled career portrayed by various American TV series. It is actually a life of unimaginable drudgery and boredom, filled with nit-picking and an anal obsession with detail, finding problems where none exist in order to justify your pompous existence. It involves sitting in a room all day and occasionally all night, piled high with papers, *the* most boring books ever written, poring over contracts in an alien, unreadable language which, if you do your job properly and no one ends up suing anyone, no one will ever read again. It also involves dealing with someone else's lawyer, who will inevitably also be an anally-obsessive lover of detail who just happens to adore nit-picking and whose imagination stretches only to envisaging life's worst possible outcomes so that he or she can draft a clause to cover such a possibility. And then, of course, you have to argue with the other lawyer, just in case the worst possible outcome actually occurs and your client sues you because you agreed to the inclusion of the word "hereinafter". On the plus side, the job earns me enough money to enjoy all my outside activities, and in the meantime I'm saving some money each month to retrain in a new area – once I have decided what it is that I would really like to do.

Having said that it is not *that* important that I find a man, in terms of being with any old geezer and in terms of sitting at home wailing and self-mutilating about my failure to secure a satisfactory love situation, it is nonetheless a major preoccupation and a substantial proportion of my social life is devoted to trying to find a suitable cock-owner. In fact, I have been so immersed in my search over the last few years that I simply have not had the time to consider why finding a man is of such paramount importance to me, apart from the understandable wish to have sex on a regular basis with someone with whom I get on reasonably well.

Admittedly, being Jewish does not help matters. First of all, if I want my parents to continue loving me as much as they currently do, I need to find someone who is also Jewish. On the basis that Jews make up approximately 0.8% of the population in the UK and bearing in mind that of that 0.8% I must exclude the aged, the women, the already attached and the ultra orthodox, the search for a single Jewish man is somewhat narrowed. I can't really hold my parents entirely responsible for the necessity to find a Jewish man; I am an adult now and can make my own decisions about who I would like to end up with (obviously overlooking the brain-washing I've received). It's just that I would like to meet someone who shares the same cultural and religious background as me. Meeting someone Jewish also means that I am able to avoid jokes about stingy Jews, which make my blood boil and ensure lifelong hatred against the fuckwitted joker. It would therefore be a shame if the joker turned out to be my husband and the father of my children.

In addition to the statistical limitations of finding a Jewish man, there is also the importance placed by Jews on the cult of family. "Settling down" is of such paramount concern to married members of our community that I no longer dare to attend a wedding in case I hear the words, "Please God by you."

But "Please God by me" is what I privately think too.

The Support Network

———⟳◇◇⟳———

I'm not the only one left you know, and I am sure it is no coincidence that my closest friends are also single. Rather conveniently, my closest friend, Claudia, seems to meet men and split up with them at the same time as me. For some reason our relationship clocks coincide almost to the hour, and this avoids a situation in which one of us is bemoaning the fact that the lover of our lives has just left us while the other wishes to describe their night in the sack with Mr. Huge Cock in blow by blow (and I use these words deliberately) details. This would clearly put the friendship under some strain and so, seemingly unconsciously but nevertheless very conveniently, we seem to fall in and out of love at the same time.

Claudia cannot understand why she is single. Neither can I. She is very pretty, with large, somewhat doleful green eyes (and just a hint of "please hurt me" around the edge of the irises), a perfect rosebud mouth that can pout to great effect, and a nose nearly large enough to qualify as possessing character. She has short, curly, brown reddish hair, which I have been dying to blow-dry with a round bristle brush for some time and to which offer she has stubbornly declined to succumb. Claudia is extremely tall, and slim, partly due to us sharing the same attitude to eating; we both tend to see it as an inconvenient physical necessity rather than an act of pleasure. Claudia is obsessed by her tits and, rather annoyingly, will bring them into any conversation, often as a complete non sequitur. We could be discussing a troubled relationship that I am suffering at work and, as I describe the latest incident, I can see the signs of an imminent breast invasion. Despite seeming otherwise involved in my dilemma and offering useful insights, Claudia's hand is wandering across the top half of her T-shirt in a caressing motion and I know that in the next five minutes I will be invited to offer comment on her burgeoning breasts.

"I really think this new pill is doing wonderful things to my tits," she says. Silence. Then, "Don't you think?" she adds with menace.

I now have two options: I can either answer enthusiastically and mentally prepare myself for a five-minute discussion of the miracle of her growing breasts; or I can ignore the question completely in which case the T-shirt will be removed and two fairly small but perfectly formed breasts will appear as proof that the new pill really is increasing her cup size. Claudia sprouted breasts at the late age of twenty-six and they are now a constant source of marvel for her and, if she's lucky, a boyfriend, who invariably seems to be chosen for his enthusiasm for tit sucking.

Personality-wise, we are talking a bit of a live-wire with a slight hint of hysteria. In public, by which I mean at work and at parties (to which she has a compulsive addiction), she manages to be loud and occasionally vulgar, without being coarse and offensive (something I have yet to mistress). She is also witty, talkative, sharp and flirtatious and adores being the center of attention. If all this sounds a bit much, may I also tell you that she is hilariously self-deprecating and opens herself up to immense amounts of teasing, all of which is taken extremely well. She sees the funny side of most things, particularly her love life, which she can discuss with equal measures of wit, pathos and pure tragedy. The only time her sense of humor offends me is when I tell her something that is making me feel particularly tragic and I hear a stifled snigger and the beginnings of a jokey comment, designed, I am sure, to cheer me up, but which nevertheless pisses me off as an inappropriate reaction to my sadness. I then have to sound all school-marmy and say something in a stern voice, like "Claudia, this isn't funny." Apart from these small incidents, her humor brightens up my life, and most conversations we have are peppered with chuckles at the very least.

In private, I sometimes see another side of Claudia. As is the way with witty, talkative, sharp, flirtatious women who adore being the center of attention, she is also insecure and extremely vulnerable. If you pressed me up against a wall for a reason as to why Claudia is still single and I was in a psychoanalytical mood, I would probably tell you that it is her vulnerability that unconsciously holds her back from committing herself to a relationship with prospects. That and the fact that she hasn't met the right man yet.

I love her for all the above reasons and because we are very open and honest with each other. I can tell her anything and she nearly always understands how I feel, and if she doesn't understand she tries to empathize with me anyway. Claudia is the person I go to with all the emotions and feelings I would be too ashamed to share with others (apart from my sister). She is a great listener, and although not a natural giver of compliments, when the chips are down and I ring her up with declarations of self-hate, she says things to me that are so loving and warm that I can get quite choked up with emotion when I think about them.

And just to complete the picture, you ought to know where she lives and what she does for a living. Well, she's in advertising – an account manager for a very good agency based in Soho where, despite her paranoia, insecurity and vulnerability, she is highly competent and well respected. She lives in a bizarre combination of elegance, comfort and squalor in Kilburn and she's twenty-nine too. Now you can enter her details on your database.

I also have two other very close friends who just "happen" to be single: Jasmin and Gabriela.

Jasmin's public persona is very different to Claudia's. Although she also craves male attention at parties, she achieves this by being the slinkiest, sexiest, most feline creature in the room, and remaining mysteriously aloof. Jasmin has thick, lustrous, shiny, straight dark brown hair, which can be self-consciously and unnecessarily flicked from her face as she sucks in her cheekbones to devastating effect. Her hair alone makes her a suitable object for desire, however, she is also fortunate enough to possess an alabaster complexion, a stunning bone structure and dreamy dark brown eyes (which can transform from dreamy to penetrating, thus suggesting a darker, more animalistic side, if you get my drift). In addition to her natural gifts, her interest in personal grooming also means that she has a wicked way with Chanel eyeshadow and MAC lipstick. Her designer clothes reflect both her good taste and the money she has spent on them. In other words, she looks fabulous, and now that she is a size eight I do admit to sometimes feeling like the ugly mate when we go out partying, grateful for any of her leftovers.

She is very demure whilst cleverly, albeit innocently, managing to avoid appearing prudish, which she most definitely is not. In fact, she's a wondrous mixture of fascinating contradictions: coy and demure, yet seethingly sexual; independent and financially successful, yet dizzy and occasionally helpless. I think she must appeal to men's "daddy" instincts as she has a stable of admirers, all of whom would do anything for her, from buying her dinner, giving her lifts around town and bringing her cigarettes, to massaging her feet, tidying her apartment and fixing her car. Men adore her. She's one of those women that you could learn an awful lot from if what you really wanted was a stable of admiring men and you could be bothered to hide your authentic self and act demure and coy.

I can see that you may not yet have a complete picture of Jasmin from what I have just told you. Perhaps you think that, with the good looks and designer lifestyle, she could be a bit on the shallow side. This, however, is not the case at all. In fact, when I first met her I initially withdrew from friendship as she struck me as being far too deep and meaningful. Within minutes of being introduced to her at a friend's dinner party, we were discussing our respective fears and phobias and I thought the whole scene too intense and heavy. However, our mutual desire to find out what life is all about is what really connects us as special friends and we just talk and talk and talk. Jasmin is extremely interesting and thought-provoking, with perceptive and wise theories on just about everything to do with life, friendship and relationships.

We are very honest with each other about our friendship, which means that arguments are a regular feature, but without sounding too corny I do think that the disagreements strengthen the bond. There are no festering resentments boiling away under the surface with Jasmin and I. They all bubble away in the open until we decide to disagree and make up.

Disagreements tend to center around our fundamentally different characters. I am very upfront, she is more demure. I can be very bawdy, which she adores in private but apparently finds offensive in male company. She's probably right in practice, judging by her success with men, but she does not understand that I have a feminist struggle to fight and I consequently refuse to be ladylike and coy. What I find difficult to understand about her is her constant desire to be what I call a chronic people-pleaser. She is a girl who can't say no. She wants everyone to think well of her, hence her need to look and act perfectly when in a social situation. Thus, a typical Saturday night argument between us might center around the fact that she has invited two dweeby girls to go out with us, who she knows I don't like and, if truth be told, she is not too keen on either, but who she has nonetheless been unable to let down.

The conversation may go something like this:

"I hope you don't mind, but I've invited Shelley and Tania out with us tonight."

"Who the hell told you to invite them?"

"Well they've got nothing to do."

"I'm not fucking surprised. They are boring and mean-spirited and that Shelley ignored me last time I saw her at a party."

"I know, but they invited me to a party a couple of years ago and they've got nothing to do and I feel a bit sorry for them. Tania hasn't had a boyfriend for seven years and she really wants to meet someone."

"In that case, they are definitely not coming. I don't want their sad and desperate vibes rubbing off on me."

"Well, what am I going to do? I don't really want them to come either but I have already arranged for them to come around to my apartment for drinks at nine."

"Ring them and tell them you are ill."

"I couldn't do that. It wouldn't be nice."

And finally: "Why do you have to be so bloody nice all the time? Why can't you be nice to me and not invite them?"

You want to know why she's single too, don't you? Well, my theory is that she doesn't know what she wants. She thinks she loves being free to party with abandon and she thinks she would also love a fulfilling relationship. She sort of wants a safe, steady, rich daddy figure while also pining after a wild, reckless and dangerous man with good taste in designer clothes or maybe a deep, intense, philosophizing psychiatrist would be nice too. And, of course, she hasn't met the right man yet.

Finally, I suppose I ought to tell you some concrete details. Jasmin works as a recruitment consultant in the City which suits her compulsion for networking (however there is also a contradictory wish for weeks of solitude) and she lives in a beautiful apartment in Primrose Hill. She's thirty-one.

And then there is my baby, Gabriela, who shares my apartment in Highgate. Gabriela is only twenty-six, and her age, combined with the fact that she is not Jewish, means that she is not preoccupied with finding a husband. In fact, her views on relationships are quite radical. For Gabriela, finding a man is inextricably linked with needing sex and money. Don't get me wrong, she's not completely cynical and calculating. But she has decided, some may think sensibly, that rich men are more attractive than poor ones. Gabriela's attraction to rich men could be connected to the fact that she is a student and constantly broke, but then she also claims to like powerful older men, which, conveniently for her, often means rich and generous too.

When she told me the other day that she wanted a man, I commented that romance never seemed to be a factor for her when considering a potential relationship. She was straddled across my back at the time, giving me a white-chocolate-flavored massage, so I could not see her reaction. Instead, I heard a wistful sigh. The massage stopped temporarily.

"Of course I want romance too. I also dream of running across a beach with my ideal lover. I just don't think English men are capable of being romantic." That was the cue for us to sigh wistfully in unison.

I met Gabriela in Italy and, quite frankly, we had both been spoilt rotten by the men there. Yet while I am still pining for an English, Jewish lover with the heart and sexual technique of an Italian, Gabriela is being pragmatic, but pessimistic.

Whereas Jasmin is cat-like, Gabriela is kittenish – small, compact and lithe yet compulsively huggable. I'm telling you, we can't stop cuddling, and she's short and light enough to bounce up and down on your lap. She has enormous energy; she can whizz around a dirty kitchen, and in a matter of minutes everything is gleaming. She studies hard, works to support herself, runs to the gym four times a week for an advanced class in back-breaking, high-powered aerobics, entertains her coterie of admirers, applies for jobs, meets her friends in rich men's bars and still seems to have time to rustle up exotic meals for us both, which are mostly delicious, if a little oversalted.

Gabriela is Czech, and although she does not like it, her accent is agreed by all to be very cute and sexy. The shoulder-length blonde hair also increases her pulling power, as do her very large, liquid, dark brown eyes and deep, suggestive, easy laugh. Men think she's sweet and fluffy, but what they don't realize is that she is actually also highly intelligent, extremely determined and impressively resourceful, at times to the point of ruthlessness.

But it's not all high energy, drive and determination. Sometimes it's tears, jars of Nutella and days in bed. Gabriela occasionally suffers from what she calls "low energy" and she explains to me that this low energy is connected to the weather conditions. I smile back at her and nod, while privately thinking that I'd be in bed for a year if I lived through one of her high energy weeks.

She's very supportive to me and I am very supportive to her, and it is the same with Claudia and Jasmin. I sometimes refer to them as my Support Network; I can count on all three of them emotionally, physically and financially and I have never been let down by them.

I also have some very good male friends, namely Matt and Nick. Matt is adorable: witty, cute, bumbling, intelligent and warm, a delightful mix of sincerity and complete phoniness. In fact, he is a little like Woody Allen: plenty of self-doubt with neuroses ranging from pimples, varicose veins, lack of sleep, low energy, career stagnation and, up until I introduced him to his fiancée, his lack of any long-term relationship. Matt and I have known each other for over ten years and, before he met his fiancée, I would not have hesitated to describe him as my soul mate. He knows me better than anyone and I know him better than he knows himself. We've nearly always been there for each other (and I have just about forgiven him for the times he wasn't there, even though he hasn't forgiven me for the way I acted at his law firm's Christmas dinner when I tried to describe my last Ecstasy experience to his uptight boss). We make each other laugh and we've made each other cry. Now, if you want to know why we didn't just get it together, seeing as we get along so well and love each other so much – well, he did want to go out with me and asked me on and off over the past ten years. I am afraid that there were several impediments to a future together: I didn't fancy him; he just wasn't my type; he smelled wrong to me. What can I tell you? We'd probably have been very happy together and my unwillingness to give it a go will no doubt torment me in years to come.

Through Matt, I have become very friendly with his buddy Nick. Nick is also witty and intelligent, which for me outweighs his other overpowering characteristic – self-obsession. On Planet Nick, everything that happens is directly related to him, with Matt, myself and others mere satellites circling his orbit. His first response on hearing that one of his closest friends had got engaged was, "What about *me*?! How could you? You're leaving *me* alone and single. When is it *my* turn?" Apparently, the customary congratulations were over-looked for the first ten minutes of the conversation while Nick wrestled with the question of what his friend's engage-ment meant to him and his life.

Nick's narcissistic egomania infuriates Matt from time to time, but I don't mind, partly because he is so funny and interesting the rest of the time, and partly because it's nice to have my own focus taken off me for a while so I can feel all passive and self-righteous about what a generous character I am. Nick is a very successful barrister and I can see why. His mental dexterity is astonishing and he can philosophize on practically any subject with knowledge and wit. That is why I enjoy his company so much. He really is the kind of person that you can talk to all night without getting bored.

Declaration of Love

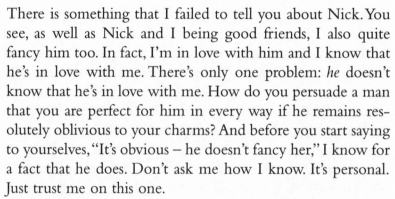

There is something that I failed to tell you about Nick. You see, as well as Nick and I being good friends, I also quite fancy him too. In fact, I'm in love with him and I know that he's in love with me. There's only one problem: *he* doesn't know that he's in love with me. How do you persuade a man that you are perfect for him in every way if he remains resolutely oblivious to your charms? And before you start saying to yourselves, "It's obvious — he doesn't fancy her," I know for a fact that he does. Don't ask me how I know. It's personal. Just trust me on this one.

So what would you do if you were me? Hang around till he gets it? I haven't got the patience anymore. After months of misinterpreting signs and driving my friends mad with constant analysis, I decide there's only one thing for it. I have to declare my love. Lay my cards on the table and if he doesn't want it, then at least I know one way or the other and I can plan the rest of my life accordingly.

So we're on the phone and he's moaning about his girl-friend again. Oh yes, I forgot to mention the girlfriend. I'm not saying I see her as an inconsequential nuisance, it's just that I care about Nick and she is an impediment to his future happiness – with me. So I can't afford to be sentimental about her. Anyway, I say, "Nick, I'm in love with you, and have been for ages. How about it?" Or words to that effect. I hope that is what comes out, however I had taken a cocktail of alcohol, Valium and a large joint while rehearsing my lines, which is a bit of a nuisance as I have been fielding calls from the Support Network all morning and they are desperate for news of his response. We've all been building up to this for months. It isn't a no, but it isn't an overwhelming yes. It is more of a definite maybe.

"Could it work?" he says. "We need to discuss this at length." Well, it's a start. I have put the seeds of an irresistible idea in his head; it is just a matter of time before he sees the light.

I spend the week in comfortable anticipation, so sure of my love for him, how could he possibly not feel the same for me? You must have gone through that before – when you feel so strongly about someone, you can't believe that it's just a one-way thing. The signs look good. Constant phone calls from him, suggestions to meet as soon as possible, he even drops around a present for me: a copy of his favorite book. That night I dare to think of "the future" with my love. I know that daydreaming about a happy future is risking fate; it isn't in the bag, he isn't even in my bed. But I am quietly confident.

Nick and I can't discuss the matter at the weekend as he is off to Leeds to visit his mother. This has its plus points. Claudia is begging me for information as to how Nick gets on with his mother as she is convinced this will indicate his attitude towards women and will thus be crucial in determining the success of our union. I happen to be of the Freudian school, so this makes sense to me. How adorable, I think, he's going all the way to Leeds for the weekend to see his mother, for no particular reason, just because he loves her and wants to spend time with her.

The next day I go for a walk with Matt, who has no idea of my feelings for Nick. As you know, Matt has asked me out for the last ten years or so and I suspect that he would be deeply disappointed that I fancy his best mate and not him. As we begin our long stroll on Hampstead Heath and Nick's name is mentioned, Matt casually confides, "Of course, you know why Nick has really gone to Leeds?"

My stomach leaps, my heart sinks, every intuitive fiber in my body is screaming: Bad News Alert. My eyes are already prickling with tears when I say hopefully, "To see his mother?"

"No," comes the reply. "He's gone to declare his love to Andrea Stein."

Only a hint of a bleat creeps in when I ask, "But what about his girlfriend?!" And then caringly, "God, what a bastard!" And then nonchalantly, as if the subject is of no further interest to me, "So, how was work this week?"

I spend the next hour of the walk fuming. My pace is fast and furious, marching up and down hills, my friend Matt remarking on my amazing zest and energy. Meanwhile, I am so wound up my stomach is in labor with an ulcer and the reason I'm walking so relentlessly is that if I stop for a moment, I'll collapse with disappointment. I'm devastated, yet Matt has no idea at all of the impact of his breezy disclosure and continues to chat away, oblivious to the pain that I feel in my heart.

The first thing I do when I get home is track down Nick in Leeds and tell him how I feel about him. Only this time it ain't love I'm declaring. You don't get many opportunities in life to scream profanities at someone, but on this phone call

I get away with it. I slam the phone down. Three minutes later it rings.

It's Matt: "What have you said to Nick? I've just had him on the phone and he's furious with me for telling you about Andrea Stein. Why did you call him? He's really upset and he says you've been shouting at him. What's going on with you and Nick?"

Not sure whether I've been rumbled and he knows everything, I nonetheless attempt to bullshit. "I just think he's being really unfair to his girlfriend. It really upsets me to see her treated in this way. I think he's being a real shit to her." I feel only very slightly guilty that I have been actively plotting her demise for the last six months; for the first time the girl has actually been of some use. I wait with nervous anxiety to see if Matt buys it and I realize with disbelief that he has.

Eventually I put the phone down and I am administered a stiff drink and an emergency beta blocker left over from a previous crisis. Friends arrive, the horror is recounted, and before we know it it is time to get ready to go out. I am in a wild, murderous mood – perfect for a Saturday night out on the town. I promise you, men are the last thing on my mind as I set out that night. But don't they say it always happens when you least expect it?

Tummy Tickles

I literally bump into Rob at a party in West Hampstead that very Saturday night. While making my way to the kitchen to dump the cheapish warm white wine that I have brought with me and, instead, fill my glass with wine bought by someone richer, classier and more generous, I have to invade a cluster of bodies, comprised of three males. As I squeeze past one of the bodies, I look up at the face to apologize and catch sight of these beautiful, dreamy eyes. I gasp both audibly and dramatically, but genuinely involuntarily, I promise.

"God, you are absolutely gorgeous," I blurt out.

A bit unsubtle and a bit forward, I know, but I do believe that credit should be given where credit is due. The guy *is* gorgeous. Thick, dark, lustrous hair with accompanying thick, dark, lustrous eyelashes. His eyes are so dark that they look liquid. He is very well dressed and very well built. Apart from the fact that he is tall (I normally like short and stocky – just the right size for a comfortable 69), he is absolutely my type.

He laughs and says something corny like, "You're not so bad yourself," to which I reply something like, "Well, it's always nice to receive confirmation," and he laughs again while I feel myself compelled to stare adoringly into his dark eyes.

His friends sigh and regroup away from us while Rob introduces himself. I am in absolute wonderment that this divine guy has been wandering the planet unbeknownst to me. He accompanies me to the kitchen where he helps me find a bottle of rich, classy looking wine. He finds me a clean glass, gets himself one, pours us both a drink and proposes the toast, "To us." I swoon, naturally, and drink the wine in one go. He pours me another glass and suggests we find a quiet corner, in which to become better acquainted. We go back into the lounge and find an armchair. He sits down and pulls me onto his lap. Of course, the only comfortable way to sit is sideways, with my arm around his neck and my nose touching his.

When you get to a certain age (and I would put that age at twenty-six and over), it is not the done thing to make out in public at parties, especially with someone that you have only met ten minutes earlier. But I do not let this unspoken convention stop me, and very soon we are openly and shamelessly smooching. I have seen neither Jasmin nor Gabriela since arriving with them at the party, and the only thing stopping me from being completely absorbed with the gorgeous guy whose soft warm tongue is inside my mouth and whose hard cock is throbbing through his jeans and pushing into my thigh, is my overwhelming desire to share news of this exciting experience. Gabriela eventually finds me, thank God, and I can show her who I've picked up and then gloat. She is suitably impressed and goes to find Jasmin so that she can have a good look too.

Buoyed up by my easy victory, I decide to work the party a bit and flash my charm. I need to be a little bit cool and unpredictable, after all. I explain to Rob that my public needs me and I take my social responsibility to entertain seriously. He looks slightly concerned, so I tell him he's gorgeous a few

more times and arrange to reconvene in the armchair in
fifteen minutes. I then find Jasmin and Gabriela and call an
Extraordinary General Meeting. We meet in the loo. I pro-
pose the motion, "Fucking gorgeous, or what?" The vote is
unanimous and the resolution is passed. Jasmin is in a panic;
two of her recent ex-boyfriends are at the party. She is understandably stressed as she has told both of them that she is "not
looking for a relationship at the moment" and "needs her
space," etc., and she is therefore forced to flirt as furtively and
discreetly as possible to avoid hurting anyone's feelings – one
of her major aims in life. The problem is that Jasmin actually
goes out with guys that she neither likes nor, even worse,
fancies, because she doesn't want to "hurt their feelings." I try
explaining to her that by going out with them and being
thoroughly charming and adorable, she is going to *really* hurt
their feelings when she finally gets around to telling them
that it isn't going to work out. After all, let's face it, it's much
easier to be thoroughly charming to someone that you don't
actually fancy. You don't need to hate them in advance for
breaking your heart.

The only guy Gabriela has spoken to at this party is a
sado-masochistic freak who has already revealed his desire to
peg her tits and who has also confessed that he would not be
averse to her putting a bulldog clip on the end of his dick.
Seeing as he is not a rich, sexy Italian, Gabriela is not inclined
to enter this guy's sick world. We vote unanimously that she
will not be going back to his place tonight and close the
meeting by reapplying another coat of lipstick.

Rob is waiting for me on the armchair. He has got me
another glass of wine. He is really very adorable and as I am
now already tipsy, I am not analyzing the situation and weigh-
ing up the possibilities of us getting married, although when
he suggests smoking some hash I consider proposing to him

myself, such is my love of hashish. We smoke, drink and kiss
for the next hour or so, with conversation limited to an exchange of compliments on our respective physical attributes.
Jasmin and Gabriela reappear at one point with news of their
intended imminent departure. Jasmin is feeling restricted by
the mournful looks of her exes and Gabriela's S&M guy is
getting out of control. He has mistaken her scientific interest
in the lifestyle of fetishists for embracing enthusiasm and does
not seem to want to take no for an answer to his invitation
to shackle her to the torture rack at his place.

I don't like leaving parties without Gabriela and Jasmin
and I point at Rob and ask them if I can take him with us.
Gabriela nods enthusiastically (she lives very much in the
present). But Jasmin shakes her head. I decide to go with Jasmin's advice on the basis that she has never been dumped,
whereas Gabriela's recent track record in love has been
uncharacteristically but seriously ego-bruising (I did tell her
not to sleep with the dyslexic millionaire on the first date,
but, as I said, she lives in the present and decided to ignore
the long-term strategic implications). I tell Rob that he lost
the vote and that I am going home without him. A pen
appears as if by magic and my number is taken.

In the taxi on the way home, I am pumped furiously by
Gabriela and Jasmin for information on Rob. I suddenly
realize that I know very little about him, apart from the fact
that he has the most gorgeous eyes, he is twenty-seven and
Jewish. And with my thirtieth birthday looming, he could be
the perfect antidote to my ageing crisis. There were no meaningful, soul-searching conversations between us. I fancied
him, he fancied me and I feel rather blasé about the whole
thing.

With good reason, it turns out. Rob calls me the following morning asking if he can take me out for lunch. As I don't

really "do food" with potential love interests, I suggested afternoon tea instead on the basis that I won't look too weird if I don't eat.

"How about a walk on Hampstead Heath first?" he suggests.

It's a fabulous idea and I agree enthusiastically despite the fact that it is difficult to dress seductively for a hike over the Heath.

Perhaps it is because he is several years younger than me, or perhaps because, in a sense, I picked him up, that I feel very much in control of the situation. I do not feel like a passive soon-to-be victim with Rob. I am not too nervous before the date, perhaps because I am also still slightly drunk and stoned from the night before.

When I open the door to him, I gasp once again and tell him that I had forgotten how gorgeous he is. He loves it and pulls me close to him for a hello kiss. We ramble over the Heath and every time we come to an area enclosed by trees, he pulls me against him and we start kissing. Conversationally, we deal mainly with the superficialities: where we work, where we go out, where we've been on vacation this year, where we shop and where we score. It is all delightfully frothy and the conversation, when interspersed with such passionate kissing, makes the afternoon fly by. He wants to see me in the evening too, but I have arrangements to see friends and I am not, repeat *not*, the kind of girl who cancels friends for a new man, or indeed any man.

"How about dinner tomorrow night?" he suggests. "I'll pick you up from work."

He is either in a big hurry to consummate the building passion or he really likes me. Who knows? It's probably both.

Within minutes of him dropping me off at home I am on the phone to Jasmin. She listens quietly while I relate the events of the afternoon. When I am finished she asks the simple question, "Tummy tickles?"

A tummy tickle is the feeling you get in your stomach when you *really* like a guy. I don't mean really fancy, I mean *really*, *really* like and *really*, *really* fancy. The tummy tickle turns your stomach over when you think of the guy in question. The tickle can spread upwards to a flutter in your heart and it can shoot downwards to cause a sensational tingle in your groin. A tummy tickler of a guy can cause you to take a sharp intake of breath when you think about him, while you sway slightly with longing, desire, nerves and excitement. Four men in my life have caused me substantial tummy tickles. Admittedly, I met three of them before I was twenty years old, which sometimes causes me to believe that tummy tickles are a youth thing. Maybe when you are young, fresh and impressionable, it is easier to find a tummy tickler. Despite this, I am still holding out for another man who gives me the tummy tickle sensation.

"Tummy tickles?" Jasmin asks.

"No," I reply.

"Why the hell not?" she demands.

I reflect for a minute on Rob's gorgeous eyes and his sexy, forceful way of pulling me to him and kissing me. Yes, I feel a tingle, but it is definitely limited solely to the genital area.

"I don't know." There is something missing that I can't put my finger on, but I am enjoying the whirlwind nature of our affair and if I start figuring out what it is that is missing, I might just find something wrong with the guy and that would be highly inconvenient, especially as the affair has not yet been consummated. "I'm having dinner with him tomorrow night," I tell her. "Maybe it is too early for tummy tickles?"

She says nothing, but we both know that if the tummy

tickles ain't there in the beginning, there is a slim to no chance of them ever appearing.

Rob appears on Monday night to pick me up and he looks as gorgeous as ever, until I catch sight of his feet. He is wearing *sandals*. Now I don't like sandals on men at the best of times, but these were particularly revolting, with black soles and thin black straps that fastened with Velcro. They were the kind of sandals that are only acceptable under very limited circumstances, such as when worn by children, or in a kibbutz in Israel where there are no concessions to demands of fashion.

I stumble back in horror. Surely this is some kind of sick joke.

He asks me what is wrong.

"You are wearing sandals," I say.

He starts to get all defensive and I start to feel all mean so I pretend that I am joking and ask him whether I can suck his toes later to cheer him up. But I am privately thinking that here I am, someone who spends a lot of time, money, effort, thought and energy on my appearance, and now I am forced to blow it all by stepping out with someone in sandals. Hopefully he will take me to a restaurant with long table-cloths so that I will not have to see the offending foot attire and I won't be caught out in public with a sandal-wearer.

Thankfully he does, and the evening starts to improve. I schmooze him like mad in order to make up for the fact that I have been bitchy about his sandals, and once his male pride has been restored he starts to schmooze back. The Italian restaurant obviously has a slack dress code as no one makes any reference to the fact that he is wearing sandals. He evidently knows the place as we are ushered to a secluded table at the back which has clearly been reserved by request. Wine and food ordered, we sit back to relax and enjoy the evening.

We talk about our respective days. Then we talk a little about our families. Then we talk about the merits of cell phone networks. Then the food comes and we eat, while talking about his fitness regime. Then we discuss his work as a computer something or other and by the end of the evening I know conclusively the reason for the absence of tummy tickles. Yes, he is gorgeous, but could he also be a bit boring? My attempts to take the conversation on to a darker, deeper level are very firmly resisted, and before I know it I am being drawn into a discussion on the layout of supermarkets.

To make matters worse, I also suspect a severe sense of humor failure. Attempts at irony, such as when I express my desire to adopt an old-age person when I get married as I don't like children but I do like the elderly, are taken at face value and he advises me that he does not think it is possible to legally adopt an old person. Although he is still technically "gorgeous," he becomes less attractive to me. Call me old-fashioned, but I do like to have a bit of personality too. It is all slightly frustrating but sadly liberating in that I now do not need to worry whether he will go off me. I have gone off him.

Nevertheless, I decide to continue to act adoring just in case he develops a personality on the way home, and because, to be quite honest with you, I really, truly do not know whether I am being too fussy in demanding conversational compatibility; isn't having a good-looking, all-round adorable boyfriend better than having no boyfriend at all? He invites me back to his apartment and I accept. His apartment is actually rather cool and the sandals obviously a peculiar lapse in what otherwise appears to be a man with very good taste. With the cool white decor, real gas fire, large sofa and panoramic views of London, you have a setting highly conducive to seduction. Rob gets us both a drink, puts on some old soul and pulls me on top of him on the sofa. He tells me how unbelievably sexy I am and, more importantly, he stresses how interesting he finds me.

I tell him how unbelievably sexy I find him and leave it at that. He seems content and the conversation over and done with, he seduces me. As I lie in his arms, gazing over London, I think how wonderfully perfect this would be if Rob was someone I really, really liked instead of someone that I just really fancied. I feel so sad at that thought. If I was with someone that gave me tummy tickles, I would be so unbelievably happy; but being here with Rob I feel empty – as if I am just going through the motions, playing a part. I yearn to feel real intimacy with a guy who I feel understands me and who I understand and appreciate. When is it going to happen? I ask myself, as I prepare for a rerun with Rob on the sofa.

I continue to see Rob for a while until my boredom turns into impatience which then turns into suppressed anger and downright cattiness. Sometimes I forget that he does not have a sense of humor and I will make a joke, which I inevitably follow with the weary words, "It's a joke." He is strictly a "missionary" man (and I don't mean that he preaches in his spare time). He is also a "towel" man, by which I mean that minutes, and sometimes seconds, after ejaculation takes place, he jumps out of bed to fetch a towel "to clear all the mess up." I do not feel inclined to tell him that I actually rather like "the mess" as I reckon that if he does not have the initiative to smear his cum over my tits, I'm not going to enjoy his disgusted expression when I do it myself. It is all quite methodical. Meal, wine, sofa, hang up clothes, bathroom, teeth brushing, towel by bed, sex (lights kept on at my request), clean up, kiss good night, cuddle and lights out.

At the same time, he is also very nice, kind, generous, Jewish, good-looking, with a stable job and a banana-shaped cock. If I had less understanding parents, they would pressure me into marrying him. I keep asking myself if I am being too picky, whether my perfect man exists, and if he does is he even single at this stage of the game? But I never really believe that I will settle for someone who does not stimulate me mentally as well as genitally.

Of course, the more distant and uncommitted I become, the keener Rob becomes, until I decide the kindest thing to do is to put him out of his misery. I telephone him with the news, in accordance with my "it's kinder to dump over the phone" policy; it allows the rejected lover to lose control of facial muscles in private and thus affords a minimal amount of dignity in an otherwise humiliating scenario. Despite his protestations of feeling distraught, I know he will be snapped up by someone else.

And so it turns out. Only one week after splitting up with me, he is spotted at the same Italian restaurant at the table at the back, staring into someone else's eyes and looking to all intents and purposes like a man very much in love. When I am told this news (by a male friend; a good female friend would know better than to deliver such news), I experience a brief but powerful moment of regret. He is lovely, he deserves to be happy.

But don't I?

Dreams Come True

Now that I have returned to single status, my old male friends come crawling out of the woodwork. It wasn't as if I dumped them while I had a boyfriend. It was more that my male friends look to other single female friends to hook up and flirt with in their spare time. Nick has heard from Matt that I have broken up with Rob and he apparently decides to pluck up the courage to call me. After my experience with Rob, I am so pleased to speak to a man with interesting things to say that I soon forget all about Andrea Stein (who wasn't interested in him, you will be pleased to hear – well, I'm pleased anyway) and six months have passed since our screaming match on the phone, and I have actually really missed him. Our relationship blossoms over the next couple of months into what is clearly a platonic friendship, despite the fact that I still have occasional daydreams that Nick declares his love for me.

In proactive romantic terms, however, I decide to finally give up on Nick. There are two main reasons for this, apart from the small but undeniably crucial fact that Nick has consistently denied any romantic feelings towards me for some time.

Firstly, and don't judge me too harshly on this one, I had my tarot cards read by Lucia, a Czech friend of Gabriela who also happens to be a white witch. Lucia has been so accurate for me in the past that she predicted my last shag practically down to the moment of penetration. When I asked Lucia about my long-term prospects with Nick, she consulted the cards and I noted with alarm that her face set into a stern frown. I immediately suspected that she was not going to predict a short joyful engagement followed by a long and happy marriage. She waved the Liar card in the air and for the first time in the reading sounded convinced by one of her own predictions. She shook her head mournfully. Not only were we not going to be married, but any relationship would be short, unhappy and ultimately completely doomed.

I took this information on board with a mixture of disappointment and, surprisingly, relief, because it was actually more convenient for me on a practical level to be told that Nick was not my soul mate, in view of the fact that he was refusing to admit I was his.

My second insight into the Nick situation came during a meditation, when a voice deep within me cut through the crap that normally fills my mind and told me in no uncertain terms that Nick was not the man for me. I do believe that we hold all the answers to life's more meaningful questions within us and my revelation felt both true and profound.

So I give up. I accept that Nick and I are not destined to be together and this now releases me to (a) be his friend and (b) find someone else who feels the same way about me and who will hopefully be good-looking. I don't think I mentioned this before as I didn't want you to think I was shallow, and because love *is* blind, but Nick does face certain challenges in the looks department.

As you get older you will notice that people always tell you that looks are really not important. You will hear plenty of reasons for this. Good looks fade with age when *everyone* looks ugly. And before they fade, everyone will fancy your man, and try, perhaps successfully, to steal him. Nobody will try and steal your ugly husband. Oh yes, and a good-looking man will be vain and take up more space in the bathroom cabinet than you. Compromise on looks, they say and concentrate on finding a rich man instead.

I'm not sure I agree. Plain men are much more insecure. They are more likely to be flattered by female attention as they will have a greater need for an ego boost than a good-looking guy who's had no problem pulling women in the past and has nothing to prove. Ugly men are also more likely to be unfaithful as they will try and make up for lost shags in their youth, when looks were universally regarded as important and consequently they lost out. They will probably be quite unable to say no as they will remember all the times they were gagging for a yes.

And to be quite honest with you, darling, I'd rather have a pretty face to wake up to in the morning. Wouldn't you? Be honest.

Meanwhile, the rich guys are either self-made, which probably means they are psycho workaholics, or they inherited their wealth, which is worse, as they will be spoiled brats and you will almost certainly be regarded by their family as money grabbing and unworthy. I reckon the best solution is to earn your own money and team up with someone you fancy.

In light of the above, therefore, I feel I have no reason to cling to any vain hopes of romance with Nick; what with the Liar card in my tarot spread, inner wisdom and constant rejection by the man himself, my decision has been made for me. I go about the business of life much happier and with a lighter and more open heart.

Time passes and my relationship with Nick settles into a very happy friendship. Now that I am not constantly trying to get him to love me, the strain is off. I'm relaxed and we're enjoying each other's company more than ever. After all, we started off as friends.

It is Saturday night, and Nick and Matt ring me to ask if I would like to go to a party. I call Claudia who has, I think, only once been known to decline an invitation to a party, and invite her along. Despite having had three hours' sleep the night before and a family lunch the next day, she is predictably up for it.

You know some nights you go out and you just know you look great? You may have worn the same outfit before to no avail, but on this night, some special chemical has been released that makes you irresistible. Weeks later when no one at all in the whole world fancies you, you torment yourself trying to figure out what the hell it was that night that gave off the right signals and how on earth you can replicate it. Well, this is one of those nights. And I *know* it has nothing to do with the fact that I've had four glasses of house panty remover and two lines of Bolivian marching powder.

The party is being held at a bar in town and I soon clock a man who I know and vaguely fancy (or is it vaguely know and really fancy?) called Michael. I decide this is going to be his lucky night and I make my way towards him.

Meanwhile, in another corner of the bar, Claudia and Nick are having an intense discussion about me, apparently initiated by Nick. Despite Lucia's predictions and my own

inner revelation, Claudia is unconvinced (rightly) by my pro-
nouncements of having given up on Nick, and she recog-
nized the happy flushed excited look that lit up my face
when we arranged to meet up with him for this evening. It
is unspoken between us that, sadly, deep deep down in the
darker recesses of my heart, I still hope that Nick will come
to his senses and ask me out.

Nick tells Claudia of his fears of getting involved roman-
tically with me. He thinks I am too hard and he does not
think he can be vulnerable with me as I would just tease him
(true, but what is wrong with that?).

Claudia explains that the hard woman act is just a very
superficial exterior and that actually I am like an avocado
pear: tough on the outside with a soft interior. She neglects
to mention the hard stone in the middle.

He talks of his tendency to date completely unsuitable
women who often live on other continents. His current amour
lives in Australia.

Claudia suggests that this may be connected to his fear of
commitment and Nick reluctantly agrees that she may have
a point. She deals with each of Nick's anxieties in turn,
including his belief that I am fickle and fancy everyone at
some point. Having completely convinced him that I am in
fact still seriously and, in her opinion, a little sadly devoted
only to him, they resolve to come and find me immediately.

When they do find me, I'm busy. I am rammed up against
the bar making out with my victim, Michael, like an animal
unleashed from years of captivity (for captivity read celibacy),
completely oblivious to the good work Claudia has just put
in with Nick on my behalf. And unfortunately completely
unaware of Nick and Claudia standing, watching, immobilized by the floorshow that Michael and I are providing. After
an indecent amount of time, Claudia quietly ushers Nick

away on the grounds that it would be voyeuristic to remain a second longer.

The irony is that although I am busy kissing Michael and enjoying it enormously, I can't help wishing it is Nick that I am kissing. So much for my declarations of having given up on the guy. I realize I still have extraordinarily strong feelings for Nick and decide that I just have to find him and simply transfer my passion to the man I love (but not before politely making my excuses to Michael and giving him my telephone number – I always try to have a back-up plan).

In all the time I've been nuts about Nick, I have never made an actual move on him and decide to waste no further time. En route, I meet Claudia who excitedly gives me a quick resumé of her free therapy session with Nick. The bar is crowded but I instinctively make my way straight over to him and melt into his arms. We kiss on the cheeks and then our lips meet for a second. Nick pulls away. "Not now," he says, "you've just been kissing someone else." His "not now" floats into the air with the surely undeniable implication of "but later definitely." I can wait. We know that. I've been waiting for the past two years.

I stayed with Claudia that night, dissecting the evening's activities with relish. Claudia is convinced she has made serious headway with Nick. I cannot sleep despite Claudia's desperate efforts at five o'clock in the morning to give me some lavender night cream to combat my insomnia and allow her to return to sleep undisturbed. As I wearily apply the cream I think that it is going to take a lot more than a bit of scented moisturizer to quell my intense excitement at the climax of a two-year wait.

The next day I feel dreadful. Hungover, tired and anxious. I go home, return to bed and stay there all day, too ill to move. I really want to escape the telephone lying next to my bed. I've never been the sort of girl to sit by a phone waiting for it to ring. Going out and ringing in every half an hour for messages is more my style. The day goes so slowly it is torture. There is nothing on TV and my head hurts too much to read the papers.

At around 5:30 pm the phone rings. It is Nick. Do I want to go to the movies? I don't but I say I do. He asks whether I have spoken to Claudia. I have but I say I haven't. Life's complicated, isn't it?

He hurries over and we study the film guide. I can't focus due to nerves and lack of sleep, so Nick peruses the options. While we are cozily planning our evening's entertainment, his cell phone rings. It's Laura, a female friend of his, and I listen with horror while he arranges for her to come to the movies with us. I cannot believe it. This guy's either got a sick sense of humor or he's so out of touch with reality that I ought to report an alien encounter to the Ministry of Defense.

Not only do I not get it, I just don't think I can go along with this anymore. He is seriously bad for my health. When he gets off the phone, I politely inform him that I won't be coming to the movie and that I'm going back to bed.

He follows me upstairs and lies down on the bed next to me. Suddenly, my hopes are raised again. We lie there facing each other for a while in silence. He then asks me if I mind if he goes to the movie with Laura. I don't know whether to slap him around the face or start crying. So I say no, I don't mind. Suddenly, he leans over and kisses me.

I kiss him back and he kisses me again and I kiss him back again. This goes on for five hours. It is magical. Delicious, fun, sweet, sexy, romantic, relaxed and affectionate. Every time I look at him he has a massive smile on his face and he tells me that I'm smiling all the time too. Do you know, this is the first time since I was eighteen that I haven't been tipsy or stoned when I've got it together with someone. And the funny thing is that I don't even feel like I need anything. Our intimacy feels pure, it feels like a soul connection. I am relaxed and happy. I light the candles, turn down the lights, put Van Morrison on the CD player, draw the curtains and lie in bed with the man I've been crazy about for years. I don't feel smug, just very very happy. It feels right. It was a long struggle, but it was worth the wait. It all came good in the end.

P.S. For those of you worried about poor Laura, he cancelled her after the sixth kiss.

Shpilkersville

Nick calls me the next day and wants to meet for lunch. Unfortunately, my new boss is hovering over me and I can't speak, neither can I meet for lunch. I am initially delighted that he has called. The delight lasts for about ten minutes until a horrible new thought forms in my mind. What if he wants to meet for lunch to tell me that last night was a terrible mistake? I swing between delight and horror for the next fifty-eight hours and thirty-seven minutes until we next speak on Wednesday evening. It is pure torment.

Now you may say that sixty odd hours is a long time to be contemplating such a thing, and probably not very accurate as I am including sleep time. Well, believe me when I tell you that I slept very little on the Monday and Tuesday night and when I did I bloody well dreamt about him. And I wasn't even distracted by food because I wasn't eating either. So, I'm tired, I'm starving, and very soon I'm ill as well. My resistance is low and I come down with the flu. Once again, I am unwillingly lying in bed, unable to move and waiting for that goddamn phone to ring.

There is also the mystery call late on Monday evening to consider. Apparently, someone, a man, called for me at 11:15pm while I was out, and hadn't left a name. This event has since led to new house rules on phone-answering techniques and Gabriela is now instructed to: (1) *first* ask who is calling, (2) *then* reveal that I am out. Although to give Gabriela her due, she did dial last number recall only to find that the mystery caller had withheld his number. The withheld number paranoia fits into Nick's personality profile and therefore affords me some hope that the call was from him.

When I finally get to speak to Nick on Wednesday night, he is adorable. We have a languid late night chat and arrange to see each other on Friday night. He tells me that the reason he wanted to meet for lunch was that he couldn't wait to see me after our magical evening together on the Sunday. Unfortunately, I don't sleep on Wednesday night either as I'm too excited.

The following evening, I have a nightmare. I am hanging out at Danny the Dealer's pad smoking some weed with some of my single friends. I buy some heroin from one of my friends (note: this is still the dream – I have never done and certainly do not plan to introduce heroin into my life as I'd probably like it). But anyway, in the dream I buy the heroin and my friend puts it in a brown paper bag for me. I then decide to go across the road to the shops to buy a few things, intending to return to Danny's place. When I come out of the shop, the road outside my friend's apartment is surrounded by heavily armed police who are planning to raid the place. Needless to say, it is a pretty scary scene, especially as I am clutching my brown paper bag stuffed with a class A drug. But I then realize that the police don't suspect me, and as my car is parked outside I ask the police if I can leave the area. They allow me to go but I feel extremely guilty about leaving my friends to get busted. But worse than the guilt is the underlying feeling of unease that I bought the heroin and I am going to use it. Why have I bought something that I know is highly addictive, very, very bad for me, that is ultimately going to ruin me, when I know all this in advance?

I wake up and immediately realize the significance of the dream. And if you've worked it out too, you can skip the next chapter. I try to get back to sleep and in the morning I push the dream and its implications to the back of my mind.

Nick comes around on Friday night. We have a quiet night in and we get on fabulously, despite a mild disagreement about who is kissing whom the most. I feel adored by him. He displays all known signs of a man falling in love. He talks about intimacy and getting to know each other and the importance of communicating how we feel to each other to avoid unnecessary misunderstandings. All good stuff, I'm sure you'll agree. When he goes home at two o'clock in the morning to officially end his relationship with the girl in Australia, he leaves me lying in bed wondering what our children will look like.

On the Saturday night I have already bought a ticket to a husband-hunting ball. Although I don't believe I need to go, the ticket cost me a fortune, so I feel obliged, and my friends are relying on me to make up the table numbers. It is OK, not brilliant. The usual mix of beautiful women dressed in designer clothes and short men with glasses, with everyone too busy searching for a life partner to really hang loose and enjoy. Personally, I have lost my motivation to find a husband and am exhausted from the week's enormous emotional expenditure.

Shish Kebab-ed

I wake up on Sunday morning excited about seeing Nick again. He calls and says he is going to pop around, but he has to leave at 4 pm to let Matt into his flat to watch the football on cable. He doesn't show up until 3:30 pm and he isn't smiling when I open the door. We go upstairs to my bedroom and lie on the bed. He comes straight to the point. "It's not going to work out between us," he says.

I feel as if someone has stuck a kebab skewer through my heart, and as it pierces me I switch off and think bitterly that things just don't seem to work out for me. Happy endings are for other people. I just get months of aggravation, a week of happy aggravation then a year of depression. Some people have a boyfriend for a couple of years. The really lucky ones get one for life. I have one for a week.

He has obviously thought it through as he comes up with fifteen reasons why it won't work. As I count them it dawns on me that he's covered every single angle. If you don't mind, I'd like to list the reasons so that you can see it really is not worth my while to try and persuade him to give us a chance. It's one thing reassuring the odd concern, but dealing with fifteen separate concerns is quite beyond me.

1. The timing of our short union was unexpected and he was not emotionally prepared.
2. He has just split up with his girlfriend. You know, the committed relationship to the one who lives in Australia.
3. I'd been kissing someone else the night before we got it together and this disturbs him.
4. We share a mutual friend, Matt, and a relationship between us could put him in a difficult position.
5. We are both very intense.
6. We are both very different.
7. We have different expectations of relationships, by which he means (you'll love this one) that he is looking to get married and settle down whereas I just seem to want to take the relationship on a day-to-day basis. I explain that seeing how a relationship develops on a day-to-day basis is in fact the most conventional way of proceeding to a long-term relationship and possibly marriage. People rarely decide to get married after the first date. But he is already on to the next reason . . .
8. He needs to learn to be alone before he can successfully commit to a relationship. By this stage, I feel disinclined to bother to point out inconsistencies in his reasoning (see 7 above), but I still feel compelled to point out that he is thirty-four and if he hasn't managed to figure this one out by now, he probably isn't going to.
9. He doesn't think I could deal with his hectic work and social schedule, the constant cell phone calls, etc., always rushing from one arrangement to the next. He is probably right.
10. I wouldn't like the fact that he plays golf at the weekends as I would want to see him all weekend. Says who?
11. He has a fear of commitment but he says he doesn't want to talk about this one as he doesn't think it is relevant.

12. We'd already had an argument on Friday night (remember the mild disagreement about the kiss count?) and this could be an indicator of other possible arguments in the relationship. Need I comment?

13. He is so neurotic and anxious that I would be horrified if I knew the extent of his angst. (This one speaks for itself too.)

14. Can you believe it! There are more reasons. Although he was very happy when he was in my company in my bedroom, he confused the excellent house vibes for a mistaken belief that a relationship could possibly work between us. I can't believe it – the guy fell in love with my bedroom and not me.

15. Finally, and I left this one until last on purpose, he is worried that a romantic relationship with me will spoil our friendship.

You will note that I rarely use exclamation marks. I would love to plonk one at the end of Reason Fifteen. But I've always been told that only lazy and immature writers use exclamation marks. Really, one should leave the impact of what one has written to speak for itself.

Are you beginning to realize what I am up against here, because as he is listing the above reasons it finally dawns on *me* who I am dealing with. This guy's anxiety levels ought to be monitored for medical research.

I look at Nick while he's listing the reasons and although I have a kebab skewer lodged in my heart, my brain is still functioning perfectly well. I quietly listen to him while thinking what an idiot he is and decide that in addition to not having the energy to persuade him to give it a chance, finally, I don't have the inclination either. In fact, he's boring me and

I feel only contempt tinged with pity for this neurotic little creature.

He has to let Matt into his flat in five minutes, and as he has run out of time (for all I know he could have had a few more reasons tucked up his sleeve) he gets up to leave. He stands outside my bedroom door, I look him straight in the eye, and with a calm icy detachment I say slowly and with menace: "Never ever ring me again. And take a good long look, because you won't be seeing me again either."

Suddenly he bleats, "I told you I was right. It would ruin our friendship."

"Yeah and you've been proved right, now get the fuck out of my life."

!!!

Therapy

He's not even out of the front door and I'm already on the phone to the Emergency Services. Thank God Jasmin's in. I arrange to go around to her house immediately. While driving around there, I leave a brief nameless monotone message on various friends' answering machines, announcing simply "It's over." It feels like I'm ringing around with the news of a death, which I suppose, although dramatic, I am. I am bereaving the death of my hopes and dreams, and, more importantly, my wedding plans.

I arrive at Jasmin's bursting with energy and anger. Suddenly I am vibrant (yeah, I know, I love the drama – sad isn't it?) having spent the last week in a hazy fuzz. We get down to business immediately: coat off, drinks poured, joint rolled, answering machine switched on. Ladies and gentlemen, let the bitching commence.

Have you noticed that when you first start going out with someone, you only tell your friends the good stuff? He's so wonderful, generous, funny, cute, sexy, good-looking, romantic, caring, etc., etc. You don't mention the bad stuff: the nasty shoes, the revolting way he masticates, the cocaine habit, the inane laugh, his pimpled back, his inability to have sex unless you are wearing his ex's thigh-length rubber boots, the wife, the children . . . It's not that you've exactly forgotten to mention them, it's just that they've been shoved to the back of your mind. You don't need to dwell on small irrelevant details when he's so gorgeous and he's yours.

Now, sitting at Jasmin's, with the word REJECT stamped on my forehead, I can see no reason why I should keep the knowledge of Nick's defects to myself a minute longer. I have actually been bursting to offload my concerns about Nick's lack of technique in the sack, but thought that as I would be marrying the guy, I couldn't tell anyone as I did not want my friends to be sorry for me for the rest of my life.

Well, maybe I shouldn't repeat all the bad stuff here as it would be terribly unfair to Nick and you might just think I am bitter. On the other hand, you already know I'm bitter and you must surely despise Nick by now. You may also think that as you've come this far with me, why should you be deprived of the juicy bits. And I agree. So we'll compromise. I'll only tell you two things: he is the worst kisser in the world and he has donkey's bollocks.

Yeah, I'm serious. The worst kisser I have ever come across in the whole of my life, and between you and me, I've kissed a lot of men (and a few women) in my time, and I'm telling you, he was baaaaad. Now, *everyone* wants to know what I mean by a really bad kisser in case they are one and they have gone through life happily unaware that they are doing it all wrong. Well, if the following technique sounds like your style, I can confirm that you need to start completely from scratch and really hone up on your kissing skills. Do you . . . open your mouth very slightly, quickly poke your tongue ever so gingerly into the mouth opposite, withdraw tongue, and repeat twice or thrice. If so, you should be ashamed of yourself.

Once I get started on the queen bitch route, there's no stopping me. Forget Nick's fifteen reasons! I am on to my forty-eighth reason by now. With an impish grin (I haven't had this much fun in ages), I am delighted to unburden this one – "And he has the ugliest goddamn balls I've ever seen."

Jasmin is intrigued. "What were they like? I need to know."

"Well," I say, "they were enormous, dangly things. I would have thought he'd need a wheelbarrow to cart those sacks of King Eddies around. In fact, they were just like donkey's bollocks." And thus from this moment Nick is renamed. Donkey Bollocks. Shortened to DB for repetitive convenience.

Do you think I am a bitch? I mean, I know everyone has some physical curse about which they are extremely sensitive. I don't want you to turn against me when you've been on my side all this time. I would be mortified if someone mocked one of my physical imperfections in print. I mean, *really seriously* mortified. How then can I do this to someone whose only crime apart from being chronically angst ridden was to decide that he does not want me to be his girlfriend? I'd like to say easily, but I do feel a bit guilty and by the time this manuscript makes it to the publishers, it may be removed. If, however, it does get past the editorial, libel and conscience departments, I'll have to live with the guilt. But the fact is all my friends know, so why shouldn't you? And this is a no-holds-barred story. Or a no-hard-balls story.

When I first caught sight of his balls, I was struck by a sad irony. My last but one boyfriend, David, had a small cock but the most beautiful set of snugly fitted well-hung balls I've ever had the pleasure of licking. Of course, I did not focus on

the beautiful balls but the undersized penis. I tormented myself over the shame of future holidays with friends when it
would be silently noted by all that his trunks were not full to
capacity. Nick, on the other hand, could have walked around
on a nudist beach with pride were it not for the balls hanging
round his knees.

Jasmin and I then spend the next four hours debating
whether I should send him a letter venting my displeasure.
This is not as sad as it sounds. The four hours will always be
memorable for the laughter, the confidential stories and the
bonding between us. As we lay top to toe snugly under her
duvet on the sofa we agree it is a shame that I don't have a
penis as we could then marry each other.

I tell her that I plan to send him a postcard saying, "Dear
Nick, you said it would be easier for you if I could tell you
that I had doubts too. Well, I did. You were the worst kisser I
ever kissed. P.S. By the way, has anyone ever told you that you
have donkey bollocks?"

As you know, Jasmin is a lovely person who rarely has
bitchy thoughts, and if she does, she suppresses them on the
grounds that it's not nice or ladylike. I, on the other hand,
have been described once or twice (half-jokingly) as evil. And
although you know deep down that I am not (although deep
down, I fear that I am), I have no qualms about expressing
intense and extreme feelings, such as love and, for the purposes of this discussion, hate.

That afternoon at Jasmin's, I feel hate for DB. And a letter
seems an excellent way of offloading that feeling. Jasmin tries
her hardest to dissuade me from writing it. However, I come
up with some very convincing reasons. Firstly, it will be a
good way of expressing my anger and, therefore, releasing it.
Secondly, I will no longer be the victim in my relationship

with Nick. After the letter I had planned for him, he can now honorably take the role of victim. Why, I argue, do women always have to take it lying down. Passive and accepting. I am aware of the backlash of angry women cutting suits to shreds and although I do not particularly want to join the category of angry bitter woman, I do object to quiet resignation.

About ten years ago, my cousin was going out with this guy with whom she had fallen madly in love. I'm telling you, marriage was on the cards. Her mother had practically booked the caterers. On the Wednesday he rang my cousin and invited her out with his friends the next week, on the Thursday he told her he'd bought Wimbledon tickets for the summer, on the Friday he suggested holidaying in the U.S. for the summer, and on the Saturday he called her to tell her not to bother coming around that night as he had given the doorman of his building strict instructions not to let her in.

My cousin is emotionally delicate, and took the news badly. After a week of her crawling into her parents' bed at night, it was decided that she might need some form of professional counseling. The counselor's suggestion was straightforward. Ring him and tell him how angry you are. When my cousin came home to tell her mother of this advice, her mother, who used to wield enormous influence on my cousin, especially at times of low confidence, successfully persuaded her against this course of action. She would be lowering herself and would lose pride and face. I have always regretted this and thought my cousin would have benefited from the angry call.

We can always justify not expressing our hurt and anger and pain using pride as an excuse. But as I point out to Jasmin, I don't care if Nick knows I am angry as I don't care what he thinks of me, period. It isn't as if Nick has the mental capacity to incorporate other people's states of mind. Especially, I point out, after receiving a postcard like the one I have planned. He will have other things on his mind then. I tell her that the letter has to be carefully worded, as I don't want to tip him over the edge so badly that he actually seeks therapy as this could then result in recovery and could, ironically, propel him towards a successful relationship. Needless to say, that would be unacceptable. Bad enough to cause anguish, not bad enough to precipitate rock bottom and thus, recovery.

"OK," says Jasmin, "I've got a compromise. Wait seven days and if you still feel the same way, send the letter. But promise me," she adds excitedly, "I can have a copy." You see, the fact is that Jasmin is coming around to the idea. She reminisces about the ex who serially cheated on her and began fantasizing about the letter she wishes she'd written. But ever the well-brought-up, gracious lady, she had retreated into silence and depression instead. And when she bumps into the serial cheat at parties, she is still the well-brought-up and gracious lady who inquires after his parents.

I consider the proposed seven-day cooling off period, and to Jasmin's surprise, I readily agree. Although not for the reasons she anticipates. "Great," I say. "Imagine the material I could come up with over another seven days. I'm doing pretty well for an afternoon. I could really hone the letter to perfection in a week." And, of course, a week will give him time to feel guilt and perhaps regret and we wouldn't want him to miss out on that experience. He will probably have elevated me to the level of wounded saint by then and the evil epistle will have far more impact.

I go to bed that night single, having woken up in the morning looking forward to seeing my darling boyfriend. I'm drunk so the pain of having a kebab skewer embedded in my heart has been dulled. I know that getting drunk was a cop-out and a way of escaping my feelings. But I've had a wonderful day with Jasmin and tomorrow I know I'm not going to escape my pain so easily.

I resign myself to a full dose of the blues.

Happiness is the Greatest Revenge

I wake up the following morning and enjoy 0.03 seconds of ignorance before remembering that I am unhappy.

I get up, get dressed and go to work. By lunchtime, it occurs to me that I really don't feel too bad. Can this be right? Ought I not to be suicidal? What's going on here? When I get home, I put on some tear-provoking music and wait expectantly. Nothing. Well, I rationalize, I am famed for my ability to immediately pick myself up and dust myself down for a day or two before collapsing into a heap of self-pitying misery. This time, I promise myself, I'll experience the pain and deal with it so that I don't just unwittingly add it to my ever-increasing emotional baggage.

Days pass and, strangely, I feel better. In fact, I am having a wonderful week, discussing kissing techniques and testicle types. My appetite returns, and after a week of fasting I can tell you that food tastes wonderful. I sleep deeply and blissfully, free of tortuous dreams.

Someone mentions the letter. What letter? Oh yes, well, mmmm, I'll have to see about that. I've got a very busy social schedule and I don't think I have time right now, I say. The fact is that I think that this time I really have been cured, and I am now released from any future fantasies of a wonderful life with Nick.

Boogie Nights in Highgate

I spend the next couple of months quietly celebrating my escape from Planet Nick and a final conclusion to the matter of whether or not Nick and I would be spending the rest of our lives together. The outcome seems almost unimportant. I am just pleased to be free of the uncertainty so I can plan the rest of my life accordingly. In the meantime, I see friends and chill out. Nothing heavy. Nothing exciting. At the end of my third month of single man aversion, I start to become lonely and restless.

In fact, on a spring Tuesday evening after another dead weekend of inactivity, I start praying for a party. The conscious motivation for this fervent wish is so I can find my soul mate, relax and put my feet up on a Saturday night instead of squeezing into tight clothes, slathering on foundation and spending vast amounts of money on partying and trying not to have a bad time (I've been at this game too long to hope for a good time).

There is, however, a deep unconscious motivation at work behind the frantic phone calls to other single earthlings. And I think it might have something to do with the fact that over the last month, my bedroom has become the Unofficial

North London Porn Exchange. Although my hot water bottle scores high for warmth and loyalty, it's not all that good at rampant sex. I am quite unaware that I have become simply MAD FOR IT. Unfortunately, I associate sex with getting hurt (emotionally I mean) and I have therefore subconsciously eliminated sex with other human beings from my life. This is rather unfortunate as I do actually like sex very much. But it seems that pornography has now taken the place of human interaction and the associated risks involved.

The porn craze started about three weeks ago when Claudia held a hen night for her sister-in-law, Sandra. I used to be friendly with this girl when she was single. Sandra was sassy, lively and knowing. I'll tell you how knowing she was – she partied till the grand old age of twenty-five when she decided she'd had enough so she painlessly, effortlessly and promptly found the man of her dreams. Just like that. Weird isn't it?

I knew that she was going to be able to hang up her fuck-me-and-that's-an-order thigh boots and chuck out the foundation and trowel when Sandra told me that she had told her new boyfriend all about her dreams and he had listened with rapt fascination. Well, I don't know about you, but in my experience the only dreams I ever find interesting are my own, and the only other person I would expect to be interested in my dreams would be my analyst. The guy was clearly hooked, hence the wedding and the hen night.

I was not invited to the hen night or in fact the wedding. Sandra had a full personality bypass operation soon after her engagement. It was very sad but not completely unexpected. She had arrived. The sole purpose of her existence had thankfully been achieved and no further effort to amuse and befriend would now be required. She stayed in, put her feet up and discussed her dreams, which fortunately interested her fiancé as she no longer had any other real-life material to fall back on. I know I sound mean, but I really do hope to God that I do not join the living dead when I become a member of Couples R Us.

Unsurprisingly, the hen night was a quiet night in with a chocolate penis, a couple of ribbed, colored condoms and a male stripper who didn't strip naked (it cost an extra £10 and was thus deemed an unnecessary extravagance). Apparently, Claudia did try to spice things up by offering to do a topless tit-shaking dance.

The good news, however, was that Claudia had got hold of a porn movie from her accountant for the evening and brought it around to me the next weekend.

I mentioned to a couple of friends that a porn night was planned and the videos soon started rolling in. It was amazing how many people had got hold of the most delightfully revolting films and I soon amassed an international collection of X-rated movies.

Thus, Claudia, Jasmin and I settle ourselves down for a quiet night of pot and porn. I suggest to Claudia and Jasmin that as we have a lot of chatting to catch up on (we've only spoken twice today) we should watch the film for five minutes or so, then keep it on as background viewing. I've spent nightmare evenings watching porn films with girlfriends before, as girls tend to watch them as if they were proper movies, i.e. from beginning to end and in silence which is crazy as they are normally incredibly boring with little or no plot and lousy dialogue. But this movie is something else; even I am silent for the next two hours as we just sit in my bed sighing wistfully and quietly moaning like the horny spinsters that we are. Jasmin seems to have a weak bladder as she keeps disappearing to the toilet, looking flushed but happy on her return. Gabriela soon joins us and every five minutes or so a hilarious observation is made and followed by raucous laughter. Gabriela's brother is staying with us and he asks us later in the week what was going on that Sunday night. He thought by the long periods of silence, sighing and laughter that perhaps we were playing charades.

I suppose I should not have been surprised that the film was so stimulating – it was German, and reluctant as I am to concede that the Germans are good at anything, they do make a damn fine porn movie. The participants are normally ugly as sin and somehow (don't ask me why, please), that just makes it all the more horny.

Word soon gets out that I've got a stash of porn movies (well, from me actually) and everyone feigns curiosity, medical interest, etc., and wants to join my video club. Business is booming. However, I soon get bored with the films and decide to branch out into magazines. Unfortunately, my main supplier is a lesbian-mad man and I therefore have limited choice. However, after constant badgering for a decent porn mag, he brings me a magazine of erotic stories divided into various categories. I skip past the chapters on infantilism, depilation, fetishes (sneezing and socks) and (yawn) lesbian sex, and I plump for exhibitionism and group sex. I've always been a social animal. It really is the perfect bedtime story book.

My bedroom is festering with some serious shakti energy: there're ugly Germans screwing on the telly, Ann Summers's toys under the bed and my bookmark is wedged between the chapters on bondage and editor's choice. I feel quite smug in my self-sufficient independence, but it is becoming apparent that a man is needed. Soon.

On the Friday night I have a date to see Gareth, some fresh blood that I met at a husband-hunting ball. Gareth is a good looking forty-year-old whose longest relationship has been with his psychotherapist who he has seen three times a week for the last nine years. Gareth is also a bit of a smoothie: charming and overwhelmingly sensitive. When I met him at the ball, he listened attentively to what I had to say while quietly considering a non-judgemental empathetic response that also invariably provided insight and wisdom. You might imagine that he is perfect boyfriend material. He is interesting: he has lived in different countries and his approach to life is genuinely inspiring. He seems to view it as an adventure, while following his heart and incorporating vast amounts of personal growth into his busy schedule. A smile is never far from his lips and he has the gift of easy laughter, which makes me feel that I am, indeed, really quite hilarious. He seems to understand women so well that he almost crosses the line from man to honorary woman. He sits on the boundary between the category of men you should fancy but for some strange reason you don't, and the category of men that would make fabulous boyfriends because you can talk to them about anything and they always seem to understand. In theory, of course, I want to meet a man who is in touch with his feminine side, but, in practice, I find it counter-productively unnerving and asexual. So, although I believe that he is a great catch, I am not sure whether I fancy him.

And, more importantly, I am not sure whether he fancies me. In the good old days, on being told that someone fancied me, I would reply, "Naturally, he's a man." Recent experience has knocked my confidence and my reaction these days is surprise followed by gratitude.

He is taking me for a Japanese meal and so although I'm not sure what direction I want the evening to take, I decide the best way forward is to dress for success. I look pretty hot that night and as I take an admiring look in the mirror, I think to myself that if this don't swing it, nothing will. The doorbell rings and I race down to open the door, ready to dazzle.

But instead of an appreciative once over, I get a bear hug and a kiss on both cheeks. This one could be an uphill struggle, and after the Donkey Bollocks episode, I'm not doing any more chasing. We have a pleasant evening and the chatter, although not fizzing with chemistry, is sufficiently animated to suggest that amiable companionship may be a more sensible way of approaching potential relationships for the thirty-plus age group. When we get back to my house, he parks the car and, without waiting to be invited in, he follows me up to my apartment. He has a hot lemon tea with honey, I have a melon vodka and we head for my boudoir, where I entertain all my guests (male and female).

As we are chilling out on the bed, he asks me what book I am reading at the moment. I hesitate as we all know what I've been reading, and then decide to come dirty and hand him my erotic letters magazine. He looks at me with interest and I can see that he has finally taken note of my seductive clothing.

I tentatively decide to find out whether he is seeing anyone at the moment and ask him if he is having an affair with someone who I actually know is a platonic friend of his. "Oh no," he says, "we're just friends." He should have stopped there but he goes on to add, "But I am sort of seeing someone else." My mask slips for a micro-second into a twisted grimace, but only for a micro-second, and I force a bright-eyed, bushy-tailed, slightly disinterested smile (this is extremely difficult, but I'm a professional pride merchant). I nevertheless decide to enquire further.

"Does 'sort of seeing someone' mean that you are emotionally involved and not sleeping with her *or* are you sleeping with her and not emotionally involved?" I ask. But the strain of putting on a devil-may-care attitude has taken its toll, and while he is answering I retreat into a mental sanctuary to recover from the impact of the revelation that I will not be having any action tonight. Never mind, I think, he is too old anyway and to be honest, the only ten-year age gap I am interested in is with a twenty-year-old and not a forty-year-old with a hairy ear problem.

And, of course, I am still praying for a funky Saturday night party.

Cockism

So here I am on Saturday afternoon, hammering away on the phone and beavering away in my address book, gagging for a party. I even go out and buy some new underwear in hopeful anticipation. A male friend tells me that men like cheap tarty underwear; gaudy pink fake satin, for example, so I compromise and buy a lilac lace set which is more expensive than it looks.

Five o'clock and still no sign of a party. Finally, at seven o'clock Jasmin comes up trumps. She's found a birthday party in town. I am initially optimistic until she tells me the name of the birthday boy. I vaguely know the guy. He loiters unwelcome in my memory as the guy with the worst pick-up line I've ever heard: "If we are both still on our own at the end of the evening, let's get it together." It took a while for the implication of what he'd said to sink in, so instead of coming back with a cutting retort, I simply smiled and agreed, although you will be pleased to hear that I did pair up with someone else and I smugly flounced past him at the end of the evening, new man in tow.

So, it's his birthday. Yuck. I know the crowd; the girls have blonde bouffant hair and square French-manicured fingernails, and the boys come up to my waist and lookswise we're talking German porn star standard (fine for sick fantasies, not OK for sitting outside cafés in Hampstead). And Mr. Charm, the birthday boy, is Nick's golfing partner, so I'm bound to bump into old Donkey Bollocks as well.

I ring my sister to ask for guidance and it turns out she's going too. There's absolutely nothing else doing, so I reluctantly agree to go. Once I've squeezed into my snakeskin hipster fake flares, please-fancy-me knee-length boots and slinky top that makes my double-D boobs look like the weapons they are, I'm actually in the mood to party. My new friend Gareth is invited on the condition that when we see Nick, he puts his arm protectively around me, gazes at me adoringly and laughs at everything I say.

"Will it be necessary for me to stick my tongue in your mouth?" he asks, with some relish.

"Yes," I reply briskly, "if the occasion demands it."

So, we are all set to go. I turn up at Jasmin's with a bottle of melon vodka, ready to party, and she's in turmoil. It turns out that she is wearing a G-string body stocking under her trousers and she is deeply concerned that when she dances the body stocking rises and reveals an inch of flesh above her trousers. She's flapping round her apartment desperately looking for some tape to stick the body stocking to her leg so that it doesn't shift.

"Why risk it with tape?" I inquire with impatience and suggest that she staple the body stocking to her leg and be done with it.

The doorbell rings and it's my rent-an-escort, Gareth, who looks suitably dashing. We run through the adoration procedure, swig a bit more vodka and pile into his car. The party is at some lame bar in the West End and, as predicted, there are no sexy men there to get the party adrenaline going. Well, there are some sexy men there but I've been out with most of them and the few remaining unknown sexy men are surrounded by bouffant blondes with square French-manicured fingernails. Even the Nick plan fails miserably when it turns out that the one person Gareth knows out of the two hundred party guests is a mutual friend of both his and Nick's who knows for a fact that I am not Gareth's new girlfriend. I decide within half an hour that I want to leave, but the others want to stay, much to my horror and incomprehension. Am I the only one with standards around here?

Jasmin mentions another party in Battersea, a friend of a friend. I've been to one of this guy's parties before and the male–female ratio is 80–20, which would be great were it not for the frighteningly overwhelming testosterone atmosphere. But tonight I reckon I can handle it. I find a couple of people who want to come with me and we get the hell out of there. When we get to the party in Battersea, I see a friend of Claudia's called Steve who is renowned for having the second biggest cock in Manchester. He is also a big drug user, which is strange as men with very big penises do not usually have any fundamental insecurities which they need to numb with drugs.

Folks, I have a confession to make here. Well, you know some people are sexist. And some people are racist and some are ageist. Well, I happen to be cockist. I like my cocks large and thick. "Don't we all!" you are saying. But the thing is, I'm very cockist. To the extent that the last time I thought I had found my soul mate and I discovered that he was peniley challenged, I seriously considered calling the whole thing off. Common sense prevailed and I continued with the relationship, but I did enter a period of mourning, followed by a period of resignation, and although we did have a fabulous sex life, I never really reached the acceptance stage. When the relationship finally ended, I comforted myself with the hope that my next soul mate would be great in bed and have a large penis (as well, of course, as being kind, intelligent, funny and sensitive).

I toy with the idea of seducing Steve, but I toy too long. He starts chatting up someone else, and Steve's friend assures me that within five minutes of Steve chatting to the woman they will be on the dance floor, and within five minutes of dancing they will disappear for the night and Steve will then not resurface for twenty-four hours.

His friend Rick and I decide to find a seat and rest our weary legs. It turns out Rick has just returned from a vacation in Goa that morning and decided to spice up an otherwise tedious flight by taking acid. He looks tired and he is not in a communicative state. This is a shame, as he really is quite sexy in a handsome but debauched druggy kind of way. He is short and stocky with a well-built manly frame, a closely cropped hairdo and a good-looking face, despite or perhaps because of the dark bags under his eyes and disheveled unshaven look. I have also just about given up on the evening and am too tired to try and persuade someone to fancy me. I slink further into the seat, mournfully reflecting on the sorry events of the evening.

Steve comes over to let us know he is hitting the dance floor with his new lady friend. Rick looks at his watch, raises his eyebrows and says, "I told you – five minutes exactly." There goes my chance of experiencing the second biggest cock in Manchester. It is time to go home.

Rick and I arrange to share a taxi. While I pick up my coat from the cloakroom, Rick rolls a joint outside. I notice with some surprise and a little alarm that he has started being nice to me. I quiver with excitement, then panic; I have forgotten how to respond to attentive men. I play it cool and decide to revert to my "I've only slept with one man and it wasn't very good" demeanor. It is not difficult; it has been a long time and I do feel coy. Actually, I enjoy feeling coy; it takes me back to my youth when I had a waiting list of guys eager to go out with me. Hang on – there is probably an important connection here. Innocence must be a turn-on, but with my knowing eyes, it's quite hard to fake unless you are dealing with someone whose perceptive powers have been substantially diminished by acid and pot.

Whilst we are in the taxi, he casually suggests that I come back to his house to chill out for a while. I am feeling very woozy from the joint by this stage and the thought of lying down is very appealing as long as I don't have to be active once I am lying down. In fact, I am out of my head and feel instinctively that any decision I make at this stage will probably be a bad one. I don't have my cell phone on me and anyway it would probably be inappropriate to ring my sister to ask her what *she* thinks I should do. Here is a chance to exorcise the porn demons with a real-life man, as requested by me in numerous heartfelt prayers to the Angel of Lust over the past ten days, and can you believe it, I'm wondering what to do. Do I go back to a sexy man's house on a Saturday night for sex and drugs, or do I go home to my hot water bottle and a porn movie?

I agree after some gentle persuasion to go back to his house, and I don't suppose the hesitation does me any harm in his eyes. Aren't men supposed to like a bit of a fight and it obviously supports my "I've only slept with one man and it wasn't very good" act. So we trundle into his house and I feel strangely relaxed and happy, considering I'm in a complete stranger's home and I'm out of practice. He apologizes for being a lousy host, which, in my book, is simply an excuse for being lazy and selfish.

I get the feeling he is summoning final emergency energy reserves to set the scene as he whizzes around the flat in that "I'd better do all this while I am still standing because when I lie down I don't think I'll be able to get up again" rush. Music, candles, incense, pot, whisky (maybe he's not such a lousy host after all?).

As we lie on his bed, we start talking for the first time since meeting two hours earlier. We chat easily. He is intelligent, interesting and he is making me laugh. This is an added bonus: I did not expect to like him. For the first time this evening, I am enjoying myself. Actually, really, *enjoying* myself – a foreign and strange sensation and all the more joyous for its rarity. I feel like a normal, attractive, sexually active person and think to myself, hey, I can do this too! It's quite easy.

We start kissing and the passion quickly mounts. Two weeks of porn fantasy and three months of celibacy unleashed, uninhibited by the pot and semi-naked in bed with a man. It's heaven. And I am so glad that I like him as a person as it doesn't feel like a mechanical exchange of body fluids. Suddenly he pulls away from me and huskily whispers, "I want to lick you." Before I have time to argue (who am I kidding?), he slides down the bed and pulls my panties to one side.

It is the best oral sex I have ever had in my life. He is absolutely incredible. He must have been a woman in a previous life. As I lay panting on his bed, recovering, I look at him with a mixture of gratitude, awe and respect. What a guy! What a host! The evening is really turning out very well indeed . . . I could not be happier.

As a sign of my gratitude I decide to return the favor, and the minute I put his cock in my mouth I want to go home. Immediately. His cock is not big enough, and due to being an ignorant cockist I completely stop fancying him. It is tragic. As I bob up and down, at least I have time to think, and he can't see the expression of horror on my face (there's enough room in my mouth to register an expression – that's how small it is).

Everything suddenly makes perfect sense to me. Of course, *that's* why he is so fucking brilliant at oral sex. *He has to be.* And he has got to do it first thing as well before anyone grabs his cock and leaves. Another piece of the jigsaw falls into place – the constant drinking and drug taking to cope with his understandable insecurity. Poor guy. If I was a man and I had a small cock I'd be on heroin.

I realize I have to wait a decent amount of time before throwing on my clothes and running out the door. I don't want to hurt his feelings, especially after he has been so kind to me, and I feel incredibly guilty, but I just have to get out of there.

I pretend I am freaked out by the intimacy and then I complain that I am freezing and tired. He gets the picture. I quickly get dressed like some shitty man running back to his wife after a sneaky lunch hour shag. As I run around his room looking for my bra there is a ring on the doorbell.

It's Steve. He tells us he didn't score with that woman after all.

Oh my God. I could have had the second biggest cock in Manchester instead.

Cumuppance

A few weeks pass and another Saturday night and its attendant party is looming. An outfit must be planned. A new, sexy, full-length silver skirt is acquired which, when worn with a G-string, gives a free-floating-buttock pantyless illusion. I team the skirt with a little red vest top and Nike slip-ons. Okay, so I look like a teenager but who cares. I think I look gorgeous.

I meet up with Jasmin, Karen and Claudia. Karen is a good friend of Jasmin and is great fun. Despite the fact that she is a beautiful, glamorous Jewish princess, she has a raucous sense of humor and is positively the crudest girl around, often making men blush with her explicit descriptions of her various sexual encounters. We set off to meet Steve (proud owner of the second biggest cock in Manchester) in a pub in Primrose Hill and then we all head off for the party fueled by a few tequila slammers to numb our fears of rejection and feelings of isolation. As we approach the party, Steve tells us that some friends of his will be there, one of whom, he says, with a grin on his face, I know.

Now, to be honest, I had actually suspected that Rick, King of Oral Sex, might be there, and after another three weeks of celibacy the idea of some top-class licky-licky seems very appealing. I decide I will see how I feel when I see him. Maybe I can overlook the rather delicate matter of his penis size and enjoy his remarkable skills instead. If the worst comes to the worst, I can always have sex with him in return. After all, I reason, I won't feel a thing. I have actually contemplated ringing him before on several occasions. When I told Jasmin what I was planning she suggested that I wait till I bumped into him one Saturday night. Well, tonight's the night.

We are all outside a club in Fulham: me, Steve, Jasmin, Karen and Claudia, and assorted friends of Steve including the King of Oral Sex himself. Steve makes the introductions and I look shyly at Rick who I last saw at 3 am three weeks earlier, looking bewildered as I bolted for the door.

As we make our way to a table in the club, Jasmin whispers to me that she thinks Rick is gorgeous. I must admit, he is really rather cute and perhaps I was foolish to have run out of his house that night. Never mind, I think, I'll make up for it tonight as I have already decided that I will *definitely* be going back to his place. We all chat and mingle and I can see him looking over at me out of the corner of my eye. I confidently whisper to Jasmin, "He's *crazy* for me and I'm going back with him tonight." Rick approaches and asks me what I would like to drink. It's a sure thing.

Only he ain't playing ball. As we sit opposite each other at a table in the corner of the bar, I ask him coyly, "Do you remember me?"

"I was wondering whether you would remember me. One minute we were having a wonderful evening, the next thing I knew you were bolting for the door. Why did you rush out on me like that?"

"I was freezing, I was tired, I felt emotional, I was incredibly hungry. Basically, I was far too stoned. I'm really sorry. All I wanted and all I could handle at that stage was my bed." I think it sounds very convincing, but Rick looks unimpressed.

"Anyway," he says, "I've had enough tonight. Now all I want is my bed. I'm going to get a taxi and go home."

Hang on a minute. Did he say he is leaving? He must mean he wants me to go with him. "Do you really want to leave now? Why don't we stay for another half an hour and then leave?"

A look of disdain crosses his face. "No. I want to leave now." And there's no suggestion that I leave with him. Something really strange is going on here. It appears that he is seriously planning to leave and go home to bed. Without me.

Out of nowhere a female friend of his suddenly appears and sits on his knee. Initially, I am anxious for her to leave so I can humiliate myself and plead with him to reconsider, but as they laugh and joke, I am glued to my chair, immobilized by a sickening sense of *déjà vu*: Nick coming around two days after a wonderful night together to tell me that it wasn't going to work out between us, Greg coming back from Spain to tell me he had a new girlfriend and would not be requiring my services any longer. Tom, the love of my life getting married. I could go on but I won't.

The thing that I find most difficult about life (and I admit I do find life something of an uphill struggle) is when situations don't go according to plan. I am supposed to be going back to Rick's tonight for some casual sex, and there he is walking out the door, looking defiantly triumphant.

I know logically that it is a sign of true maturity to accept that life does not always go according to plan and that the challenge of life is to take the rough with the smooth and that we learn from our suffering and that there are always people worse off and Que Sera blah blah. But it still annoys the fuck out of me. I am supposed to be rich, successful and adored by now. *What is going on around here?* It isn't supposed to be like this. Someone, somewhere, anyone, anywhere, must surely want to come back for more?

So here I am, slumped once again in a chair at a party on a Saturday night wondering how I manage to fuck up so consistently. I must come to terms with my cockism before I attract someone with a penis the size of a toothpick so that I am forced by the Universe to learn my karmic lesson. But it's not just my cockism; I fear it may be more serious. I think I may need a complete personality transplant. The one I've got at the moment doesn't seem to work very well.

As I sit absorbed in disbelief at the evening's outcome, someone, a man, is hovering around me. Without any encouragement from me, he proceeds to come on to me. I really cannot be bothered to start all over again with someone new at this stage of the evening, particularly someone with no proven track record in oral sex. He's chatting away to me and although I am looking at his mouth moving up and down, I am miles away and I hear nothing. After a while his mouth stops moving and I guess from the expression on his face that he has asked me a question. I switch off the self-recriminations and turn my attention to him.

"Look, I'm really sorry, but I haven't been listening to a word you've been saying. I am afraid that at the moment I cannot focus on a word anyone is saying as I am currently coming to terms with the fact that I will not be having the best oral sex of my life tonight as planned and expected." He gets a quick résumé of the Rick situation.

"I am absolutely brilliant at oral sex," he assures me. "I bet you that I am much better than Rick."

"How do you know?" I ask. "Have you competed at national level? Anyway, I can only find out who is better by setting a practical examination."

He nods enthusiastically. "I would be more than happy to undertake a practical. What time does the exam start?"

"Before I enter you as a candidate, there is a small matter of basic entry requirements. In my experience, the men that are really talented at oral sex have got small cocks. They hone their oral sex skills to perfection to make up for the fact that their cocks aren't big enough. It's the small cock compensation theory," I explain.

"That theory doesn't apply to me. My penis is massive."

"Well then," I remark dryly, "perhaps we can do business."

For those of you shocked by the intimate nature of our conversation, please be aware that we are both quite drunk and I'm in one of my "I don't give a shit" moods. Perversely, I am rather good company and wish I could meet someone as entertaining as me, although this guy is doing pretty well. We have an animated discussion on what makes oral sex good. He tells me that he loves it and can go on for hours; I point out that this is meaningless as he may love it but nevertheless be crap and his stamina will therefore be counterproductive. There's nothing worse than someone giving it all they've got and, meanwhile, all you want is a cigarette break.

I end up confessing that I actually give the best blowjobs in town and I give him three very good reasons why:

1. I have sucked my thumb every night for the last thirty years and I am therefore an experienced sucker. My sucking muscles are basically what you would call toned and are thus perfect for imitating the walls of a fifteen-year-old's vagina.

2. I used to be a man in many previous lives and therefore know exactly what I would like.
3. I love it.

It is at this point that he introduces himself to me. "I'm Mark, by the way. Would you like to come home with me tonight?"

"I'll let you know at the end of the evening," is all I will commit to at this stage.

I mull over Mark's business proposition with Jasmin and Claudia over a couple of tequila slammers. I quickly weigh up the pros and cons. On the plus side, he is lively, intense and completely unfazed by my brazen hussy act. He asked me if I wanted to know why he fancied me. "Was it because you heard I had the cunt of a fifteen-year-old?" I asked.

"No," he said, "it was your smile."

Now, I don't care if compliments like that are true or false. You're never really going to know in the beginning whether you are being spun a line or not, so predicting motives at this early stage is pretty pointless. You will only really know for sure whether all the lines were bullshit once you have had sex. And in fact, you can narrow that down to the five-minute period after you've had sex. If within that five minutes they are up and dressed and cheerily waving you goodbye, you know you've been had good and proper.

Even then, one or two can pass that hurdle only for you to discover that this type are even worse. They stay for a cozy breakfast, continue to charm delightfully and then wave goodbye, promising to ring. OK, so he doesn't ring the next day, he doesn't want to be too keen. That's fine. It's forgivable but let's be honest, it's not ideal. The second day that passes without a call, you're surprised but still hopeful. Another day passes and a weary resignation sets in. Day Four is anger day, the fucking bastard. Once the official five-day waiting game is over and you've lost, you realize you would have been better off with the honest user who left first thing. And the funny thing is, he is normally a better shag anyway.

Personally, I like men who actually bother to pay you a compliment. And believe me, there are plenty of guys out there who don't realize how far a little charm, flattery and a well-timed compliment can take them. If you are going to sink to the depths and have a one-night stand you might as well be told by the guy that you are beautiful, desirable, great fun and give the best blowjob in town. And if only Englishmen realized this, as their Italian counterparts do, they would actually get a better performance out of you. At work, managers are told to give positive feedback to staff as it makes commercial sense – the staff will work harder and be more productive. The same principles apply in bed.

So this guy Mark pays compliments, and as explained above, I like this. Some people are unable to accept compliments and I have always thought this rather sad. Why deny yourself the luxury of basking in someone's admiration? Enjoy, respond and spread a bit of happiness, that's what I say.

Ooh, I've got a nice smile. You see, even a relatively mild compliment like that can work wonders. See guys, it's so much easier than you think. We like our men nice, thoughtful and charming with only the tiniest dash of bastard for a little added bite.

However, with all this said, I still tell him that I am going home alone. But he is rewarded with my telephone number and a confirmatory goodbye-see-you-again kiss.

The fact is that I've got a headache and I've had more than enough excitement for one night. I need to be alone to mourn the disappointment of Rick not wanting a rerun with me. Jasmin and I get a cab home and in the car I have a good wail. Jasmin's not much help. When I try and dwell on the positive side of his rejection, namely the fact that his cock is tiny and he takes so many drugs, she tells me she could happily live off fantastic oral sex. Oh God, I cry, I think I could have put up with it too. With the onset of summer, I imagine languid pantyless boat journeys up a river, walks in the woods and alfresco 69s.

Shit.

How could I be so shortsighted? I didn't have to marry the guy. A fling is just what I need before my planned forthcoming sessions with a new therapist will make me fit for a real relationship. Let's face it, there is no way I can have a meaningful relationship until I have been completely reprogrammed.

Listen to me, wallowing like a victim. It's not too late, I tell myself. I'll ring him and charm him back. He's been hurt and I'll kiss him better. I'll make it up to him. His pride has been hurt and a bit of groveling from me will surely help. So, it's one all at the moment. He's made his point. But I can change all that.

I tell Jasmin that I'm going to ring Steve and that I'm going to get Rick's number. I've made a terrible mistake. I've been a bitch and I've been punished, but it can't end like this. I want a second chance.

I decide to leave it until Monday evening to make the call. I don't want to appear sad, mad and demented by ringing within twenty-four hours. Early Monday evening, Jasmin calls me.

"You are never going to guess who has left a message on my answering machine."

"Who?" I ask excitedly.

"Rick. He's left a message. Last night. Asking me to give him a call."

I am delighted. He has obviously been having the same thoughts about me. He has punished me and now he is ringing her for my phone number. I excitedly tell Jasmin my theory.

"Listen sweetheart, that is possible. But I mentioned to Karen that he called and she thought that he might be calling for her."

"Why?" I ask. "Why on earth should he be calling for her? They barely spoke to each other at the party on Saturday night." I feel a bit queasy.

"Well, they did speak for five minutes and she thought he was pretty gorgeous actually. The truth of it is that I don't know why he was calling, but I'll ring Steve to find out."

"Well ring him *now*," I say. "I *need* to know."

Steve is out and she leaves a message. Needless to say, I wait up all night for her call but hear nothing. I go to bed feeling a little forlorn but am comforted by the fact that as my feelings are so strong, his must be too.

Jasmin and I speak the following evening. I skip the pleasantries.

"Have you heard from Steve yet? Has Rick called again?"

"No, I've not heard from either of them."

"Look," I say, losing patience, "why don't you just ring Rick up and find out what, or should I say who, he wants?"

"I just haven't had time to call him back."

"But it would only take a minute," I start to whine. "How can you be so mean and selfish? Please just find the time and ring Rick back and put me out of my misery."

She eventually gives in and agrees to ring Rick. He is out too so she leaves a message.

Another waiting game.

I am quietly confident, but due to the unpredictability of life I do not want to be conscious while I wait, so at 8:30 pm

I take two sleeping tablets and down three herbal tranquilizers (the label says one to two tablets, but I reckon my complicated sex life warrants an extra tablet, just to be on the safe
side). I am asleep by 9:00 pm.

When I wake the next morning, I feel wired. I will know
today whether I have fucked up and whether this God bloke
really has it in for me. I go shopping during my lunch hour
and find myself trying on outfits that will look good on
languid pantyless boat journeys up a river. I hold up something sexy, look at myself dreamily in the mirror and wonder
whether Rick will like me in it. I decide to act hopeful for
once. This is going to be my lucky break. This time, the toss
of the coin will turn up heads rather than tails for me.

After lunch, I ring Jasmin.

"I'll get straight to the point. Have you heard from Rick
yet?"

"I can't talk right now, I'm with a colleague," she tells me.
So fucking what? I think. Just put me out of my misery.

"Well, have you spoken to Rick or Steve?" I ask, my
aggression slipping out.

"Rick," she says, "but listen, can I ring you later? It's difficult to talk right now."

I'm beginning to run out of patience.

"Look," I say, "just tell me. All you need to say is one
word. Did he call for me or Karen?"

"Karen," she says.

I then have to reassure her that of course Karen must go
out with him. No, I don't mind. No, really. It's just one of
those things. He obviously likes Karen and not me. What can
you do?

It kills me, but tell me, what can I do, realistically? I

cannot veto Karen seeing him. That would look really sad and you can't get away with the "him or me" ultimatums at this age, and besides, although I am friendly with Karen and have known her for some time, she is really Jasmin's friend and owes me no loyalty in this department whatsoever. We're supposed to be desperate and so you take it where you can. Dates are few and far between. Apparently, Karen fancies him too. I had my turn with him. I fucked up. Now it's her turn. She has the advantage of being pre-warned as I have told her about his small cock. No nasty shocks for her at three in the morning. She's been emotionally prepared by yours truly. Well, I suppose it's nice to have been useful. The night I spent with him served some purpose. Although I must admit, I didn't imagine for one minute it would have been to do the groundwork for a relationship between Rick and Karen.

I just cannot believe the fucking shit irony of it. Not only does he tell me to piss off; OK, fine, I can deal with that. All right, he meets someone else; not ideal, but I don't need to know about it. But now that he has asked Karen out I do know about it, and what's worse, I'll have to hear all about it and, most difficult of all, act pleased, or at the very least unconcerned when I next see her. Now tell me, is that unlucky or what? It occurs to me that he is calling her as some type of sick revenge on me. But Karen is beautiful – and great company, and she can match me blow for blow on the old cock-sucking technique. She once demonstrated her know-how on a vibrator for us one evening around at Jasmin's, and let me tell you, she knew *exactly* what she was doing. She even taught this old dog some new tricks. The girl's a pro, believe me. He'll soon get over his unpleasant experience with me.

I'm beat. I lost out again. *And it's all my fault.*

You will, I'm sure, be delighted and not at all surprised to hear that Karen's date with Rick went very well. When I accidentally bumped into her at Jasmin's flat she asked me whether I wanted to hear about it. A mixture of masochism and intense curiosity made me unable to say no. Apparently, he'd taken her out for dinner to a lovely restaurant in Notting Hill. The evening ended up in her apartment with them chatting, smoking and bonding. I can't tell you more, as I'd be breaking a confidentiality agreement, but suffice it to say he asked to see her again and his dick was reported to be a respectable length and width. Karen had undertaken some research on the subject and had been informed (accurately, it transpired) that acid reduces a man's penis substantially.

When I left Jasmin's place that night, I felt like a boiling kettle whose off switch was broken. Busily boiling away, fuming, puffing and steaming out of control until I feared an electrical explosion. Get me to a therapist. Quick. I think that poisonous thing lodged in my heart is spreading. It's grown two heads and is pregnant with twins.

Look Nice, Be Nice, Go Home

Mark, the oral sex guy I met at the party, calls me on Wednesday night. Do I want to go out Friday? Why not? I need cheering up.

He's picking me up at eight o'clock. I'm quite looking forward to it as we had a good laugh on the phone, but due to a possible lack of physical attraction (he's a wee bit wide and bald), I'm not sick with nerves. It makes a nice change. Anyway, I only have one beta blocker left and I'm saving it for an emergency.

We go to a bar and he gets me drunk. I can get a bit weird when I'm bombed and I think I might be losing him when I start telling him that lately I've been wishing I was a man and fantasizing about fucking fifteen-year-old girls with short skirts that I see on the bus. I realize I may have misjudged the mood slightly and revealed a little too much of my shadow side. In fact, he looks rather alarmed at my confession and I fear another "no thanks" at the end of the evening. I must do something fast. This cannot happen to me again. I refuse to be rejected by anyone else, especially someone less attractive than me. So I surprise him by lunging at him across the table with a passionate kiss on the lips. He responds (thank you, God). I've made a comeback.

He celebrates by buying me another drink which I then, in my drunken clumsiness (or whatever Freudian reason you want to come up with), spill over him. I tell him it's time to go and before I know what's happening, we're in a taxi on the way to his place.

The minute we get inside his apartment I become a bitch. I don't know why I do it. I have no control over it. I know I'm doing it; I can hear myself, cold, indifferent and, worse, taunting. I make a mental note to consider this behavior pattern in the privacy of my own head the next day. It could be an important clue as to why I have been single for so long. Who knows? Just a thought.

He remains nice, however, and even though I'm not sure if I fancy him, I am drunk and horny and therefore soon find myself naked and sucking his huge cock. He didn't lie about the cock. It is magnificent. This is more like it, I think, as my lips are stretched to capacity. He was, however, sadly mistaken about being better than Rick at oral sex. There is no contender to the throne after all.

I feel remarkably relaxed in his company, and as we lie entwined in each other's arms I feel warm, snug and comfortable. So when I get up to leave at about 2 am, he expresses dismay that I do not wish to stay the night with him.

"Please don't go," he says. "Spend the night with me."

"I'm sorry but I just cannot understand why someone would want to spend the night in bed with a stranger," I tell him. "For a start, what if they snore?"

"'They' don't snore," he reassures me.

"No one owns up to snoring and I have an overwhelming fear of lying next to a snorer at four-thirty in the morning, wide awake and resentful as hell that the person is fast asleep, blissfully unaware that it is *his* defective nasal passages that are keeping me awake. And, of course, I can't get up to leave at four-thirty in the morning or I look all weird and anal. 'Just go to sleep,' they say impatiently. 'Aren't you tired?' But I just lie there, too sullen to answer so that when morning comes, I hate their guts, no matter how many wonderful orgasms they gave me the night before. Anyway, even with the best case scenario of all-night sex sessions and confessional intimacy, the next day is a complete wipe out as I'll be completely exhausted."

"That doesn't matter. We can just chill out in bed together tomorrow."

I look at him as if he is nuts.

"What?" I ask incredulously. "You mean not leave straight after breakfast?" Weird.

He orders me a cab.

"I'll ring you on Tuesday or Wednesday, unless you want to ring me tomorrow." he tells me.

"Get real," I tell him. "I'll speak to you when *you* ring *me*."

I get a disturbing call midweek from an ex-blind date, Lawrence, who wants his socks back. He'd lent me a pair a couple of months ago when I'd been chilling out in his apartment and my feet were cold. Where do these people come from? This man lives in a five-bedroom mansion flat in Mayfair, filled with *objets d'art*, and he is prepared to ring me two months after we officially cease contact (I hadn't returned his third message and he officially got the message) for a pair of lousy socks. Well, to be fair, they aren't lousy at all.

They are actually really nice, thick, gray woolen socks and he's not getting them back. Especially as he'd failed the friendship test I'd set him.

Lawrence and I were set up on a blind date and the minute I set eyes on him I knew for a fact that we had absolutely no chance of a future together, however good his personality turned out to be. He just wasn't my type. He was blond and I like dark. He was tall and I like short. He was slim and I like solid. He had a smattering of golden chest hair (this is a wild guess, by the way), and I like a pelt. I just did not fancy him and a relationship was therefore not up for negotiation. The good news was that he was a gynecologist and I reckoned he could be a useful person to know. In addition to which he was one of those people with a view on everything, which made him great company.

And he also professed to adore me and it was about time I had a bit of adoration in my life. In return, his life got to feature me and my wit occasionally. I thought it was a fair deal. Only problem was that he became a bit soppy, despite the fact that I told him fair and square after the first date that although I was flattered that he fancied me, I did not feel the same way about him. Admittedly, he hadn't actually told me that he fancied me, I just assumed that he did. I was right. But given the option, he declared he was prepared to settle for a platonic friendship.

Anyway, as I said, he was getting a bit on the sad side, wanting to hold my hand in the cinema, trying to kiss me good night on the lips, and even daring to make suggestive comments about physical intimacy with me. I laughed along for a while. I did not want to be cruel by brutally explaining that I was not sexually attracted to him as I know how much this can hurt. I thought it was obvious when he pounced on me one night while we were watching TV on his sofa and my lips and legs automatically clenched tightly shut. The flattering comments, once so gratefully received, were rapidly losing their charm and he had become irritating. It was time to say goodbye. A platonic friendship was clearly not going to work.

I gave him an ultimatum one night on the phone. It was unplanned but nonetheless it worked a treat.

"Lawrence. I have an interesting proposition for you. You have a choice of two situations. Think carefully before you choose. You can either (a) continue with my friendship but there can be no more innuendoes, attempted hand holding or clumsy lunging. In fact, with this option, mere talk about our possible future together would thereafter be forbidden. Or you can go for option (b) where we have sex once and never see or speak to each other again."

I was interested to hear his choice. I could practically hear him stiffen with excitement at the thought of option (b). The breathing quickened and he was obviously not going to need any time to mull it over. A weak, hesitant voice piped up, "Please can I go for option (b)?" Every man I have since told this story to knew without hesitation which option Lawrence chose.

"That's interesting, but disappointing," I said. "Of course, I'm sure you realized the whole exercise was hypothetical, but it seems that, nonetheless, you are not interested in my friendship at all, all you want is one quick opportunist fuck."

He started blathering, but my point had been made.

"Well, goodbye, I have to go now," I said. "See you around."

★　★　★

Mark calls and I tell him a guy I knew briefly has just rung me to ask for his socks back. He cringes at the story and we agree the guy is a little on the sad side.

"What did you get up to at the weekend?" he asks.

"Well, on Friday night I went out on a date with this guy called Mark who took me out for a drink but not for dinner, then shamelessly got me drunk, and when I was feeling weak and vulnerable he lunged at me in a public bar."

"What happened next?" he asks.

"It's all a bit of a blur," is all I will say. "What did you get up to over the weekend?"

"Well, I also went out on a date with this girl who borrowed my sweater. She pretended she was cold, but I knew it was just an excuse to wear my sweater. Then she leaned over to kiss me – it was more of a lunge actually – and I felt kind of duty-bound to respond."

"Didn't you want to respond?" I ask.

"The thing was that she was wearing my sweater and I wanted to make sure I got it back that night as I didn't want to be one of those sad fucks who rings up weeks later to ask for its return. It was quite funny actually as the girl thought I was checking out her tits, but all I was really doing was staring at my lovely sweater, desperately thinking how I could get it back without ripping it off her. I decided the safest thing would be to invite her back and then at least I would ensure that the sweater got home safely."

"Of course," I add, "that explains why you were so anxious to rip the sweater off her the minute she got into the apartment."

"That was, of course, the reason. I want to see her again this Friday. Do you think she'll say yes?"

"Actually, I think she will."

The scenario with Mark feels strange. We've been out on

a date and he still seems to like me. In fact, he wants to see me again. I am not quite sure what I am doing right. Then I remember Gabriela's top tips for alluring men and I realize that I've unwittingly been following them with Mark. The tips certainly work for her, and after the fifth bouquet of flowers arrived for her within two months, I begged her for her secrets. I get a lesson a day and so far we're up to number five:

1. Listen to what they say and be enthusiastic and interested. I've always screwed up on this one as I'm too busy trying to dazzle them with my personality. OK, right, so I need to let them shine. Could be frustrating but I'll give it a go. Gabriela, on the other hand, appears to be totally fascinated by the minutiae of a love object's life, asking detailed questions, listening intently to the answers and then probing further. It is not until later that she confides in me, "Oh why are the rich good-looking ones *so* boring?"

2. Let the child within you come out. Be playful and cute. I think I remember how to do cute. This one is easier for Gabriela who is small, bendy and blonde and whose Czech accent and grammatical errors are disarmingly child-like.

3. Don't care. This one is hardest to fake. It's alright for Gabriela who has reluctantly decided that men's main charms are sexual and financial, while I am still searching for a Prince Charming to make everything OK.

4. Flirt. I like its simplicity.

5. Compromise.

I think tip number five might be even harder for me than tip number 3. I've waited this long for Mr. Right to turn up and I'm not about to start dropping my standards. I have trawled through enough crap, I am really not happy about settling for anything less than perfection. I'm not shallow; they don't have to be rich or good-looking. But they *must* be funny, intelligent, sensitive, cultured, kind, sharp, (preferably) Jewish, popular, socially integrated, non-possessive, easy going, accepting of me and my past, able to deal with my neurosis and chronic insecurity, reasonably well dressed, sophisticated, generous, well read, not too druggy but into the occasional dabble with pot and coke, excellent at sex, with a high sex-drive and, of course, at least an average-sized cock. Now, you tell me, are any of these requests unreasonable? Isn't each of these qualities essential? How can I compromise? It's not like I'm desperate. Listen, really, I'm not.

Actually, Gabriela is so successful that she's now having to turn suitors away. I ask if I can finish with one of her boyfriends for her. I've been dying to do some dumping for a change and I reckon some vicarious rejection is just what the doctor ordered. She's only too happy to relinquish the burden of breaking another man's heart, especially as she detests confrontation. I realize I am in a stronger bargaining position than I originally thought. I suggest that she does my bathroom cleaning rota for a week and, in return, I'll get that dickhead Robert off her case. She thinks it's a fair deal and she asks me what I'm going to say. I want to go for the jugular, not being at all squeamish about confrontation myself and determined to enjoy the experience of telling a man to piss off. I offer to explain that he is crap in bed, his spunk is bitter-tasting and that Gabriela wants to cease all contact with him before he puts her off sex for good. She likes its accuracy and agrees it will be effective. He will be unlikely to bother her again.

But, of course, it's all talk. I want my own man to dump. And the irony is that I think I've found him. And guess what, the thought of it is making me ill. I actually don't want to hurt this guy's feelings. What the hell is going on? I've been dying to do a bit of rejecting for a while yet I can't seem to bring myself to do it. Yes, Mark is good fun, he's lovely to me, I can be myself with him, he makes me laugh, but I just don't fancy him. Even with a cock that would put a German porn star to shame.

We go out to dinner on the Friday night and I just feel sad that here is a guy who appears to really like me, but whom I just don't fancy. Apart from anything else, Jasmin very kindly called me before Mark picked me up to give me an update on how wonderfully things are going between Rick and Karen. By the time Mark arrived, I was seething once again with anger and bitterness.

As we sit in the restaurant, he asks me what is up. I cruelly tell him that I am still pissed off about the Rick situation and basically how I feel the whole thing is completely unfair.

Look, even I realize that telling a guy who has kindly taken you out for dinner that you would much prefer to be with someone else is slightly cruel, but at least I am following Gabriela's tip of not giving a shit. And the whole point is that even if I am unsure, I have to try and keep him keen (a) in case I change my mind and start falling for him too, and (b) so that *he* doesn't end up rejecting me. And there's no point saying, "What a bitch," because all the women I know are exactly the same: you must keep them sweet. Just in case.

I feel completely in control over dinner as I sit opposite this doey-eyed guy, who, it seems to me, cannot help falling in love with me. We discuss game playing.

"Do you believe in playing games with women?" I ask.

"I'm definitely anti," he says.

"Well, to quote Seinfeld – "If you don't play games, how do you know who's winning?"

"Who is winning at the moment?" he asks.

"Me, obviously," I reply.

"What's the prize for winning?" he asks.

I consider his question. "Going home alone," I reply triumphantly.

I must admit, as I hear myself say the words, winning doesn't seem such a great option after all.

Despite the fact that I do not fancy him, I realize that these aren't the signals that I am giving out. When we get back to my place from the restaurant, we go straight to my bedroom. My skin-tight trousers are giving me a stomachache they are so tight and my crotch area is so hot and sweaty you could base an hour-long wildlife program on the flora multiplying in my G-string. So within minutes of sitting on my bed, I tug off my trousers and, naturally, my panties just seem to peel away with them. So, although I don't fancy him, we end up having sex anyway.

Left Luggage

Despite, or perhaps because of, my new involvement with Mark, I have dreamt about Tom every night for the last two weeks, and in each and every dream he rejects me. The setting and circumstances of each dream are different, but I always get dumped in the end. I suppose this is better than dreaming that we are together again, as the moment of reality upon awakening would be too painful. Maybe if *I* got to dump *him* in the odd dream that would be OK, but it never happens. It's a real bore being rejected every night and I decide that I must undertake some demanding emotional work to deal with the demons left by Tom.

I met Tom, the love of my life, when I was eighteen and we were together for six years. Meeting the love of my life was so easy that I assumed that when we broke up I could just go out and find another one.

As we know, it has not been quite that straightforward. I am beginning to doubt whether I will ever find that kind of magic again. Perhaps I am lucky to have found such a special love once in my life and I should be grateful for that; I am sure many people never experience it at all. But I just feel that now I know what it is like to feel the intensity of true love and passion, I just can't settle for second best. Then I ask myself whether everyone who is not Tom will be second best. Is it true that you only have one true love in your life? In which case should I just give up now?

Of course, I was a different person when I met him. Then I was innocent, trusting, open and vibrant. Although I already had emotional baggage, it was more of a handy travel vanity case as opposed to the crates of pain and paranoia now lodged in cold storage.

I reckon the reason I have accumulated so much baggage is that I do not deal with pain as and when it arises. Instead, you may have noticed, I put on a brave face, convince myself that the man in question is too screwed up, too old, too hairy and/or his cock too small and I am better off without him. But the truth of it is that I don't think I can handle the pain. I don't think I will survive it. Perhaps I will fall into the depths of a dark depression never to return as a fully functioning individual. Or maybe, in my darkest moments, I believe that I will literally not survive − I won't be able to carry on and suicide will seem the only sensible answer to a life filled with disappointment and rejection.

When I was seventeen, I met a guy, Greg, who although way above me on the social register in terms of looks, popularity and coolness, took a real shine to me. None of the bitches at school could understand why he was going out with me and they kindly took it upon themselves to write me letters to tell me as much. I didn't even know if I liked him and I wasn't actually sure that I fancied him after I watched him cut a large piece of dead skin from the sole of his foot one afternoon and proudly pin it up on the notice board in his bedroom. But I was certainly flattered and it was great fun pissing off the school bitches.

A couple of months after we met, he went away for a month on his summer vacation to Marbella. My own summer was a little less glamorous due to the fact that I spent it working in the laundry department of a home for the elderly where I developed acne on my forehead from daily exposure to steamed piss-soaked underwear. The only thing that kept me going that month was the return of my beloved boyfriend from the playground of the rich and beautiful. I counted the days.

I guessed that our reunion was not going to be quite as pleasurable as anticipated when he canceled twice at the last minute. When we finally did meet he informed me that there would be a slight change in the dating arrangements. He explained that in Marbella he had met a rich and beautiful girl who, unfortunately (for him), lived outside London. He therefore proposed that we continue to see each other during the week but unfortunately (for me) he would be unavailable at weekends as he would be visiting his other girlfriend in the country. He was either insane with arrogance or clever enough to maneuver a constructive dismissal (whereby you treat someone so badly that they are left with no alternative but to resign). I resigned.

When he left, I ran up to my bedroom and weighed up the options. I could either (a) collapse with disappointment, cry and confront the fact that I had spent a month yearning for an arrogant asshole, or (b) not let that arrogant asshole be responsible for one precious tear and remove all trace of him completely from my mind.

I remember consciously deciding to take route (b). And I've taken route (b) ever since. Except that while I may have managed to expunge an arrogant asshole with strange taste in bedroom decor from my mind, in retrospect, what with the recurrent dreams of rejection by Tom, it may not have been the most sensible response to the breakup of a six-year relationship with someone I loved with all my heart and soul.

When I did split with Tom (he met someone else, by the way) I refused to admit to myself or anyone else that I was the slightest bit upset: the break up was mutual; I would find someone else quite easily; it was time to spread my wings; we were very different people; I didn't like his sister, he was the wrong religion, he had done me a favor.

Instead I came down with chronic bronchitis and lost my voice. I did not connect the breakup with the illness. After I eventually recovered from the bronchitis, I picked myself up, dusted myself down and I'm still trying to start all over again.

So, here is the task I have set myself: to cry, to mourn the end of a relationship. Six years late admittedly, but – it seems – inescapable. The pain has become poisonous inside me and needs to be expressed, experienced and, if all goes according to plan, released once and for all.

To start the process I go to my parents' house to collect photos of Tom and grocery bags stuffed full of love letters from him, all festering in a box under my old bed. I am convinced that sitting and reading and remembering will lead me to the Land of Tears where I bravely plan to check in for some time before I consider release and redemption. I will complete the cycle by entering the mourning stage.

As soon as I have the letters and photos in my possession I feel as if a sharp, heavy object is lodged in my chest. As I sit on my bed, sifting through the bags, memories come flooding back to me.

Our first kiss. We were both at a student party. I was wearing a red dress and he called me "my scarlet love." It sounded so romantic that I pretended I was drunk so that he wouldn't feel shy about taking advantage of me. As we kissed on the stairs, with people jostling around us, he moved my face to one side and kissed me gently on the lips. He then stopped and held my face in his hands as he kissed from another angle. I thought the interruptions were adorable but infuriating as I just didn't want to stop kissing him, even for a second.

The first night I spent with him I woke up in his arms and, while he was still sleeping, I leant over and gently kissed him on his chest. I felt his arm around me pull me close to him, and he said softly, "That's the nicest way I have ever been woken up." I remember that feeling of joy, trust and the excitement of new beginnings with such clarity and tender-ness that it hurts me. From that night on we always slept entwined.

Tom had to get up early on Sunday mornings to play foot-ball. We were living on the same campus at University and I decided that after spending one Saturday night apart I would bring him breakfast in bed. I got up early, borrowed a tray, prepared a bowl of cornflakes, some toast, a little jar of flowers and bought the Sunday papers. I then carried the tray over to his hall of residence. The place was like a ghost town. No one surfaced before midday on a Sunday and I sped through the campus with this tray, grateful no one could see me.

As I approached Tom's door, I practically collided with the football team captain who was about to hammer on the door to get him out of bed. I suddenly felt embarrassed and shy and asked him to take the tray in for me while I scurried off back to bed. He was too taken aback to say no, and Tom awoke that Sunday morning in a state of confusion. Instead of being woken by an irate football player banging on his door shouting obscenities, the guy knocked on his door and brought him a tray with breakfast, flowers and the Sunday papers.

The first time he told me he loved me, it was the most conditional declaration of love I'd ever heard, but still the most beautiful. We'd been together only a month or so and we were lying on the bed facing each other. I could see that he looked slightly puzzled and asked him what was going on. He said to me, "You know I really like you . . ."

"Yes," I replied smiling, encouraging him to continue.

"Well, I think I might be beginning to love you a little bit."

He thought, he wasn't sure. He might be, but he might not. He was only beginning to, not quite there yet. And it was only a little bit. But I knew. And he knew. He did love me. And I loved him too.

That was the strange thing about our relationship. The love crept up on us, surprising us both. When my friends heard that we had got it together, I remember everyone saying, "We give it a week." I thought pretty much the same myself. I had a boyfriend in London who I thought I was crazy about. Going out with Tom was an experiment for me; I had never dated a non-Jewish guy before and thought I would try a few out before settling down after college to married life in Hendon. I thought he was incredibly cute and that our relationship would be short and sweet.

There were loads of gorgeous guys at University and I thought I could have the pick of the bunch. In fact, I kept a list of guys that fancied me which was very embarrassing when news of the list got out and guys wanted to find out if they were on the list and kept coming up to me to ask whether they fancied me. My plan was to have a couple of flingettes then settle down with a nice Jewish guy. How could

I know that I was going to fall in love with the first one I met and that twelve years later I would not have met anyone else to match him?

I loved him with such passion and intensity that even after six years together I was still flustered with excitement each time I saw him. I don't think he felt the same way at all during the last year, only I didn't want to see it at the time. I now think Tom had been trying to get rid of me for a while, but as he was one of those people who are terrified to be single for five minutes, he cleverly lined up a successor before removing the present incumbent. He told me one sunny Sunday afternoon that we weren't making each other happy anymore, and then he told me that he had fallen in love with somebody at work and said he hoped we could be friends.

I still feel a numb pain and anger that he has moved on and met someone else. He's even had the cheek to marry her, so I hear. But as I sit with the letters, poems and photos there are no tears. Nothing. Perhaps it's too late. My friends all have their suggestions: Gabriela urges me to get rid of what she calls "the pus" by seeing a therapist; Jasmin says I'm morbid and I should leave the past behind and move on. She points out that she cried her eyes out when she split up with her long-term boyfriend and look where it got her – she's still single. Claudia comes around to read the letters with me and *she* ends up crying. Karen suggests watching the film *Ghost* to oil the tear ducts while Matt suggests pinning pictures of Tom around the kitchen and peeling onions.

I decide to follow the therapy route, despite my last experience when I cried in therapy and the counselor told me to stop being so self-pitying and pull myself together. Gareth recommends a lady who he assures me is compassionate and won't shout at me.

Fucked Up and Mad

I wake up on Tuesday and jump out of bed filled with a rare *joie de vivre*. I am so excited, I can't wait for the day to begin . . . I've got a sizzling hot date tonight at 7 pm. With my brand new therapist. I am ready to let the healing begin.

I've got it all worked out. Explain about the Tom blockage, get the therapist to make me cry, mope for a month maximum, and then watch out guys, the new me will be unleashed. A new model, baggage-free.

I confidently predict that it should take about four sessions, and at £35 an hour I'll soon recoup the outlay. I mean, dinner for two at a nice restaurant is equal to the cost of two sessions. And once I have a boyfriend I won't have to do all the driving – halving my gas costs per year is worth at least all four sessions. Let's just say it's an investment, in every sense of the word.

The first time I saw a therapist was about six years ago when I was twenty-four. I had a few tricky things going on in my life, what my friend Paresh, who is a personal motivator, calls "challenges."

I once spoke to Paresh after a six-month break in contact

and asked him how life was treating him. He said he was currently dealing with "some interesting life challenges."

"Oh," I said, "tell me more," eager to hear that someone else's life was not turning out as planned. His challenges turned out to be leaving the wife who had changed religion and thus alienated herself from her family to marry him, and dealing with the aftermath of a dodgy investment that had left him £100,000 in debt. Mmmm, I thought privately, you call that a challenge. I call it a fucking nightmare.

The "challenges" in my life the first time I decided to seek therapy included finally admitting to myself that I actually hated the career for which I had spent the last six years training. Please don't ask me why, but at the clueless age of seventeen I decided that I was going to become a lawyer. I had no idea what this involved, but it was suggested by school and family alike, I suspect, simply because I was good at arguing; they probably thought that if I was arguing on behalf of other people I would be too tired to continue arguing with them. When I went away to University, I can tell you that studying was the last thing on my mind. What I was studying was irrelevant, as long as I had fun. In fact, I was so busy having fun that I didn't notice how much I hated law.

Challenge number two: my younger brother was in the hospital recovering from a burst appendix. I remember driving back from the hospital in the pouring rain, having seen my kid brother in the most incredible pain, and feeling helpless. My parents were on vacation and were unaware that their son was in the hospital. My sister and I were visiting him the whole time as he also happens to be phobic about hospitals.

The night before, I had been at Matt's brother's party, and in my desperation to seek solace I ended up irresponsibly kissing Matt with a strange passion. Strange because I didn't actually fancy him in the slightest. It felt so cruel because I knew that Matt was in love with me and had been for years. I felt guilty for leading him on and acting as if I was crazy for him by spending the night with him. If only I was a one hundred per cent bitch I could have just used him and left in the morning and felt no pain. Instead I felt that I had given him false hope and I was panicking that he would tell me to fuck off once he discovered I had just needed affection. Women often do that. They end up having sex when all they want is a naked cuddle.

So there I am driving back from the hospital late on a Sunday evening; tired and emotional, severely distressed at seeing my brother lying immobile and in pain in a hospital bed, filled with self-disgust at spending the night with someone I did not fancy, worrying that I had ruined a wonderful friendship and finally facing up to the disastrous career choice I had made and dreading another week at work in a deadly dull law firm. It is hardly any wonder that as I sped down a winding hill in the pouring rain, blinded by tears, driving was the last thing on my mind. The car soon spun out of control and ended up in a ditch at the side of the road. To add to my problems, I had now written off my brother's car.

I managed to get home to find a message on the answering machine from Matt's brother, Stephen. I was convinced that he was ringing me with the news that the gorgeous, sexy, cynical guy I had been chatting to at his party before I paired off with Matt had rung him for my number. I was basically prepared to convince myself of anything, especially as said gorgeous guy had witnessed me stuffing my tongue down Matt's throat. Surely nobody's day could be this bad. There had to be one sliver of silver lining in a day this shitty.

I was obviously in shock from the car accident and should have been speaking to someone comforting. Instead I picked up the phone to ring Stephen, with whom there had always been a mutual attraction. I once had a dinner party to fix him up with a friend of mine and ended up smooching him myself in between courses. I never took it further as I knew it would have killed Matt to see me with his big brother, and as I told you, I am not a one hundred per cent bitch. So I rang him and tried to sound normal, rather than like someone who ten minutes before had been lying in an upturned car in a ditch. I forced a bemused giggle when I heard that he and his new beautiful, rich, confident girlfriend were lying in the bath together drinking champagne.

Once the pleasantries were over with and I assured him that it was not the start of something beautiful between me and his kid brother, while privately worrying that it was more likely to be the start of something ugly, I asked him why he wanted to speak to me, ready to hand out my number to the guy who was going to rescue me from all the shit in my life and make it worth living again. So, why had he called?

Did I buy him the penis-shaped candle, he wanted to know, as he and his girlfriend were sorting out which presents were from which guests. Actually, I hadn't bought him a present at all, so as well as it being intensely disappointing it was also rather embarrassing. I could hear the girlfriend in the background slurping champagne and splashing around playfully in the bath and decided that I simply could not bear to be on the phone to these happy, successful people a second longer.

"Look," I said, "I've just had a car accident and I think I need to sit down," and quickly put the phone down. Still no tears, by the way. Just shock and misery.

For some even stranger reason, I then rang my neighbors who were some of the most unsympathetic people in the world, coming from the "Life Is Shit And Then You Die"

school of thought. Before I could stop her, the wife neighbor
announced that she was coming over. She turned up with her
husband, by which time I couldn't actually stop the tears. I
told them what had been happening (leaving out the Matt
débâcle – wrong generation), tears and snot pouring down
my face. The husband promptly told me off for crying and
impatiently urged me to pull myself together. I was then subjected to a series of unhelpful recriminations, such as why
were you driving so fast, don't you know you should drive
carefully in the rain, and how do you think your brother will
feel when he comes out of the hospital and realizes his car has
been written off? Hasn't he been through enough with his
operation? How could you be so irresponsible? You know,
helpful sympathetic questions like that.

My hatred for the neighbors momentarily revived me
and I managed to politely persuade them to leave, ever the
nicely brought up young lady, rather than chasing them out
of the house with a sharp kitchen knife and obscenities as I
would dearly liked to have done.

But underneath all the stress of my brother, my career and
Matt, there lay a deep but unacknowledged pain that Tom
had left me. Just before my brother was admitted to the hospital with his burst appendix, a friend "kindly" told me that
Tom had already moved into a flat with his new girlfriend –
they had been together less than a month. Without wanting
to dwell on Tom's new happiness without me, certain disturbing thoughts and ideas were floating around my head.
For the last six months of our relationship, he had been withdrawn. When I used to ask him what was wrong, he would
tell me that he was dissatisfied at work. He worked in advertising and wanted to make the switch from liaisoning with
clients to the creative side of things. I was only too pleased to
put his moodiness down to work. When he then told me

that he wanted a break from our relationship for a while, I sympathetically provided him with the space he said he needed. I thought it could be a good idea; we had been together so long, all through the period of youth when other people were out screwing with abandon. Maybe we could separate for a bit, each have a fling and then reunite for a long and happy marriage. But within two weeks of our separation, Tom rang me to tell me that he had met someone else, and wanted to give it a go with her. It turned out his new woman worked for the same advertising company, in the creative department. He said that his new girlfriend had insisted that he have no further contact with me if their relationship was to stand a chance. She was obviously a smart woman. Tom and I never spoke again.

I smoked myself into oblivion the night I crashed my brother's car and woke up the following afternoon in a still-stoned hazy fuzz. I made an appointment that day with the family doctor, ostensibly for some minor ailment but within minutes of sitting down and the doctor gently asking after my brother, I started wailing that my life was shit and I wanted to die. The doctor was adorable, nodding and murmuring sympathetically, and suggested cutting down on the pot and making an appointment with the surgery counselor.

I was also handed a prescription for anti-depressants, which sat in my bag during an interview later that day with an organization to whom I was applying for a post as a voluntary counselor on a late-night helpline. I had decided that listening to other people's problems would take my mind off my own depression; if I could immerse myself in other people's misery, I could keep running from my own. The interviewers at the help-line asked me if I was happy and settled. Yes, I lied, the prescription for three months' anti-depressants seemingly glowing and vibrating in my handbag, ready to be handed in at a pharmacy the minute I left the interview.

I turned up for my appointment the following week with the surgery counselor, Gerald – a large, pot-bellied African in his fifties – and immediately noted with some alarm that a copy of his newspaper was lying next to his briefcase. I was supposed to be receiving wisdom on how to live my life from a man who read a *tabloid* newspaper. At one point in the session when he confronted me with a few uncomfortable home truths, I was pissed off and cheeky enough to point out that we were bound not to agree on my identity as a woman as he read a trashy newspaper which depicted women as bimbo morons. He found this very amusing, probably because he had completely unshakeable self-belief having been through considerable therapy himself.

I started off the session by telling him that I had recently completed a depression questionnaire in a medical hand-book, and that when I had added up my score I had done really well, comfortably falling in the *This person is in immediate danger of harming herself* category. This piece of information did not have quite the effect that I anticipated. He looked at me astonished and wanted to know what sort of person sat at home filling out depression questionnaires. Mad, unhappy people like me, I explained. Self-pitying, self-obsessed people, he said. Yeah, that as well, I agreed.

My experience with Gerald is memorable for two things. Firstly, he irrevocably altered my view of my childhood. Before seeing Gerald, I believed that I'd had a perfect child-hood. I had an adorable playmate sister and brother, close in age to myself, loving parents who provided me with toys, pretty dresses and summer vacations. I went to an idyllic pri-mary school where I spent lunchtimes playing kiss chase with sexy seven-year-old boys around the willow trees. Ten ses-

sions with Gerald later and I was convinced that I was subjected to systematic emotional abuse from which I am unal-
terably damaged. Great.

And the second memorable thing? I fell in love with him.
Of course. He was witty and charming, he listened to me, he
constantly told me I was beautiful and intelligent (which I
now understand is quite unorthodox behavior from a therapist, who should really remain as neutral as possible), and,
quite frankly, if he had asked me to elope back to Ghana with
him I would have gone in a flash. I used to turn up at the sessions in full make-up and button-up dresses, which would be
half-unbuttoned before the session began. Of course, he
figured me out and challenged me, asking me what kind of
games I was playing with him. I denied everything but we
both knew I was lying. God, it was *so* embarrassing. *Cringe,
cringe*. He never did ask me to elope with him, by the way.

By the end of the ten sessions, Gerald had also convinced
me that my only salvation would be to leave the country and
start all over again somewhere else. Again, to be so direct to a
client is also very unorthodox, I now understand. But at the
time, his word was the absolute ultimate gospel and emigrat-
ing scared the shit out of me. I didn't want to leave the
country and start all over again, I just wanted a rich boyfriend
who would bring me breakfast in bed. When I used to tell
Gerald what I really wanted he sighed and warned me that
this would be the worst thing that could happen to me.
Disaster would surely follow, he warned.

The whole experience therefore left me in considerable
turmoil. As well as feeling forced to leave the country or face
certain disaster, I also now hated my parents. The good news
was that I no longer believed I was nuts. Now I was officially
"damaged," although to be quite honest with you, I am not

sure which was worse. At least nuts was fun. Damaged just felt sad and rather pathetic.

The second experience with a therapist was more recent and less damaging simply because I only saw the woman three times and I was older and considerably more self-aware. I soon realized that she was, in fact, much, much crazier than me. I was mildly stressed out by my new relationship with Rob, worried that my self-destructive urges would sabotage the delicate new seedlings of our affair. I thought I would seek paid help during the relationship rather than risk returning to single status again. Quite sensible, don't you think?

Anyway, this therapist was cheap (I soon realized why) and local, so I thought I would try her out. Firstly, she insisted on sharing details of her own life with me and I was too polite to tell her that I didn't give a fuck about her life, it was me I wanted to talk about. Secondly, she persisted in trying to give me advice on how to play the relationship, something I was very wary about after my experience with Gerald. I wanted someone who would help me to find my own answers, rather than pay someone to help them feel powerful and benevolent.

I was particularly perturbed when she urged me to heed her advice on how to act with Rob when she uttered the following reassurance: "Listen, I know *all* about relationships, I've been divorced three times." I looked at her with horror and thought: in that case, what the fuck am I listening to you for?

The sessions used to last for hours. Whatever happened to boundaries? Even I get bored of talking about myself after two hours. When I arrived at the second session she seemed a little shaken. It transpired that her last client had run from the room screaming. By the end of the second session, I was beginning to understand how they felt.

As I left the third and final session, having already privately decided during the session that I would definitely *not* be coming back, no matter how cheap and local she was, I was in no doubt that I had made the right decision when she waved me off at the front door with the words (shouted out loudly by the way): "Don't you dare fuck up with him tonight, or you'll have me to deal with."

But here I am, ready to try again with a new therapist. This one is local, but she is also relatively expensive and comes highly recommended by Gareth, who as we know is something of an expert when it comes to therapy. And, as I said, this time I am arriving with a specific request. It's quite simple: all I want to do is have a good boo-hoo over Tom and get on with the rest of my life.

I get good vibes when she comes to the door. She looks happy, together and has kind eyes. I am ushered up to her consulting room and note with approval that there are no tabloid newspapers. The books on the shelves are quite impressive, the sort of thing I might read. I know immediately which chair is meant for me as it has a box of tissues next to it. She sits down opposite me and waits silently and expectantly for me to disgorge. That's just how I like my therapists on the first date; legs crossed and their mouths shut. So far, this bird is perfect.

I give her the run down on Tom and tell her I want her to make me cry. Instead of agreeing, she hands me a box of crayons and a large pad of paper with the instruction to draw something that symbolizes the essence of me. I hate art and I particularly hate art therapy. She reassures me that this exercise will be very helpful for both of us. Better get it over with quickly then, I think, and I grab a dark brown crayon and draw a jagged thunderbolt shape. I can't be bothered to pick up another colored crayon and color in the shape, I just want to get back to what I consider the proper process of therapy.

But she wants to discuss my drawing. She evaluates what the drawing says about how I feel about myself (nothing good, by the way) and concludes that I am a "good case for therapy."

Is that a euphemism for "really fucked up" I want to know?

She hums and hars and talks to me in therapy lingo about needing to grow and develop and confront shadow sides, and how it simply means that if I am willing to surrender to the process I will greatly benefit.

Yeah right, I think unhappily, that definitely means "really fucked up." And the tragic thing is, she's probably right. By the end of the session she has convinced me that my nightly dreams of Tom are a symptom and not the cause of the current difficulties I am experiencing. Back to square one. Now I'm going to have to find a seriously rich and generous boyfriend to recoup the outlay on the sessions, which could last for some time according to her prognosis.

The thing is, unlike you, I am not cynical about this therapist. I feel instinctively that she's not trying to rip me off. I am pretty perceptive and reckon I can sense the charlatans in this game, and once we've haggled over money, we arrange for me to return the following week. She gives me homework – to read a moving book about a little boy who recovers from a horrific childhood through therapy.

Will it make me cry, I ask.

She nods in such a way as to say, "Yes, even you, with your hardened bitter heart, you will cry."

I buy the book the next morning and read it in one sitting, patiently waiting for the tears to flow. And guess what, my eyes don't even glass over. It is rather disappointing.

By the time the next session arrives, I am three dates down the line with Mark and still not quite recovering from the impact of hearing that Karen and Rick have settled into a fulfilling relationship. I settle myself in the hot seat and ask her whether I can get personal. She nods enthusiastically so I launch straight into the small cock/big cock situation. I tell her about Rick's sensational oral sex performance, my subsequent horror at his small cock, my failed attempt at a replay and my consequent rejection, the arrival of Mark at my moment of despair and my overwhelming desire to dump him, despite his warmth, humor, intelligence and massive cock.

She listens intently to the story (looking as though she hasn't had this much fun in ages) and then succinctly delivers her verdict. I am terrified of intimacy and I will always find a reason to run. Could be the wrong religion, could be the wrong-shaped nose, could be the wrong age, could be the wrong size and shape of cock. And with Mark, despite the fact that here is a guy with whom I can relax and be myself and have fun, I have decided that he just looks wrong and I don't fancy him. She tells me that she believes Mark has been sent to me by the Good Lord to give me a second chance. Was I going to learn my lesson from Rick and not fuck and run? Was love not all about intimacy, mutual respect and affection? Could I walk away from all Mark's good qualities quite so quickly?

Could it be true, I wonder. Do I always find a reason not to get involved with a guy just to avoid heartache? Perhaps she is right. I leave that session determined to give Mark another chance.

You can Take a Horse to Water, but You can't make Her Drink

I am due to see Mark this afternoon and as I await his arrival, believe me when I say I am full of good intentions. I have pre-arranged the welcome scenario with Gabriela, who is to answer the door, present herself as the warm-up act and assess Mark's fuckability status. I will then float downstairs, the main attraction, encourage Mark to use the toilet facilities before we set off for the afternoon's entertainment, and in his short absence, debrief Gabriela.

All goes according to plan, and once Mark has been encouraged to disappear and Gabriela has expressed her horror at the sweatpants he is wearing, she pronounces her verdict. "A good family man," she states.

"Fuckability zero, then?" I inquire. But Mark has returned and she is unable to answer.

Mark and I go for a long walk and I *really* try to like him. Honestly, I do. But as he is so perceptive, he has now become insecure. He knows I am not sure and I reckon he subconsciously senses that the pressure is on to persuade me that I do actually like him. Unfortunately, once you get insecure with someone, and it can happen to anyone, conversation becomes a real bore. In your fervent wish not to say the wrong thing, you often end up not saying anything at all. Paranoia builds inside you and transforms even the most mild of exchanges into a series of little digs and put-downs. Well, that's what happens to me anyway.

And during this walk with Mark, I suspect that it may be happening to him. He is annoyingly quiet and the burden of providing light, fluffy, entertaining conversation falls on *moi*. And, of course, because he is so quiet, the mild conversation *does* turn into a series of digs regarding his non-communication. In fact, I even suspect that as well as being uncommunicative, he may also be BORING.

Now you may think that this is an arrogant assumption; that it takes two people to provide an interesting conversation. How can I say with any certainty that it is him that is boring and not me? With some confidence, actually.

I have known for a fact since I was fourteen years old that I am not boring, and to be honest with you, I have not tormented myself on the question once since then. I had the most powerful revelation of my life on a bus when I bumped into the then object of my affections, Tony. I thought he was the coolest dude in the universe. He had the right floppy haircut, wore the right shoes (very important at any age, but especially then) and he liked the right music (well, I assumed he did, as I had rarely heard the names of the bands he threw into the conversation, which automatically made them cool). He was a fairly tortured soul; I think he wrote poetry and he was definitely in a band in which he was the lead singer, bleating lyrics that were probably very profound if you were only deep enough to understand. Tony was a fifteen-year-old mini-Morrissey and I thought he ought to fall in love with me.

I was pretty tortured at the time too and spent evenings weeping over books that featured isolated, excluded individuals with whom I strongly identified (I could compile a really successful teenage suicide reading list if you are interested and you know any annoying teenagers). It seemed that every time I tried to talk to the guy, however, I had nothing of interest whatsoever to say. In fact, I considered myself to be a complete bore. How was it that I could be the wittiest person on earth with everyone else, but with him, my personality went totally AWOL?

I was soon to discover the answer. As I said, I bumped into Tony on the bus and as he spoke to me, I racked my brains furiously for something interesting to say to demand his attention and respect. But as he talked and talked and I dried up and my eyes glazed over, a thunderbolt struck me. *He* was boring, not me. Could this be true? As he droned on and on about his band, the alternative music scene and his latest trendy clothes purchase, I realized that it was beautifully and simply true. Not only was the subject matter and style of delivery tedious, he also displayed the classic characteristic of a bore – he was not interested in a word anyone else had to say.

There is really no excuse for being boring; all you need to do is be interested in what others have to say and a dialogue will follow. It is the closed mind of a person that makes them a bore. They have nothing to discover about anyone else. They are only interested in themselves. All this dawned on me in a micro-second on the bus and it has stood me in very good stead ever since. I now live by the motto: If I Am Bored, The Person I Am With Must Be Boring. It has been a great comfort to me over the years and although I have had to remind myself of it once or twice, I have never doubted its validity. I have always believed that I have enough personality for two people, so if I am bored, the person I am speaking to has got to be a real yawn.

So there I am on this summer afternoon walk with Mark

and, horror of horrors, I am bored. So bored in fact, that when we get back to my house, I am forced to give him a blowjob as a conversational get-out. I can hardly talk with my mouth full and he must be relieved to switch off for a while too. Soon after the deed is done, I politely inform him that I have evening arrangements for which I need time to freshen up.

It all sounded so right when my therapist spoke of me being given a second chance with Mark. And yet, it all feels so wrong. Aren't you supposed to want to kiss the man you are with rather than giving him a blowjob so that you don't have to speak to him anymore? It may be true that I am scared of intimacy, but I really do not think that this particular fear is relevant to the Mark situation. It's tragic, but there it is. Back on the shelf. The last turkey in the shop. Single once again.

Fuck 'n' Dump

Before Mark left that Sunday, he cleverly pinned me down for another arrangement.

"Do you want to see me again?" he asked.

"Well I suppose we ought to have a major sex session at some point," was all I could come up with.

"Don't make it sound so enticing," he said.

"I'm offering you my body aren't I?"

"Yeah, and that's all you're offering," he replied. "I want you, not just your body."

Yikes.

You see the thing is that although penetration has occurred, it's never been for very long. I always end up feeling wrong about the whole thing and calling the proceedings to a halt. We haven't therefore had a real major multi-orgasmic romp, and with a cock like his it would be a shame to miss out on one big blow-out session before I say goodbye, especially as I don't know when I'll be getting it again, if ever. I've been through such long periods of celibacy that I actually become convinced that I will never again have sexual intercourse. And he's right, this is all I want to offer him. My body. In exchange for a night with his.

So I agreed to see him in nine days' time, and in my mind I formulated a quick, easy, painless (for me anyway) plan. Go around to his house the following week and fuck 'n' dump. I told him that I was out every night until then so there was no point ringing me before the date. He looked sad, but agreed not to ring.

I have a busy social week and a relaxing weekend by the sea in Brighton and by the time Sunday evening comes around again a strange urge to ring Mark has arisen. I go to pick up the phone for a chat and put it down again. It's not fair on him, I think, to ring him and make him think that we have something going. He will only be even more upset after I've fucked and dumped. But my fingers hover over the phone, twitching to dial. I really do want to talk to him so I decide to go with the feeling and ring him anyway. He sounds delighted to hear from me and we chat easily about our weeks. As I put down the phone, I think what a shame it is that he has to go. He really is so nice. But a girl's gotta do what a girl's gotta do. Meanwhile, he has promised to provide some pot for me for Tuesday evening. I don't want my mind to be present while I abuse my body and soul.

I turn up on Tuesday night and for some reason I am in a great mood. Tonight I will offer up my body for an evening of good old hard core porn. As I sit in his living room rolling a joint, I warn him of the two personalities that could result once I have smoked it.

"I will become either very nice or a complete bitch. That's what happens when I smoke. It's either Miss Affectionate Talkative and Lots of Laughs, or Paranoid Evil Weird Bad-Tempered Bitch. It can go either way and you can never predict the outcome."

He seems unalarmed. "I think I would prefer the bitch," he says.

That throws me, so just to be awkward I say, "Well, in that case I might just become nice."

Then he says something that really throws me. "Yeah, you could be nice to me and I could be nice to you and we could have a nice evening and you could go home happy."

It takes a while for the impact of his suggestion to sink in. It is the most radical concept I have heard in years. I actually need to excuse myself, and as I sit on the toilet I marvel at how far out the suggestion seems; I am nice to him, he is nice to me and we have a nice evening. Do you know, that thought had never occurred to me. A nice evening? Going home happy? Being nice? Was it really that easy? Could it be so simple?

I return to the lounge, where Mark puts his arm around me and kisses me. He looks so happy to have me there in his arms. As I take a long drag from the joint, I realize I am turning into the nice incarnation of me. I kiss him back. We chat and he listens attentively as I blabber on in my stoned "I am endlessly fascinating" ramblings. Every now and then I kiss him and he gives me two kisses back. It is easy being nice to him and it feels wonderful to receive his affection. When he suggests going to bed, I skip along happily to the bedroom, eager to carry on being nice to him in a sexual way.

And guess what, I go home happy.

Nice Weird

Following on from the success of Tuesday evening, we make arrangements to see each other on the Thursday. I turn up at his place again, wondering whether we will be able to recreate the feelings of the previous date. He must be thinking the same thing as he offers me a glass of champagne soon after I arrive, just to make sure he gets me in the right mood.

I highly recommend a champagne/pot combination to any man trying to get his woman into a loving, open, affectionate, sexual mood. It certainly works for me. As I lie in his arms in bed, giggly, chilled out and turned on, I realize how weird this feels. And the reason it feels so weird is that it feels so fucking good. I haven't been held or kissed or cuddled like this since Tom and that was years ago. Instead I have meaningless, but technically excellent (on a good night), sexual encounters. What I have missed is the warmth and affection and fun of lying in bed with someone I like.

It is also weird because it was not supposed to happen like this. I was supposed to go around to Mark's on Tuesday evening and either enjoy meaningless but technically excellent sex and leave pretty much straight after, or, even worse, go around and not be able to fuck so just dump instead. But here I am, two days later, competing in a marathon kissing exchange and enjoying the most superb sexual skills I have ever encountered.

As I lie in bed recovering from my second multiple orgasm, I think to myself that if Rick hadn't turned me down, I would not have started chatting to Mark. Instead, I'd be getting a sore ass on the back of a bike, and although my groin would be receiving the shuddering vibrations of his Honda 650, I wonder aloud whether his oral sex skills alone would have been enough. I think of Rick's hacking cough as he lit his tenth joint of the evening and thank my lucky stars that the guy blew me off. This time it really does seem that second best has turned out to be best after all.

It's very weird, Mark and I agree as we lie entwined in bed. But this time, it's nice weird.

Temptation

After a weekend in bed with Mark, everyone says I look beautiful. My skin is luminescent, my eyes are shining, my pheromones have come out of hibernation and are multiplying furiously. I'll tell you how beautiful I have become – I actually look wonderful without make-up, a very strange phenomenon at my time of life. Men in the street keep whistling and waving at me. Even the miserable old bugger in the corner store has started smiling and winking at me.

Jasmin says she never realized my eyes were so green. She says she wants to meet someone and fall in love so that she can look this great too. She has just split up with Toby, the hippie she met when he came around to landscape her roof terrace garden. It wasn't only the begonias and tulips in the new flowerbeds that blossomed when he offered to deal with the weed situation by rolling a joint. The relationship soon wilted, however, when she realized that gardening, sex, smoking dope and the Grateful Dead were the only things in life in which he had any interest.

Jasmin is in some ways the typical Jewish princess, with her one-to-one tennis lessons, her therapist, her manicurist, her aromatherapist, her designer clothes, her apartment in

Belsize Park, her stockroom of Clarins products, her take-out laundry service and her constant dining out. I once had to accompany her to a supermarket when she had a party. I soon realized she had never been to one before when she asked me whether we could take the car. I explained that supermarkets provided parking facilities and regarded her with a mixture of astonishment and grudging admiration as she smiled with relief.

Toby needs a druggy hippie chick to keep him happy and although Jasmin is a druggy chick, she simply doesn't do hippie.

Anyway, back to me. Yeah, I have become beautiful again and the wonderful thing is that I don't even realize it so I can be nice and modest with it.

Soon after we've officially fallen in love, Mark goes away for a male bonding session in the country. Meanwhile, for me it's a friend's thirtieth birthday party at a bar in town. I dress up in my usual flirtation gear and look forward to socializing with my new non-single and thus non-desperate status. The minute Jasmin and I enter the bar, I feel the party adrenaline buzzing. The party is packed with *gorgeous* men and suddenly the evening seems full of wonderful new opportunities.

I also realize that this is the bar in which I had the fastest sobering experience of my existence. About two years earlier I had been incredibly drunk, and as I stumbled to get my coat from the cloakroom, I suddenly realized that the bar was twice as big as I had originally thought it was. That meant there were still men I hadn't chatted up. I perked up. There was hope for the evening yet. I could still have my number taken and/or meet my future husband. As I strode down the bar with purposeful relish, I noticed a girl walking towards me. She was wearing exactly the same lime green satin shirt as me, although it looked a hell of a lot better on me, I thought smugly to myself.

As I came face to face with the girl, I stopped her to point out our identical shirts (I do occasionally talk to other women at parties). As I started speaking to her, she started talking to me too, but I couldn't hear what she was saying as the music was so loud. When I stopped speaking, I noticed she looked confused. And then I realized that it was me who was looking confused. I was standing in front of a mirror.

Praying to Goddess that no one had seen me, I scurried to the cloakroom. Have you noticed that you can be bombed out of your head yet can function perfectly well and be having a truly wonderful time, *until* you realize that you are actually bombed out of your head? And the minute you realize quite how far gone you are, which I find is when I am left on my own for a minute, you suddenly want to collapse or puke or cry and go home, but not in that order, in fact you're lucky if you have a choice over the order of events.

Well, once I realized I'd been engaging myself in conversation in the mirror and that the disheveled drunken mess opposite me was actually me, I started to sway, topple and feel pukey.

Tonight, as I realize this is the same bar, I make a mental note not to make the same mistake. In any case, tonight the bar is chock full of horny bastards just waiting for me to make their night, and it appears that I do not need a mirror illusion to create more of them.

I locate a gaggle of sexy young men sitting in the corner of the bar and I'm soon nestled in between them, holding court. With the knowledge that I have a man somewhere in the UK who is crazy about me, I can strut my stuff with confidence. Soon, one of the guys (name, Jeremy) and I become involved in a deep and meaningful conversation. Really, I mean it, deep and meaningful. He has lived in Asia for three years and has a very attractive Buddha detachment about him. He seems to incorporate all of the Buddhist qualities that some people spend their free time chanting *om* for. He is completely calm and serene while at the same time intense and passionate. He is soon besotted with me and gazes at me with wonderment, adoration and lust. I must admit, I feel pretty much the same way about him.

I realize that I may have some sort of magic about me and after an hour or so of mutually rewarding conversation, I excuse myself. I want to see if the magic is real and whether it will work on anyone else. As I make my way to the loo, I am repeatedly grabbed and blockaded by men, eager for me to be theirs. They can't get enough of me. One ex-boyfriend who barely bothered to acknowledge my existence at a party a month before, lines up to pay homage. I initially take great pleasure in looking straight through him, but when he starts hanging off my skirt, I extricate myself with an exquisite snarl. After half an hour or so of a complete *bella figura*, I see the Buddha, Jeremy, waiting patiently for me at the back of the line. Get this – this guy has come to find *me*. Instead of me running around a party desperately trying to track down a guy who I mistakenly understood was mildly in love with me so that I can persuade him to take me home for the evening, tonight the man is tracking me down. What a result. As we take a seat to resume our acquaintance, I am constantly bombarded by men I know or even barely know who seem to want to kiss me and bask in my aura. I don't need to tell you how wonderful this is for me, do I? You know what a fabulous evening I am having. After a year of feeling invisible at best and repellent at worst, this is totally delicious.

Jeremy and I are hitting it off to such an extent that when

his friends decide to leave the party, he wants to stay behind with me. As we sit together in the corner of the bar, I realize that this is make your mind up time. If he stays, I will be duty bound to kiss him at the very least. If I let him go with his friends, I will be missing out on the opportunity of experiencing an extremely cute guy who also happens to be fascinating company. It sounds as if I am in a real quandary, but I'm not. Yes, he's gorgeous. Yes, I'm horny. Yes, he's very definitely up for it. But no, I am not going to leave with him.

I don't want to cheat on Mark. Not even a kiss.

With poignant bittersweet regret, I tell him that I have a boyfriend. He then goes and spoils it all by telling me that he has a girlfriend. Not so Buddha after all, but who cares?

Thank God, this time, I don't.

Finally, Perfection

The following weekend I spend thirty-six hours in bed with Mark. He is perfect. You couldn't wish for a more perfect boyfriend. I am smothered in kisses, cherished, adored and fucked good and proper.

He makes me scrambled eggs on toast in the morning. He runs me a bath, buys me newspapers and cigarettes, and lets me watch MTV. Later, during the day, while he watches a video, he brings me in the phone and a glass of wine so that I can chat with my friends and crow over my perfect new boyfriend. He orders in take-out and we spend the evening watching a film, while kissing every few minutes. I reckon we must kiss about two hundred times an hour. The total kiss count for the weekend must be well over two thousand.

Occasionally, I become disorientated lying in a relatively strange man's bedroom for hour after hour, day after day. Mark is in the living room watching a boy's film involving a lot of gunplay and annoying, simpering women who stay at home while their men save the world (the sort of film that makes me want to buy a gun and shoot the audience for enjoying the film). Every half an hour, I totter from the bedroom to ask Mark two questions:

1. Who am I?
2. Do I like you?

He answers:

1. My girlfriend.
2. Yes.

And I trot happily back to bed, satisfied with the answers.

I am so relaxed that as I lie in his arms that night, my head nestling on his broad, hairy, manly chest, I feel my heart melting.

Help! Every Man I Meet Wants to Go to Bed with Me

The following week it is Claudia's thirtieth birthday party. As it is on a school night and Mark's job is becoming increasingly demanding, he isn't coming with me. Besides, he will not know anyone there and I want to be free to socialize without hindrance.

Claudia started having heart palpitations about three weeks before the party, not least because all of her admirers are coming, most of whom know nothing of the others" existence and all of whom expect to accompany her home afterwards for a birthday shag.

She had been so determined to make sure that there was a shag option at her party that she had been furiously networking to this end for the previous four months. She attended every single social event she'd either been invited to, heard about or even overheard about. Blind dates were solicited from everyone from grandparents to the payroll department at work. But her efforts paid off and now she has ten eager suitors on her back.

I sympathize with Claudia's concern at turning thirty and her stress at hosting a party, and indeed beg her to sort herself out with some beta blockers. There is no need for her to suffer unnecessarily, as I had done. Claudia is not averse to using artificial means to regulate her moods and she is anxious to avoid the same fate as me on the big day.

I don't mind admitting that I completely fell apart when I turned thirty. I also had a party, a cocktail party at my place, and I spent most of the evening in my bedroom receiving one-to-one counseling from close friends. I languished on my bed, surrounded by presents, unable to have a cocktail to calm my nerves as I had not eaten for a week due to stress and I didn't want to spend another party quietly vomiting in the toilet as I had the year before. I was too paranoid to smoke any pot, which was a shame as one of my friends had bought me a bag of top quality skunk.

At about 1:30 am, I decided I had just about had enough and announced that the party was over and could everyone please go home. No one took the slightest bit of notice. I was the only one not enjoying myself, apart from Jasmin's friend from Manchester who looked positively green from mixing his Sea Breezes with his Whisky Alexanders.

Rob and his banana-shaped cock were floating about somewhere in the party, probably wondering what the hell was wrong with his previously confident, assured new girl-friend. In retrospect, having a very good-looking, young, sexy boyfriend sending me a dozen red roses on my birthday was not quite the tonic it should have been. I felt too old and haggish to deserve him and knew that I would soon self-destruct and fuck it up. Quite frankly, I didn't need the added pressure of a gorgeous new lover at that moment in my life, and it was a pain having to quietly freak out in my bedroom rather than wail and gnash as I could have done in front of my friends, who are used to it and know how to deal with me.

The panic attacks started a good month before my birthday. I had already started turning the lights off when I got into the bath so that I would not accidentally catch sight of my ageing body in the mirror. And apart from the physical implications of growing old, I also had the metaphysical implications to contend with. About six months before, I had read a book about the psychic contracts we make with our parents.

I'd better explain. A psychic contract is a subconscious agreement that we make with our parents early in life which we unknowingly adhere to, despite the limitations it places on us.

I racked my brains for any psychic contracts I had entered into with Ma and Pa, but despite contemplating the issue for some time, I could not come up with anything. Yet I knew there was something nagging at the back of my mind.

About a month later, I was walking up the escalators on the way to work and I suddenly remembered my psychic contract. It hit me like a thunderbolt. Only it wasn't just a psychic contract; I had actually signed a written contract with my father when I was about eleven years old, promising that "I will always remain a little girl." When I told my friends of the contract I had signed, they thought my father was a little odd, but it was just his weird sense of humor. He loved his little girl and didn't want to lose her. Most daddies are probably the same, they just don't ask their young daughters to sign a contract. When I was eighteen, I had to give him what he called "a cast-iron guarantee" that I would only marry a Jewish guy, but by this time I was secretly dating a non-Jewish guy so I mentally crossed my fingers behind my back. I no longer felt bound to comply in order to retain his love.

By turning thirty, I was going to break the contract that I was unwittingly bound by. You can't be a little girl aged thirty.

It doesn't sound right. I had managed to remain a little girl quite successfully up until then. Remember my therapist, Gerald? When he asked me what I would have if I could have anything that I wanted, I decided on a rich boyfriend who would bring me breakfast in bed. I didn't want to grow up and accept any responsibility for making my own way in life; I wanted another daddy to look after me. It's quite a common syndrome, you know. It's called the Cinderella Complex and the bad news is that you can get away with it until you turn thirty when you will suffer a complete identity crisis.

And finally, as if that wasn't challenging enough, I had absolutely failed to achieve any of the things you were supposed to have achieved by this particular milestone. No marriage under my belt, not even a failed one. No kids. No home of my own. And to make it worse, my career was in the doldrums. I was going nowhere slowly. I didn't fit into either category: I hadn't sacrificed my career for the satisfaction of motherhood and a settled loving relationship. And I couldn't blame my child-free single status on lack of time due to forging a wonderfully successful, financially lucrative career. It seemed to me that all I had achieved at age thirty was considerable sexual know-how. And where had that got me? Sure I could make money out of it, but who wants to put that on your resumé?

Do you ever feel that the world is full of overachievers? Every time you pick up a newspaper or a magazine, there are articles, interviews and features on people who have created successful companies with just luck and timing on their side. People who have signed multi-million pound record deals, people opening restaurants, art galleries and night-clubs, people writing bestsellers, producing award-winning films, designing buildings and winning marathons, etc. It's even worse when you recognize the people involved, especially as when you knew them you were both at roughly the same stage in life. I felt sick when I saw a contemporary of mine had become a member of Parliament, a close financial adviser to Gordon Brown and a mother since the last time I had seen her five years ago. One day when I was feeling particularly down on myself for being such a non-achiever, I opened a magazine only to find a feature on someone who had worked as a trainee lawyer with me and who was now launching a fashion house with his model girlfriend selling clothes to Harrods. I reeled from overwhelming feelings of inadequacy, jealousy and bitterness.

Why can't newspapers and magazines run a few features on losers so that the rest of us mortals can rest up and stop berating ourselves for not becoming high-flying super humans? We've got success thrust down our throats the whole time – why can't we read a bit more about the underachievers to lessen the dissatisfaction we feel with our own small lives? Am I depressing you now? You were quite happy with your life until I started going on about people who are more successful, rich and beautiful than you. But do you know what I mean?

So that was what was going through my head as I turned thirty: ageing, growing up and failing. It was time to return to the doctor, who gave me some beta blockers to calm my nerves and slow my heart rate down so that I could start eating again. When I'm stressed, I don't eat. Comfort eaters, such as Gabriela who is currently on four Viennettas and two jars of Nutella a week, envy my ability to crash diet in this way. But the thing is that I am still hungry and my stomach is rumbling and beginning to digest its own lining and I feel weak from lack of food; I am just too churned up to eat. All my clothes start falling off me and my trousers go baggy around the bottom. Believe me, it's no fun.

So after I explained psychic contracts to the doctor and we agreed that my current diet of three cookies a day for ten days wasn't as nutritious as it could be, he prescribed me a small bottle of beta blockers which I have since discovered are the most wonderful little pills legally available. All they do, basically, is slow your heart rate and thus stop you panicking your guts out. Once I had swallowed a couple of those babies, I was able to progress to chicken soup and I was soon on to solids again.

And so the crisis passed, the relationship with the sexy (but boring) Rob ended and I managed to get back on track again. I just didn't want Claudia to go through the same shit as me. But she's a Valium girl and has sorted herself out with a couple of these for her birthday.

I have been really looking forward to her party. It makes such a nice change to be invited to a party rather than crashing one and then wandering around not knowing anyone apart from the sad single mates you've arrived with. Claudia looks fabulous, with a Wonderbra'd cleavage that earns admiration and respect from both sexes. The rule is that before you speak to her you have to first kiss her cleavage. I don't mind burying my head between her lovely tits for a wee while, not that I get to speak to her much as I am a woman and am not therefore much use to her during the evening. Which is fair enough, I reckon. If I had ten men after me at a party, I wouldn't waste time talking to my best friend. And anyway, I am in hot demand myself. The magic has intensified after the thirty-six-hour love fest with Mark and I am practically having to fight the men off, and all this in spite of the fact that I am wearing sneakers and my own magnificent cleavage is not on show. If one more person tells me that I am beautiful, I'll scream. Well, not really. But the frequency with which men are cornering me is alarming. Apart from a louche film critic, who is apparently incredibly debauched, I'm not tempted in the slightest.

Until I meet Nico.

I am at the bar, which has closed, trying to persuade the bar person to sell me some cigarettes. I actually only want a couple and they only have strong disgusting brands left. A man sitting at the bar offers to sell me his half packet of my brand at a bargain price. I am used to this kind of thing happening by now. But as I turn to face him, I gasp. He is absolutely fucking *gorgeous*. I mean, seriously and utterly divine. Almond-shaped sparkling blue eyes, a beautifully upturned nose (but not too small to arouse cockism fears – there is a proven nose/cock connection, you know), full, red, cruel lips, neat white teeth, sharp, tidy sideburns, soft, curly, light brown hair, exquisite bone structure. He is quiet, deferential and charming. He invites me to sit with him and we just gaze at each other in wonder, absorbed in the other's sheer fabulousness. To add to his all-round attractiveness, he has also spent time in Italy and we coo to each other in Italian, the sexiest language in the world. I think he might be the most ideal man in the world. In my drunken haze, I do perhaps overlook some character failings that threaten to mar my prince's perfection, such as a hint of sneering arrogance and condescending chivalry, along the lines of "what a lucky girl you are to be talking to me."

When he asks me where I am going after the party, I realize that this is temptation at its most ruthless. Lost in his beauty and charm, I cannot believe how severely my fidelity and commitment are being tested. Why the hell am I meeting this perfect specimen after getting it together with the lovely Mark?

And yet, I tear myself away and give him one long, lingering, lustful look before exiting through the door with my friends for the cab ride home, slightly wistful, but pleased with my resolve and the strength of my feelings for Mark.

Pissed Off

'Blessed art Thou, O Lord our God, King of the Universe, who has not made me a woman"
Jewish prayer to be said every morning by Jewish men

I see Mark a couple of days after the party and I get fucked so good and hard that when I go to the loo the next day I recognize the stinging burn of cystitis. That's the down side of having a boyfriend with a big cock. Cystitis. Cystitis is the pits of the earth. Especially when you have to go to work. The loo is miles from my work station and I have to walk down miles of corridors, settle myself on the loo and painfully piss, wait another five minutes and painfully piss a bit more. Wipe, wash and return to the office only to sit down and find that I need to go again.

Despite drinking gallons of water, crates of cranberry juice and a sodium bicarbonate mix, the symptoms are getting increasingly bad. I spend most of the working day either walking to or sitting on the loo. I awake sporadically but reliably throughout the night to trot to the loo for a two-second piss. The broken nights and consequent lack of sleep add to my mounting despondency and I am eventually forced to concede that a visit to the doctor may be necessary. But the doctor puts me on some hopeless antibiotics that fail to have any impact whatsoever, apart from lowering my immune system and making me feel leg-achingly tired and depressed.

It's a curse being a woman, and even the Jewish religion recognizes this, hence the prayer Jewish men say every morning when they thank their lucky stars they were born men. Mark fucks like a tiger, shoots his load and *I* end up having to constantly interrupt my work, fork out for a prescription, lower my immune system with crappy antibiotics and pull my panties up and down a hundred times a day. He, meanwhile, is completely symptom-free.

Any sexual activity during cystitis is, of course, out of the question. Sticking a sword in my vagina, rotating it 360 degrees and then sprinkling liberal quantities of salt over the wound would only be slightly less painful. And, of course, the worst thing is that I am still horny as hell. The tragedy of going months and years without regular sex only to have a short but exquisite taste of a passionate love life is too hard for me to bear. Because the antibiotics are completely crap, recovery is delayed and so, therefore, is the resumption of sexual activity.

I eventually have to take a couple of days off work altogether as a result of the exhaustion caused by the combined marathon toilet run and antibiotics. I basically spend two days lying in bed cursing God for not making me a man. To be fair to Mark, he does bring around a large bouquet of flowers, although apparently it was on the recommendation of a friend of his who suggested that if he got me flowers he "might get some as well."

No doubt the antibiotics will give me thrush, the symptoms of which I now recognize as cream cheese between my piss flaps and a chronic urge to scratch my genital area (this urge mostly occurs in public places, such as work or the subway). Oh yeah, and you feel really low and generally depressed as well. But get this – with men there are *no* symptoms and so they merrily go from woman to woman passing the damn fungus quite innocently and irritation-free.

Same story with the morning after pill. A month's worth of hormones pumped into your body in one go, followed by at least an eight-hour urge to vomit copiously which must obviously be resisted to avoid throwing up the month's worth of hormones, all to avoid having a baby. I find the best thing to do is lie in bed, whimper and curse God for not making me a man. However, the eight-hour nausea while trying not to puke is a piece of cake compared to the eight days of trying not to kill yourself due to twelve months of PMS rolled into one monster session that follows.

The minute you realize that the morning after pill is required (which will be after they have come and you, invariably, have not), you weigh up the likelihood of getting dumped during the post-morning after pill eight-day madness. Based on past experience, I would say there is a good to excellent chance of being dumped.

When I took the morning after pill with David (small cock, nice balls), I warned him that I might become a little moody, and possibly a little vicious too. I explained in advance that it was not my fault, but rather it was due to his inability to realize that he was about to have an orgasm. Within two days of taking the morning after pill we had an almighty row and I was given my marching orders. It was all over and he would not change his mind, despite some pretty plaintive cajoling on my part.

The next time I had to take the morning after pill was with Rob, whose banana-shaped cock became overripe and oozed and leaked when it should not have done. He tried to reassure me that it was just a bit of harmless pre-cum, and not to worry (I suppose he thought I could always have an abortion). I thought I ought to ring a doctor just to make sure that the pre-cum was as innocuous as Rob was making out. "On the contrary," said the doctor, "it's chock full of sperm," or words to that effect.

I wearily obtained a prescription from a female doctor who was extremely and surprisingly *simpatico*. As I shuffled into the doctor's office, I tried to look as penitent as possible. I've been a very naughty girl. First of all I've had sex, and secondly I was irresponsible enough not to use any protection apart from a man's reassurance while aroused that he knows what he is doing (which is no protection at all, let's face it). I expected the usual snotty lecture and was ready to offer gushing promises never to take such risks again, which I obviously fully and passionately intended to honor, at least while I was sober. Instead, the doctor ushered me to the chair and after I explained the situation, she laughed and said, "Where would we be without some good old-fashioned passion?" and promptly filled out the prescription while murmuring sympathetic "I know, I know" noises about the nausea and hormone hell to follow.

I decided to be sensible and take the day off work so that I could lie in bed and whimper and curse to my heart's content. I rang my boss, who was male, and decided, in my general irritation with men, that he did not deserve to be shielded from the curse of being a woman. I explained that I had had to take the morning after pill and I would be spending the day in bed trying to sleep to avoid puking the pill up. Unsurprisingly, he couldn't get off the phone quick enough and he avoided eye contact with me for about three days after my return to work. Maybe he had been burned by the eight-day suicidal mania and sensibly knew it was best to evade the mounting torpedo of emotions.

I didn't hear from Rob all day, which was a shame as chocolates, flowers and sympathy can actually avert nearly all suicidal tendencies. It happened once – the spunk-happy man turned up with the above and I really didn't feel nearly as shitty as I normally do in such circumstances. All you need is love, sympathy, understanding and some chocolate. They are the only known antidotes to the effects of the morning after pill. Unfortunately, in my experience, they are rarely forthcoming, hence the hormonal low which inevitably transforms into a boiling and uncontrollable rage. Just add one inconsiderate boyfriend who neither calls nor visits and you have an explosive cocktail of raging hormones, a bitter sense of injustice and martyrdom, and seething resentment that you didn't even have an orgasm. You might as well pack all the stuff he's ever left at your apartment into a big black trash bag and throw it out the window. Face it baby, it's over.

I'm telling you. It's absolutely crappy being a woman. One of my friends says she has a real problem believing in God on the basis that all men are bastards and therefore He must be too. I can see where she's coming from. Of course God is a man. You don't need any further proof than periods.

I still haven't quite got over the shame of having periods. I feel quite disgusting to men when I'm menstruating. And I don't mean in a blood-stained sheets way, I just mean looking sheepish and feeling embarrassed when I've got a Tampax up my sleeve on the way to the toilet at work. The Tampax is hidden because I genuinely do not wish to embarrass any man with the sordid facts of a woman's fertility cycle.

I am sure you will not be surprised to learn that I am not one of those women who barely notices she is even having a period. I get stomach cramps, back pain and a craving for sugar so severe that I have been known to leave my bed in the middle of the night, doubled over in pain, for a desperate run to a 24-hour store. No chocolate is safe from me. I have no morals. I will take anyone's chocolate and with absolutely no conscience I will scarf every last bit.

Every car accident I have ever had has been pre-menstrual-related. I can't park to save my life. If you ever see a parked car miles from the curb or half mounting it, you can bet your bottom dollar that the driver is suffering from pre-menstrual syndrome. For me PMS entails zero energy and a melancholia so severe that I spend a couple of days every month cursing God that I have even been born at all. The mess, the smell, the ruined underwear; worse is the paranoia that you have leaked onto your clothes and are unknowingly walking around with a large red stain on the back of your skirt. I became obsessed with this possibility when I saw a woman at work with a very large reddish-brown stain on the back of her pale yellow skirt, and as a result I have developed a twitch for a few days every month whereby my hand casually but repeatedly brushes the back of my skirt every thirty seconds.

I'm telling you, the list of female curses is endless: vaginal farts, pantyliners, cellulite, arthritis from high heels, waxing, pregnancy, morning sickness, stretch marks, ante-natal depression, post-natal depression, facial hair, body hair, no tits, droopy tits, underwired bras that cut into your skin and have to be hand-washed, primary responsibility for contraception, sperm receptacle, passive call-waiting, inability to go to parks alone, inability to piss standing up against a wall, fear of rape (and it's all our fault for wearing a short skirt), domestic violence, discrimination at work, glass ceilings, halving your number of lovers and still being called a slut, fashion slavery, pelvic inflammatory disease.

And if you think all that is insignificant, then maybe some statistics will help: although women make up fifty per cent of the world's population, they perform nearly two-thirds of all working hours, receive only one-tenth of the world's income and own less than one per cent of world property.

There is actually also a prayer that Jewish women can say every morning. We can say, "Blessed art thou, O Lord our God, King of the Universe, who has made me according to thy will." We've drawn the short straw, but we are supposed to be grateful. "According to thy sick sense of humor" would be more accurate. Listen, I know I'm being negative and I would dearly love to have written a chapter on how great it is to be a woman, but I really cannot think of one advantage that we have over men.

Apart from anything else, it's bloody expensive being a woman. I reckon we should be paid £100 more than men a week across the board. I've worked out the actual monthly cost of being a woman and it's a horrifyingly expensive business: make-up, make-up bag, make-up remover, cotton wool, toner, cleanser, day cream, night cream, exfoliator, body moisturiser, self-tanning lotion, pantyhose, Tampax, sanitary towels, pantyliners, ruined underwear, supplies of chocolate, pain killers, birth control, prescription for antibiotics for cystitis, thrush cream, thrush pessary, bras, nail polish, nail polish remover, cuticle remover, hairdressers (at least three times the cost of a barber), dye to cover gray (unacceptable for women), hairspray, electricity for hairdryer, waxing, eyelash tinting, tweezers, manicures, pedicures, blackhead removing pads (new on the market – you didn't know you needed them before now), eyelash curlers, dry cleaning, Anusol sup-

positories (for the anal sex you had last night at his suggestion and for which you alone are now suffering), liposuction,
breast augmentation, breast reduction (this is for a particularly
expensive month, I admit).

So now you can see why I am pissed off this week, and in
general.

Withdrawal

As well as avoiding the morning after pill during the initial stages of a relationship, I would go further and say "Stay away from the contraceptive pill altogether." In one way, it's quite a good test of the strength of a relationship. If you've been together less than three months and you go on the pill and you manage to stay together during the hormone adjustment period, you might as well resign yourself to the fact that you're going to be partners for life. OK, maybe I am exaggerating, but I reckon there is a great deal of truth in that statement. Some people just don't make the connection. They say "everything was going really well" (hence the step to commit to long-term contraceptive measures) and then they say "I don't know what happened – it just all fell apart." Nine times out of ten, after further questioning, I am normally able to point out the pill/end of a perfect relationship connection.

Bearing all this in mind, I decide at this delicate early stage of my own relationship with Mark to go on the pill. Reason being that I am crap at using condoms. I am not one of those sensible girls who love and respect themselves enough to not take risks with their bodies. There are a thousand good reasons for using condoms, and having suffered from thrush, non-specific urethritis and genital warts (care of Tom), I really ought to have learned from bitter experience.

After our first year together, Tom went to the States for a three-month working trip and had a one-night stand – he claims it was because I hadn't written to him for six weeks, while he was still writing biweekly. I hadn't written because I'd been busy giving blowjobs to a (nice) German on the beach at night on my summer vacation in Greece. I forgave him. I may be a lot of things, but one thing I ain't is a hypocrite. I suppose the only thing that did piss me off was when we were reunited after the three-month absence and he tricked me into confessing to a couple of kisses. I didn't feel it necessary to mention the blowjobs and he still doesn't know. He was furious anyway and claimed to have valiantly fought all temptation in order to remain true to his beloved girlfriend who was out of his sight but never out of his mind. Boy, did I get a guilt trip for a couple of lousy kisses, or what. I begged for forgiveness, which he eventually grudgingly bestowed upon me.

Two weeks later, after plenty of deep-thrust fucking, things just did not seem right down below. I went to a doctor who soon turned nasty after she had had a good poke around. She grimly informed me that I had thrush, NSU, genital warts and, possibly, herpes. I was particularly devastated about the herpes, especially as straight after seeing the doctor I had some time to kill before meeting Tom and I went to a newsstand. A card caught my eye. The front cover said, "What's the difference between love and herpes?" Inside, was the reply, "Herpes is forever." I burst into tears.

Just occasionally, I am a really cool, calm, *nice* person. I suddenly become rational, understanding, compassionate and forgiving. Normally at times when you might expect quite the reverse from me, just as Tom did when I quietly informed him of the monstrous outcome of my doctor's visit. He was forced to own up to his one-night stand with someone who I later gathered would dearly have liked to have been a prostitute had she only been able to charge for it. I unquestioningly bestowed my forgiveness upon him, as I reckoned he must be feeling pretty shitty and there's not much to choose between a blowjob and a screw on the infidelity stakes. Anyway, it turned out that I didn't have herpes, just the other things.

I had to make an appointment with a doctor at the Genito-Urinary clinic in town for a thorough examination. There was a festive atmosphere in the waiting room and it seemed that it was full of cheery regulars who greeted each other, caught up on all the news and told each other jokes as if they were at a school parents' evening rather than a VD clinic. I figured they must be the local prostitutes and while on the one hand I felt tainted to be in such a sordid environment, there was a real buzz in the place and I quite liked being one of the girls. I was a nineteen-year-old middle-class law student with very little life experience – but I didn't let that stop me from feeling like a woman of the world.

I was almost beginning to enjoy the experience until a woman emerged from the doctor's office and one of the girls called out to her, "What sort of mood is the old bastard in today?" The woman grimaced, "Not good at all," and hobbled away. The other women jeered and joked, but the exchange had wiped the smile off my face. Especially as I was called in next.

I will never forget the examination this doctor gave me. It was a little like I imagine medieval torture must have been. I was strapped to a bed, naked from the waist down (which I felt *extremely* coy about – even I hadn't seen what my cunt looked like yet) with my legs hooked into two leather (of course) stirrups. I think there may even have been a nurse holding my hands down so that I could not escape. The doctor stood in the far corner of the room, looking grim and unforgiving, as he slowly eased his hands into rubber (of course) gloves. I was watching him through the space between my legs. Then he picked up the medieval torture implement, which was a large cylindrical metal object with, *note*, a flat blunt end. In retrospect, I think he removed it from a fridge/freezer.

Now I've only ever seen a javelin-throwing contest once on TV but I am sure this guy competed at national level. He took a running jump and sprinted towards me, wielding the torture implement with the blunt edge facing towards me. I think I passed out before he plunged it into me but I do remember trying desperately to grip my feet in the stirrups to block the impact and I am sure I saw the doctor's twisted smile as I slid up the bed in agony.

After the physical examination I felt a little teary, and this soon developed into full-scale hysterical sobbing when he handed me various prescriptions for antibiotics with the instructions, "No sex or alcohol for twenty-one days." I think he may have been Muslim as he pooh-poohed my dismay at the booze ban. In any event he was very impatient with my inconsolable, uncontrollable sobbing at the thought of no sex with Tom.

"Whatever is the matter?" he demanded.

"My boyfriend and I have been apart for three months this summer," I sniveled, "and I can't bear the thought of not having sex with him for another three weeks."

He had now completely lost patience with the little slut in front of him and I was discouraged from remaining in his office a minute longer.

Anyway, the fact is that I made a full recovery and the

only reminder I have is the need for regular pap smears on the basis that genital warts can make you ten times more prone to cervical cancer. The only consolation I have is that Tom's genital warts are also more likely to reappear on the end of his dick every now and then, which does not cheer me up as much as it should.

I suppose that nowadays everything is a bit less romantic and far more sensible – you see someone for a while and if you decide to commit to a monogamous relationship then you go for a his 'n' hers AIDS test and if it's all clear then you chuck out the condoms. But if one of you is really naughty and cheats without condoms, then you're still fucked, if you know what I mean. I don't know what the answer is.

Pills

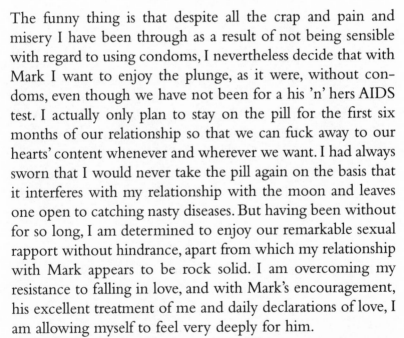

The funny thing is that despite all the crap and pain and misery I have been through as a result of not being sensible with regard to using condoms, I nevertheless decide that with Mark I want to enjoy the plunge, as it were, without condoms, even though we have not been for a his 'n' hers AIDS test. I actually only plan to stay on the pill for the first six months of our relationship so that we can fuck away to our hearts' content whenever and wherever we want. I had always sworn that I would never take the pill again on the basis that it interferes with my relationship with the moon and leaves one open to catching nasty diseases. But having been without for so long, I am determined to enjoy our remarkable sexual rapport without hindrance, apart from which my relationship with Mark appears to be rock solid. I am overcoming my resistance to falling in love, and with Mark's encouragement, his excellent treatment of me and daily declarations of love, I am allowing myself to feel very deeply for him.

After only a month of mutual blissful devotion, however, Mark starts to act a bit strange. I can't quite put my finger on it, but whereas, for example, he was always deeply fascinated by the minutiae of my existence, he is now suddenly somewhat distant. He complains of feeling tired and stressed and is no longer insistent on seeing me quite as frequently. At the same time, when I am with him I feel irritable and stressed myself. I initially put this down to the after-effects of the antibiotics from the cystitis.

Strangely, I don't feel that he is going off me as I instinctively trust him and believe his declarations of love. At the same time, however, he seems to have gone all funny after a wonderful night we spent together during which I told him that I was now one hundred per cent certain that I was indeed very lucky to have found such a wonderful boyfriend and please could I devote my life to him.

I do hold some very old-fashioned beliefs about how to act with men, along the lines of *treat them mean, keep them keen*. I feel that the minute I allow myself to love a guy, he'll be off. I know I made out earlier that my relationship with Tom was perfect, but there was a strong element of me trying to remain continuously elusive to keep him interested. And, unfortunately, that was how he wanted me. If I became too loving and just an incy wincy tiny little bit clingy, he withdrew. I remember one conversation we had near the end of the relationship that summed it all up perfectly. We were on the phone and I felt like hearing some soothing love talk.

"Say something nice to me."

"Don't be so bloody annoying."

I became angry: "Why can't you just fucking well be nice to me if I ask you to?"

"You sound so cute and gorgeous. I love you when you are angry."

The bitch act had worked, unintentionally. I had got what I wanted, but I'd had to be aggressive to achieve it.

The same principle applied in bed. If I wanted sex, I had to pretend that I did not in order to get him interested. If I intimated that I was up for it, he just wasn't in the mood. If I'm honest, once our honeymoon period was over (thankfully, this lasted two years), the cycle went something like this: he was nice to me, so I was nice to him, he withdrew, I became angry and withdrew myself, then he started being nice to me again, and so on.

Gabriela believes it's all down to the passing elevators syndrome, where two people rarely like each other the same amount at the same time. When one elevator is going up, the other elevator is going down, with the two elevators only fleetingly on the same level at the same time. Perhaps this is what is going on now between Mark and myself. My elevator is going up, while his elevator is on its way to the basement.

But something odd is going on with Mark and I don't think it is to do with me; I just can't figure out what it is that has made him shut down with me. I do ask him, but he just tells me that his job is becoming increasingly stressful and that he is desperately overdue for a vacation. He does, however, hint that he does have his own emotional baggage, darkly alluding to skeletons in his closet. He says that all will shortly be revealed. I don't want to know anything bad about him. I have finally found a wonderful man who always says and does the right thing, who gives me no cause for complaint in or out of the sack. That is all I need to know.

But the reality is that he is thirty-five and single, with no real long-term relationships under his belt. Life may be perfectly straightforward and hassle-free for certain people who have a deep, unshakeable belief in their own self-worth, but I know by now that I am not one of those people and consequently that this is not how things work out for me.

I want to remain blinkered and sheltered from Mark's problems, but at the same time I occasionally find myself dwelling on what skeletons he could possibly be referring to. You read about people who fall madly in love with someone who later turns out to be married, sadistic, or worse, unable to commit. But Mark does not seem to be afflicted by any of these curses. What the hell could it be? Why has he switched off from me just when our elevators have landed on the same floor?

What do you reckon you could live with in the baggage/ skeleton stakes? Say you find out your wonderful boyfriend has been married twice before. Is that OK? What about if he's bisexual? Devoted only truly to his mother? Suffers from impotence? Infertile? Only really turned on by whips and leather? Still hankering after an ex-girlfriend? Hooked on cocaine? A criminal record? Had sex with his sister, or worse, his brother?

So far, the only downside to Mark is that he snores like a bear.

Turns out Mark has been on Prozac – *for two years* – and after our wonderful night together when I gave him all the reassurance that he wanted that I was falling in love with him, he decided, in his happiness, to stop taking them. Just like that. After two years. No scaling down, no consultation with a doctor; basically the decision to stop was made with no forethought whatsoever. And now it transpires that he is suffering from some pretty unpleasant withdrawal symptoms, such as sleeplessness, nightmares, anxiety attacks and chronic irritability.

When he told me last night, I felt sick with disappointment and misery. I was supposed to be the fucked-up one, not him. But deep down I know the score. A happy, together person attracts a similarly mentally and emotionally healthy person. Like attracts like. This has always struck me as a particularly tragic irony. The confused people lacking self-belief actually *need* a nice, normal, stable person; the happy, together girl has got enough going for her without nabbing the best fellas as well.

But I mean, two years is a hell of a long time to be taking anti-depressants, isn't it? Loads of people I know have been on them, including myself, as you know, but only for a couple of months to assist survival through a really rough patch. What kind of person takes emotion numbing pills for two years of their life?

Once he told me, he obviously felt he had no further need to pretend that he was OK. He became completely uncommunicative. Unused to feeling full-scale emotion, he seemed to close down altogether. And that included all feelings towards me. I felt doubly devastated: my boyfriend had problems (which meant, incidentally, that he would not be available to devote himself entirely to dealing with mine) and he was no longer the loving and affectionate man who seduced me into loving him back.

To be honest, when he told me, I freaked out. I did not handle it at all well. The truth was that I was angry with him. The poor guy had let me down by not being perfect after all. I looked at him lying on the bed; he was tired, stressed, silent and withdrawn. Instead of feeling compassionate and loving, however, I felt irritated by both his lack of ability to deal with life without pills and by his irresponsible decision to just stop taking the goddamn pills without first seeking medical advice. I became bullying, harsh and unsympathetic. I started lecturing him on how he had to get his life together, get a new job, lose weight, tidy up his apartment, deal with emotions and enter therapy immediately. Basically, I was the last thing in the whole world that he needed.

We had a completely shitty evening. I was secretly convinced that the relationship was over. Mark had too many problems, none of which he wanted to deal with, hence numbing out for so long. The only person I know who has taken Prozac for so long is the author of *Prozac Nation*, the prologue of which reads "I hate myself and I want to die," which gives you some indication of the type of person who commits himself to taking the pills long term. In keeping with the mood of the evening, we went to a dark, dingy, smelly little wine bar where I drank vinegary wine and felt sick and unsettled. Mark sat there mute, transfixed by the TV in the corner. It had all gone horribly wrong. I felt like running out of the bar and into the oncoming traffic. I thought I'd need some of his anti-depressants.

When we got home, I picked on him a bit more and then decided to gather together all my belongings and go home. The thing that actually pissed me off the most was the fact that Mark had completely stopped talking. He just kept wearily rubbing his eyes and yawning. Faced with his total shutdown, I overfunctioned like mad and pestered him for reassurances that he would get his fucking life together. Un-surprisingly, I obtained no reassurances whatsoever, just Mark's tired, blinking eyes looking back at me forlornly.

I was actually a bit too drunk to be driving home, but I just had to go and I was too bombed to get a cab. I felt sick from disappointment and cheap wine and I swerved into the curb a few times on the way home, flung open my door, hung out of the car and threw up in the road. If a police car had spotted me, I would have been arrested on the spot. I didn't give a shit about being banned from driving. Instead I was thinking that not only was it not going to work out between me and Mark (who I have told *everyone* about), it also meant that I would be single again. AAAAAAARGH!

When I got home, I realized I was in the middle of a full-blown freakout; my mind was going crazy, working at a million worries a second. I felt like my brain was going to explode. I quickly rummaged about for my last remaining beta blocker and gobbled it down. I couldn't remember how long they took to work, I just hoped that I wouldn't throw myself out of the window while I was waiting. I cannot tell you how desperate I felt. I hated Mark. I hated relationships. I hated life. And I wasn't too keen on myself either.

My body then took over and decided that it needed to expel all the toxins in my stomach. I grabbed a plastic grocery bag and sat by the side of my bed, quietly puking in to the bag so as not to alarm Gabriela who was sleeping peacefully with the northern businessman she'd pulled in one of the rich man's bars she'd been frequenting on her way back from college. Whimpering over the plastic bag, I noticed the beta blocker was one of the first things to come up and I momentarily considered retrieving it, *Trainspotting*-style, but before I had time, it was smothered with a new load of vomit.

I Should Have Been a Man

I go around to Claudia's to discuss the implications of yesterday's disastrous discovery, and for some love, pot and Valium. My friend Danny also pops over and he tells me that his stepmother was on anti-depressants for twenty years after the birth of her second child, and she was a nightmare for two whole years when she came off them. I ask Danny how his father coped. Not well, apparently. There were constant threats of divorce. I know how he felt, yet at the same time feel galled at his and my own lack of support and understanding.

As we all lie under the comforter in Claudia's garden, looking at the stars and having a wonderful laugh, I realize how much I have cut myself off from enjoying my friends since I got it together with Mark. Of course, I always swore that I would not become a member of Couples R Us, but my life for the past month or so seems to have consisted merely of seeing Mark and recovering from the late nights I spent with him. I realize how much I have stopped appreciating my friends and I gaze at Claudia with overwhelming love and affection. Claudia, who has always been there for me, reveling in the good times and commiserating over the shit.

"Claudia, I love you."

"I love you too. Do you want to feel me up?"

"Tits or cunt?" I ask.

"Cunt," she specifies.

Danny pipes up from the other end of the comforter in a voice full of hope: "Can you just pretend I'm not here?"

Claudia and I always joke about having sex with each other. Particularly in front of men, to wind them up. I am convinced there is not one single exception to the all-male fantasy of watching two women together. Once, in a bid to lure Matt from his spoiled and selfish girlfriend while she was on a business trip (I'd fixed him up with her and she then told him that she didn't want him to see me anymore without her permission and presence), Claudia and I offered him a threesome. We knew that we weren't really going to do it, but it was such fun watching Matt wrestle with his conscience for all of two seconds before conclusively deciding that a threesome did not constitute infidelity.

However, the more Claudia and I talked about it, the more we got into the idea (both horny and drunk, desperate for excitement and at a party with no other male possibilities). We agreed that the only thing wrong with the proposed threesome was the presence of Matt and we decided to proceed without him. We disappeared to the loo, locked the door, giggled and fumbled, and it was with some relief that I decided that it just ain't interesting for me without a cock. I can't really see the point. It's also doubly frustrating for me as I would love to have had a cock myself. It's one of my big regrets in life. Apart from anything else, I reckon I would have been an almighty fuck. I felt like an honorary man when I lived in Italy and my southern Italian boyfriend finished with me on the grounds that he was fed up with being used as a sex object. He complained that I just liked to go out drinking with my friends and would only turn up at the end of the evening if I were in the mood for a lay. It sounded so weirdly familiar that I had to laugh.

Claudia suggests that I stay the night, which would be appealing were it not for the half hour required to clear a week's worth of detritus from her bed. I am constantly amazed at the quantity and variety of crap on her bed. Three changes of clothes, an ashtray, a razor, two old newspapers, an eyeliner, a subway ticket, matches and one of my lost lighters, a contraceptive pill packet (the last pill of which was taken four days ago), instructions to the morning after pill, a half-eaten bag of chips, a hole punch and a ruler, an invite to a party, a map to a different party, a sock, a Phillip Roth reader, a bottle of blue nail polish, a candle, two pairs of panties, the underwire from a bra, an orange and a vibrator.

As I wearily start removing the accoutrements to another of Claudia's busy weeks, I think what a great evening I've had with my friends. I am temporarily happy despite the fact that I have very nearly resolved to finish with Mark.

The Elevator Syndrome in Practice

I wake up the following morning deciding that I miss Mark and that I love him.

I reacted very badly to Mark's skeleton, partly because it touched a nerve regarding my own feelings towards how I cope with life's "challenges" (variously by drugs, drink, meaningless sex and shutting off access to my heart), partly because, immaturely, I wanted a perfect Prince Charming who was going to look after me (I am clearly still not free of my Cinderella chains), and partly because I was quietly freaking out from the effects of the combined pill. It transpires that I am on a particularly no-nonsense hard-hitting brand of contraceptive pill that takes no prisoners, both in terms of paddling sperm and emotional stability.

So, as Mark is dealing with the effects of coming off his pills, which I discover are well-known for killer withdrawal cold turkey side effects, I am dealing with the effects of going on the pill. Basically, the timing stinks. Perhaps if we had been together longer, we would deal with it better. Unfortunately, the fact is that I have not known Mark long enough to know who the real Mark is. Is he the gorgeous, sparky, loving guy who won me over? Or is that personality only maintained by a course of happy pills? Is he the morose, stressed-out, uncommunicative guy with whom I am currently dealing? Or is he the guy who two years previously felt perilously close to falling to bits, hence the decision to take anti-depressants and then stay on them? In which case, what the hell is that Mark like?

I am driving myself crazy with these questions. Instead of allowing the relationship to take its course, I feel the need to decide there and then whether this man is suitable for a long-term committed relationship. As you get older, there is so much pressure on even the shortest relationship. You spend so much energy tormenting yourself over whether or not he is The One (I hate that phrase, by the way) that there is no room left for spontaneity and discovery.

Add to all this introspective worry the effect of PMS while on the pill and I start to go a bit nuts. I can think of nothing other than Mark and his problems and whether they are surmountable. And I decide that whether they are sur-mountable or not, I am already too deeply into the guy to even contemplate ending the relationship.

However, just as my elevator is rising, it seems Mark is incredibly pissed off with me for the nasty hectoring I had given him. I plead with him for forgiveness, pointing out that I was so wound up from a week of him withdrawing from me without explanation. I also explain that going on the pill has interfered with my sanity and made me much more touchy and vulnerable than I would be otherwise. I apologize, I re-acted badly and I now want to make it up to him.

As is often the way, the more his elevator descends, the higher mine rises until I am desperate for some reassurance from him that he wishes to continue our relationship. Due to my completely unsympathetic reaction to Mark's anti-depressants, the law of karma no doubt dictates that Mark will dump me and I will end up on anti-depressants for two years. I will then meet a lovely guy who will respond unsympathetically to my medication and dump me.

My insecurity with Mark reaches a crescendo. Despite the fact that he has already told me that he still loves me and still wants me, I am not convinced. The only thing I really believe is that I have fucked up and now I am going to be dumped. I tell Gabriela that if she really loves me, she will take a gun and shoot me. I do not want to live with the thoughts in my head.

And then my period starts. I wake up bleeding and feeling normal and happy. I throw the other pill packet away. And I book a vacation. With Claudia. It is time to get away.

Non-sexual Healing

The plan is to fly to Malaga, hire a car, drive around south-ern Spain and generally hang out. The idea is to compromise my wish to vegetate in the shade and read, and Claudia's ants-in-her-pants desire to be a mover and shaker. The only thing that concerned me while booking the vacation was sharing the driving with Claudia. Being a control freak, I don't like sitting in the passenger seat, especially when Claudia is driving. She is what I would call a "hesitant" driver and she also has a tendency to tap her foot on the accelerator in time to the music. However, en route to the airport, she informs me that I will be doing all the driving as a previous motor-ing offense (don't ask) means that she is not allowed to drive rental cars for five years. I am delighted. No nausea-inducing shuddering car journeys with me loudly begging her to please overtake the car that we have been stuck behind for the last two hours.

As we trundle along in my car to the airport, we are on a buoyant pre-vacation high, aided by some laughing gas grass and a mutual desire to run from London as fast as we possi-bly can. Claudia is reeling from a disastrous date for which she had been planning and scheming for the last eight months.

I am not kidding – eight months of military-style prepara-
tion, all for nothing. She focused in on her target who she
decided would make her a wonderful husband due to the fact
that he was a thrusting young playwright who also happened
to be Jewish and single. She worked quietly at first, researching his social life and befriending his friends. She soon discovered his nightly venues and started visiting them. She
engineered chance meetings until he knew her name and
promising flirtations took place. Her *pièce de résistance* was
meeting his parents, through friends of her parents, whom she
charmed so overwhelmingly that in the end his mother
arranged the date for the two of them.

On the drive to the airport she fills me in on the details
of the date, at the end of which I have revised my first reassuring murmurs of " Well, he's obviously shy," to "Look, he's
probably gay."

Things started going awry when she casually referred to
their "date" and he reacted with astonishment. "Is this a
date?" he asked with detached amusement. After spending ten
minutes arguing and persuading him that their dinner
arrangement was indeed a date, Claudia began to doubt the
validity of her own argument. They decided to drop the
matter. He then asked her a series of such penetrating questions that she began to wonder whether he was using her as
research for a new character in one of his clever but soulless
plays. They were not the questions of a man intrigued by the
beautiful creature before him, but the haughty and imper-
sonal questions of a job interview. Where did you go to
school? What university did you go to? What did you "major
in'? (He'd been to Oxford.) What does your father do for a
living? Are you close to your parents? Who was your last
boyfriend? Was he Jewish? What did your parents think of
him? Who dumped who? Why did it finish? Are you still in

touch? What do your friends do? Do you own your apartment? Where is it? How much did it cost? Who do you live with? It was exhausting. Each time she tried to bring the conversation back to the state of post-modern contemporary London theatre (something she had been researching and revising for the last week), he would fire off another question. She didn't know whether to feel flattered or assaulted. This matter was settled definitively when he kindly hailed two taxis outside the restaurant and she went home alone.

I am delighted that Claudia has decided to take the risk of smuggling a week's worth of pot with her on vacation. She tells me that everyone has told her to carry the stuff on her through customs, rather than hiding it fully cling-wrapped in a bottle of body cream. I disagree vehemently and reckon that she is more likely to be searched than her bag. As we discuss the practicalities of smuggling the weed through customs, Claudia's previous nonchalance starts to ebb away. It disappears completely when we realize that we are being flanked on all sides of the car by three police dog-handling vans, presumably also en route to the airport bearing loudly barking German Shepherds, straining at the leash and ready to denounce us at the earliest opportunity.

Once we arrive at the airport, Claudia's nerves are not helped by my immature and hysterical giggling when the woman at luggage check-in asks us if we have anything to declare. Her nerves further deteriorate when she is subjected to a thorough body search (barring orifices) while my hand luggage is pulled to one side and carefully examined.

A couple of years earlier on another all-girls jaunt to Spain I decided to take my new toy (a vibrator) with me. Working on the same principle as above, I stashed it in my suitcase and promptly forgot all about it until I was checking my case in and I was questioned on whether there were any electrical items in my bag. Suddenly remembering the vibrator and not wanting to be responsible for a mid-air explosion (in my ignorance of aerodynamics), I blurted out that I had packed some curling tongs. The woman looked doubtfully at my very short crop hairdo and said I should take my bag to the luggage x-ray department for the all-clear.

Mortified, I shlepped my bag to the relevant department, which was manned by two cheeky looking young guys. As the bag passed through the x-ray machine, the guys started sniggering and called out disbelievingly, "Hair-curling tongs, you say." It took all the pleasure out of using the damn thing once I arrived on vacation as I was constantly reminded of my embarrassment at the airport and the security staff's impertinent jokes.

So despite Claudia's hysteria, I am just pleased not to have any sex-aids in my hand luggage. If it was a toss up between being caught with a vibrator or a kilo of cocaine, I'd choose the cocaine. *Much* less embarrassing. When we arrive in the departure lounge, Claudia watches our luggage being loaded on to the plane while I calmly read the Sunday papers. Finally, she's smiling again and I get the thumbs up – the bags are on board. The irony is that the pot turns out to be totally crappy and the week's supply only lasts two days. It really was not worth the aggravation.

We have a great vacation and, for us, a relatively uneventful one. I had not thought it possible but we manage to bond even more deeply. Claudia avoids her favorite vacation taunt, which is to gently but persistently remind me of all the friends that I have fallen out with by "innocently" asking me whether I am in still touch with someone whom I have been telling her about, despite the fact that she knows full well that not only are the ex-friend and I no longer in contact, but chances are that if we met one day we would ignore each other in the street.

I, meanwhile, invent a new game with which to affectionately taunt Claudia, called "The Claudia Richards Fantasy World." The thing about Claudia is that she tells you something categorically one day and the following day, with apparently no memory of what she has previously stated, she proceeds to tell you the complete opposite. For example, she will cheerfully tell me one day that she is *completely* over her ex-boyfriend. The following day she's on the phone crying that she is devastated that her ex-boyfriend has been on a date. Of course, it would be inappropriate to point out any inconsistency and I listen sympathetically. Or she tells you that she is really depressed and has been for months. The next time I see her she is skipping gaily around her apartment telling me what a great year it has been and how her therapy has really helped to stabilize her moods. Or she tells you that she is suffering from a chronic singles crisis and is on a constant HCA (Happy Couple Alert). A couple of days later, I overhear her earnestly telling someone that she loves her life and rarely thinks about men. Or she bemoans the fact that she does not enjoy a close relationship with her parents; a month later she tells me what a close family unit they are, and the day after that she's crying on the phone because her mother didn't ring her to tell her that her sister had gone into labor.

I recently listened with disbelief while she told me she wanted to give an ex-boyfriend a second chance as she had been so cruel to him first time around. Wasn't this the guy who she said had been a complete and utter asshole to her throughout their short, unhappy relationship, I wanted to ask. Instead, I entered the "Claudia Richards Fantasy World" with her and agreed that the guy clearly deserved to be given a second chance. I have always figured that it would be rather pointless and cruel to point out the discrepancies as I know that she sincerely believes what she is saying (and that is important) *at the time.*

But different, more light-hearted rules apply on vacation and I give her a good roasting each time she tries to lay a newly inconsistent line of reasoning on me. Claudia takes it all a lot better than I used to with the "Are you still in touch with them?" game, which truly tormented me and provoked immediate sadness and, often, regret.

Conversation centers mostly around sex, partly because I had a monster session with Mark the night before I left for vacation and I am feeling so horny that I nearly drown in one session with the shower head in the hotel bathroom. I exude sexual confidence and know-how, and on Claudia's insistence I end up imparting my Top Ten Hot Sexual Tips, which Claudia later manages, through sheer force of wishful thinking, to put into practice on her return from vacation, with confirmation to me of their efficacy. I have decided not to tell you what they are; a girl's got to have some secrets hasn't she? Anyway, maybe you already know it all and I wouldn't want to be accused of teaching anyone to suck eggs (cocks yes, eggs no). I will tell you that one of the most fundamental tips is to immediately dump anyone who will not go down on you. They are woman-haters.

The only thing that does not go according to plan on the holiday is the driving. I may be good at blowjobs, but I am absolutely shitty at driving on the wrong side of the road on mountainside hair-pin bends in the blazing midday sun in a car with no air-conditioning. Within three hours of renting the car, we've lost a wing-mirror, a side light and there are deep grooves in the paintwork along the side of the car.

Eventually the unthinkable happens. I pull in, toss Claudia the keys and say, "*You* drive." I also give her permission to unmercifully tease my driving, if she wishes. And she does.

Ever since I'd booked the vacation, I had sort of been planning to smooch with a sexy Spanish guy if the opportunity arose. And in my usual honest, open approach to relationships, I'd mentioned it to Mark (who had not fully reverted to the devoted boyfriend he was before the coming-off-the-pills-going-on-the-pill trauma and therefore deserved to be tormented). I don't think he realized I was being serious. "You won't, will you?" he said.

Feeling mean, I backtracked and reassured him that I wouldn't.

Then he said, "I trust you."

You don't know me, I thought. But afterwards his words repeat themselves in my head and I know he has said just the right thing to ensure that I keep myself completely faithful. This guy trusts me and that's all there is to it. I don't want to break that trust.

When the opportunity does arise it turns out that Mark's trust is not misplaced. Claudia and I are picked up by a couple of students from Seville in a bar in a festive little town on our last night. They challenge us to a game of pool (which we win, much to their surprise, but not mine – I'm great at pool when I'm bombed) and they then unwittingly find the easiest way to our hearts, by offering us the best dope I have ever smoked. We chill out late into the sultry night until Claudia feels far too gone to continue trying to communicate, having exhausted all the Spanish she knows about three hours earlier. I am merrily talking away in Italian, mildly hoping that if I add a lisp to most words the Spaniards will understand. They are certainly nodding eagerly and in my wonderful I-love-everyone and aren't-I-great mood, I imagine myself to be thoroughly entertaining. Claudia and I start talking about what the guys' cocks might be like, confident that they don't understand a word we are saying. It is so liberating to be talking about them so freely. We say all the socially unacceptable stuff that we would normally discuss when we go home, although I do note after a while that they are all still nodding eagerly. This either means that they do understand or that we were not previously entertaining them quite as much as we thought.

We stumble home, waving the guys goodbye. I always feel a bit guilty when I leave a guy with no going-home present, but I suppose they took their chances and it's no good making out with someone out of obligation. Especially when you have a boyfriend at home who trusts you. I fall into my bedroom and pass out immediately. We both feel surprisingly rejuvenated in the morning.

I don't think about Mark much while I'm away, except in a sexual sense. I daydream for hours about exactly what he will do to me when I return to London. I keep asking Claudia to spank me – one of the things I have planned for Mark to do when I get back – but she gets all prudish. So I spank her a few times instead and she reluctantly agrees that it is quite nice. But even my sexual longing wanes over the week and I feel wonderfully neutral about everything and everyone.

I return to London calmer, and more importantly, tan.

Treat Me Mean, Keep Me Keen

It took one month for me to get into the relationship with Mark. It takes me two months to get out of the relationship with Mark. Two months of a complete lack of effort, communication and affection on his part (for more of which, see below). Why did I put up with this shit for two months when I had only had a month of relative happiness with him in the first place?

At the time I thought it was because I loved him and because I believed we had a future together. But in retrospect, taking his behavior over the two-month period into account, this could not have been the case. I am afraid that the answer is less romantic but no less pathetic. I did not want to be alone. I did not want to revert to "single," outcast, relationship-failure status. I did not want to go to my cousin's wedding without a boyfriend. I did not want to go out manhunting anymore. I did not want to accept that my wonderful boyfriend was in fact a complete washout. I did not want to start from scratch all over again. I did not want to stop having amazing sex. And if I am really honest, I didn't want to give up on a cock that long and that wide. I was a prisoner of my own cockism. I had been hoisted on Mark's magnificent petard.

In the beginning of my relationship with Mark, I constantly marveled that I had met a man who never said or did the wrong thing. Well, once he came off the Prozac, things changed in that he never said or did anything at all, right or wrong. He never wanted to go out and he never wanted to talk.

He went from wanting to see me every night to never suggesting meeting up at all, even at weekends. He went from calling me three times a day to only calling me late at night to tell me that he was too tired and stressed to talk and would call me the next night, only to call me the following night at the same time with the same line.

The more he withdrew, the more effort I made. I started calling him more often, only to be rebuffed by him telling me that he was too busy/tired/stressed to talk. In the absence of him either taking me out or even popping around to see me, I had to go around to his house if I wanted to see him. Whereas before I had been offered champagne or wine, I now had to ask for a drink, only to discover that he had no wine (he'd drunk the beautiful wine I had brought him back from Spain all by himself, which he was clearly entitled to do but which surprised and disappointed me nonetheless). He now only bought himself beer which he drank plentifully but which he knew I did not like. Whereas before he had chased me around the bedroom, horny as hell, I now had to resort to stockings and suspenders to arouse him.

His only topic of conversation (when he did speak, which was extremely rare; any dialogue had to be carefully and patiently teased from him via a series of encouraging open-ended questions) was how much he hated work and how stressed it made him. Despite this, he continued to work twelve-hour days and six-day weeks and therefore had very little time or energy to offer me or the relationship.

I often asked him if he wanted to split up. He was adamant that he liked me very much and wanted to continue. It was just a stage he was going through, he explained, when he finally remembered how to speak. We would be fine, he said, we'd get through it and then we would get married and live happily ever after. So I tried to be patient and I tried to help. I spent a back-breaking afternoon helping him clear up his apartment, which he had neglected for months. I encouraged him to think about looking for a new job where he would be valued. I helped him prepare a new resumé. I arranged for my cousin to talk tactfully with him about job-hunting as they both worked in the same field and she had just found a new job quite easily. I tried so many times to get him to talk about his feelings (the ultimate Mission Impossible). I offered him massages and affection (refused). I invited him to early evening walks on the Heath to unwind (declined). If truth be told, I was overfunctioning like mad. I was trying single-handedly to save the relationship while Mark sat in an armchair, yawning.

I assumed that the reason he felt depressed (a feeling he denied, by the way, and which therefore made discussion of the problem somewhat difficult) was that he was coming off Prozac and therefore adjusting to feeling emotions again, and I tried to be as understanding of his needs as possible. This was challenging at times. For instance, when we had arranged to see each other one Sunday evening (don't get excited – I was driving around to his place for a takeout and a night in front of the telly). Friends had popped around to see me during the afternoon and we had had a fabulous time discussing, *inter alia*, the psychological implications of spanking, which we sadly agreed would reinforce feelings of self-loathing. I reluctantly waved them goodbye (they wanted to stay) at about 7:00 pm on the basis of my impending date with Mark. Once my friends had gone I rang Mark to tell him that I would be coming around in half an hour. His roommate told me that he was asleep. I did not hear from Mark until 10:00 pm that night. He told me he had just woken up and it was now too late for me to come over. I don't mind admitting that I found it extremely difficult to remain calm, patient and understanding under such circumstances.

Another tactic I tried was to be honest with him about my feelings and how I had been feeling over the previous couple of months. *I* went around to *his* apartment one night (see what I mean?) and told him that I wanted to talk to him about us. He groaned. I persisted nevertheless. I started by telling him that I really, really liked him and that I thought that we had something special and I really wanted to make it work. I said that I had not felt this way in a very long time and that it had taken a certain amount of trust and vulnerability on my part to allow myself to feel this way about a man again.

I then went on to add that I felt very rejected by his behavior over the last couple of months and that I was insecure and vulnerable too and that when he made no effort with me, having initially been so attentive, I found it extremely hurtful and difficult not to take it personally. I explained that I was prepared to wait for this difficult time to pass if I could only receive some reassurance from him of his feelings towards me (i.e. that he felt the same way and it was worth waiting), and if he could offer such reassurance, then could he please tell me what he wanted from me to help him regain his personal equilibrium as I wanted to help but so far nothing seemed to be working. I also gave a groveling apology for the way that I had reacted to his Prozac disclosure and asked for his forgiveness. It was a long speech, and as is the case with sentiments expressed from the heart, eloquent and emotional. When I had finished, I sat waiting for his response. He took off his glasses, rubbed his eyes wearily and replaced his glasses. He said nothing. I asked him what he thought about what I had said. He still said nothing. I asked him whether he could offer me any reassurance on the basis that I was now feeling very vulnerable. He took off his glasses, rubbed his eyes wearily and replaced his glasses. I then thought I would make it simple:

"Do you or do you not want to continue seeing me?"

"I do," was all he managed.

And that was the end of the discussion.

And then we had sex.

And then I went home (feeling like shit).

So, after two months of the above, I decide that I need to take drastic action. Mark needs a major kick up the ass. I finish with him, citing the above reasons. I say that I don't think he needs a girlfriend at the moment. He needs to get himself together. He disagrees, telling me that he wants me and makes vague references to changing things. But I am angry and, most of all, I am hurt. I feel as if he has been constantly reject-ing me and I now want him to fight for me. He looks so sad when I leave. I feel sure that he will fight. After all, this guy has talked about marrying me, how can he let me walk out of his life so easily and with so little effort?

The next day, I am in a reasonably optimistic mood and foolishly expect roses, serenading, love letters, a pleading call begging forgiveness having seen the error of his ways, wants me back, will try harder, etc.

Nothing. Niento. Fuck all. I don't hear a thing all week.

I discuss whether I did the right thing finishing with him and whether I should ring or wait for his call with a few friends (OK, OK, everyone I come into contact with over the week), the results of which are as follows: Claudia says he's a bastard and deserves it. Jane at work says it is dangerous to finish with boyfriends if you don't really mean it. Laura at work says her husband worked like a dog at the beginning of their relationship but it was worth it as she is now married to him and benefits from the (substantial) financial rewards (and she loves him). Gabriela says give him time to sort himself out and the relationship will be stronger as a result. My cousin Steven says I am too scared of not meeting anyone else and I shouldn't be as I am wonderful, etc. Danny says that it is no good trying to work at relationships; they either work or they don't. My sister agrees and says that, for the record, she had bad vibes from the start. My brother says that things must have been pretty bad for me to have finished with him. Gareth says that if it's not working after three months, it's not going to work after three years. The woman at the gym says her husband persevered with her when they first started going out when she was depressed, moody and difficult as hell and they are so happy now. Matt says that at the begin-ning of a relationship, men should put in most of the effort because if they don't do the work in the beginning, they sure as hell never will. Jasmin summarizes it rather well when she points out that I have none of the advantages of being in a relationship (weekends in bed, dinner dates, walks on the Heath), all of the disadvantages of being in a relationship (stress and aggravation), all of the disadvantages of being single (spending weekends alone) and none of the advantages (going to parties, having a laugh and coming on to guys).

Well, I listen to all of this and the problem is that I agree with all of it. But none of it helps. I don't know if I do want him or I don't. Sometimes I feel as if I love him. Sometimes I feel as if I hate him. Was finishing with him the wrong way to sort out our problems? Or was it my only option in light of his behavior? Am I going to regret giving up on him when he could turn into a perfectly satisfactory husband with a strong supportive woman (me) aiding and abetting him? Do I want to be a strong, supportive woman with a weak, tired, stressed husband? Will he always be a depressed grunter splodged on the sofa every evening for the next forty years, drinking beer and watching Channel 5?

As you can see, I am incredibly confused. Finally, clarification comes from an unexpected source: my father (who is not primarily known for his expertise when it comes to emotional problems). I tell him of my dilemma. And he makes it simple. He says:

"Darling, you are vivacious, witty, charming and intelligent."

"And pretty?" I ask.

"Very," he replies and (*key words coming up*) "you deserve better."

It suddenly all seems very simple. I deserve better. That is all there is to it.

End of discussion.

End of story.

End of relationship.

Postscript

We did, of course, get back together again.

In theory, I knew well enough that I deserved to be treated better. I knew that at least the beginning of a relationship was supposed to be joyful and not the unending misery that I had been experiencing with Mark. I just thought that if I could be understanding, patient and loving I could make it work; Mark was, after all, in the process of coming off Prozac and everything had been wonderful before he started messing with his medication. And however angry I felt towards him for not remaining the wonderful boyfriend he had been in the beginning, I honestly don't think he could help it – he told me that he didn't feel anything for anyone and that included me. That was quite painful to hear, actually

Then, one day, I remembered Julia, a woman I had met in Cornwall two-and-a-half years earlier who told me about the man she was seeing at the time. I realized with a shudder that I was now having a mirror experience with Mark. It was bizarre – it was the same story.

Her boyfriend (same age as Mark) had swept her (same age as me) off her feet and they had spent a magical first month together. Her boyfriend had then started acting strangely without explanation. It transpired that he was on medication for manic depression. He had ceased to make any effort at all with her (including acknowledging her birthday in any way), and when I met her they were three months down the line and she was still pursuing the loving, under-standing path with him.

At the time, I remember thinking very clearly that she was crazy putting up with him; I could see that she would spend her whole life looking after him and suffering his debilitating depressions, for little thanks and love in return. I was also struck by the fact that he had done nothing at all for her birthday (she had gone around to see him in the evening for a night in!) and I remember thinking that however depressed you are, it is just too mean and downright unac-ceptable not to even ring your supportive girlfriend to wish her happy birthday. Maybe I am being naive and do not fully understand the nature of clinical depression, but it does seem to me that it is only depressed men who act in this way, and not depressed women.

I wanted to urge Julia to give up on this guy before he drained all her energy. I wanted to ask her exactly what she was getting out of the relationship. But it is my policy not to offer my opinion or advice to people without them first asking. No one thanks you for telling them what they do not want to know. I find it particularly aggravating when people try and tell me what to do on the basis that they know better than I how to run my life (which may be true – but that's my problem). Asking someone's opinion is one thing, but an inter-fering know-it-all is insufferable. So I listened attentively to her story but did not offer my comments (*leave him*). And now, as I remembered each part of her story, I felt spooked, especially when I remembered my opinion of her for sticking it out with her boyfriend (*sucker*).

That night I spoke to Mark who continued to ring me every night although his sole topic of conversation still consisted of complaining how hard he was working and how little appreciation he was receiving from his boss. He flatly refused to talk about anything else, offering the same old reasons: "too tired/too stressed/too late/not now." As we were speaking I felt my energy draining from me. I had been in a relatively good mood beforehand. Now my solar plexus area was aching. Nonetheless, I persisted in asking him when he wanted to see me over the forthcoming weekend. He told me that he wanted to sleep a lot and go to work on Sunday, but how about Saturday night? I heard myself sounding initially grateful but subsequently resentful that over the whole weekend I had been designated one evening. I heard myself asking (trying to keep the whine from my voice) if we could possibly spend the whole night together, something we had not done in weeks and weeks due to Mark's need for sleep. I heard him sigh reluctantly. And then something inside me snapped. The pilot light, which had already been flickering intermittently, went out completely. Listen to me! Lively, loving, fun and interesting. Pleading with this miserable, non-communicative and cold guy. It was like I had finally been hit over the head and come to my senses. What the fuck was I doing? What did I need this for? Why did I want to spend my Saturday night with this selfish misery guts? Why was I begging? No way was this situation going to continue a second longer. I said I had to go.

He said, "What's the matter?"

"Nothing," I said, "I just want to go."

"Why?" he asked. "Suddenly you sound different."

I was enjoying this. "I'm tired and stressed." He missed the irony.

"We need to talk," he said.

I couldn't believe my ears. "Not now, I'm too tired," I said, but what I thought was, Fuck you. It's over.

And this time it was over. For good. No more postscripts, I promise.

P.S. Yes, I am a heartless cruel bitch who does not understand the nature of clinical depression and I apologize unreservedly for this. Both Mark and Julia's boyfriend deserve to be treated with more understanding from me, but as usual my own self-fish agenda of falling in love and distaste for rejection intervened. I just didn't want to go out with a clinically depressed person anymore – it was too depressing.

Life Post-Mark

I start putting myself out and about again. After all, I have research to do. First thing I agree to is a big party organized by a Jewish charity. Jewish charity parties are known unaffectionately by anyone sad enough to attend one, as "Jew Dos." They are generally regarded as the last chance saloon for the pitiable unmarrieds, and are anticipated with dread, endured rather than enjoyed, and invariably followed by a solemn oath *never* to attend another, no matter how old and lonely you become.

The pervading atmosphere at a Jew Do is desperation. You can almost hear the collective unconscious chant: I MUST FIND SOMEONE, I MUST FIND SOMEONE. You can actually smell the desperation as you approach the venue. Other people are hovering around outside wondering whether their soul will recover from another Jew Do. They think to themselves, should I just go home and curl up in front of the TV with a box of chocolates or five and save myself from what will inevitably be a supremely depressing experience? But as my sister's friend's grandma says, "You never meet anyone sitting at home."

And so you are propelled by your desire to meet someone

and you enter the bar, praying that you won't bump into anyone you know, such is your shame at attending such an event. Of course, the first person you bump into is an ex-boyfriend who will inevitably express surprise that (a) you are still on the scene and (b) you are sad and desperate enough to attend a Jew Do. You will brazen it out, of course, but you both understand the tragedy of the situation.

If, on a rare occasion, somebody approaches you (and this is rare, people seldom wander from the cliques they arrive with, unless it is to approach an ex with the question "What are *you* doing here?"), the conversation is what I would call pressured. There is no such thing as a casual conversation with a stranger at a Jew Do. Every question and its reply will be instantly and internally scrutinized for signs of compatibility. The pressure of the conversation will, however, kill off any successful flirting and the exchange becomes more of a business transaction, with both of you wondering whether a deal can be made. During the conversation, you will both be rubber-necking to see who else is about. I am on constant alert, furtively scouring the room to scope out undesirables (people from my past, usually ex-boyfriends, whom I must avoid at all costs). The guy, meanwhile, is looking over my shoulder for other reasons. He wants to see what other talent is available. It's not that he's not interested in me, it's just that a Jewish guy at a Jew Do must feel like a child in a candy store. So many smart and beautiful women dressed in their finest flirtation finery, and so few attractive men. It's a buyer's market. And they know it.

If a successful connection is made and you hand out your telephone number, you return to your friends, one of whom invariably went out with the recipient of your phone number five years ago and another of whose sister/best friend/cousin also went out with him three months ago. You are then given

a complete rundown on the guy so that by the time you go
out on your first date, you actually know everything about
him. He doesn't know that you know and you go through
the pretence of asking questions to which you already know
the answer. The thing is that he will also have done a Jew
search on you and, in my case, will have found someone that
told him that I am interesting but nuts.

The most puzzling thing about a Jew Do is seeing a
couple there. It is the weirdest thing. You think to yourself,
What the *fuck* are you doing here when you don't need to
be!?! I can only conclude that the couple are there because
(a) they want to flaunt their status, (b) one or both of them
are unhappy with the relationship and have decided to check
out the scene, test out their respective attractiveness to the
opposite sex and see if there is anyone better than the partner
they are currently lumbered with, or (c) they are freaks.

The only good thing about these events is that the bar is
usually deserted and you will have no difficulty buying a
drink. Jews are not big drinkers and you can see that the bar
staff are puzzled as to why no one is drinking. I, on the other
hand, find the only way to get through one of these events is
to drink myself past the shame barrier.

The thing that also pisses me off about Jew Dos is that
they are always incredibly expensive, which would be fine, if
you enjoyed them. You are not supposed to mind going
without food for a week on the basis that the money goes to
charity. Well, I do mind. I'm not a big one for charity in the
first place. I am the only person I know who did not give one
penny to Live Aid, an event I found irritating.

I don't believe things have changed much in the Third
World since Live Aid and I don't know much about world
economics, but I'm sure that someone really important and
influential out there knows that the First World can only

continue to exist if there is a Second and Third World. I don't want it that way and I am of course genuinely moved by famine and the conditions in the Third World, but if I were to let myself care too deeply about what horrors go on in the world, I would shoot myself.

I know that my attitude to charity is unfashionable, and maybe it's a stingy person's cop out. But I don't know why Jews can't just organize a party for the sake of having a party. Why have they always got to add the guilt factor? Remember the husband-hunting ball? After a dinner consisting of platefuls of smoked salmon, poussin, sticky toffee pudding, coffee, chocolates and cakes, we all sat around our tables, coiffed and decked out in designer clothes, and watched a video of the mentally and physically disabled. Call me cynical, but the idea was to make you feel as guilty as possible before making your donation. The organizers knew how we Jews ticked. Our primary motivation is guilt. I know I sound awful, but I can't help it. I just don't like having my buttons pushed.

But I am back on my seemingly never-ending search for that one special guy who has refused all offers and temptation, who has occasionally felt disillusioned but who has never given up hope that his dream woman is out there somewhere. And, of course, the minute he sets eyes on me he will *know* that this is why he never committed himself elsewhere. He was waiting for me. And although I am doubtful that my perfect man will frequent Jew Dos, I proceed on the basis that you just never know. "You just never know" seems to be my main motivating factor for going out these days.

Jasmin seems to think that this Jew Do will be OK (not wonderful, remember Jasmin has been to more than her fair share of these dos and she knows the score). She's met the people on this particular charity committee and they are normal. So, we buy tickets and await Saturday night with dread. The big moment arrives and the dread turns to anxiety, which can only be quenched by a full glass of vodka each. The taxi pulls up outside the venue, a converted studio, and as I approach the entrance, I think of Mark with anger and hatred. Why couldn't he have been a nice, normal guy with no major problems? It's all his fault that I am back here. I am not supposed to be going to these ghastly parties at my time of life. It's humiliating.

As we enter the bar, we head straight to the loo so that we can hyperventilate and acclimatize to the atmosphere in a safe place. A quick pep talk is needed, along the lines of "we're gorgeous and it's going to be a great night" and we burst through the door of the Ladies', heads held high. Next stop is the bar. A drink and a calming cigarette somewhere in the shadows where we can elevate our chances of getting married as a result of attending this particular party. Then a stroll around while Jasmin greets friends with a kiss and I avoid ex-friends with a blank, impenetrable expression. Finally, we find a comfy sofa in the bar area, where we ensconce ourselves. Expectantly.

The first person to approach is a quiet journalist from Finsbury Park who kicks off the conversation by revealing that he is very hot due to the undershirt he is wearing under his shirt. I try not to judge him too harshly, but if I can keep quiet about the fact that I am wearing a sanitary towel I think the least he can do is not reveal the fact that he is wearing an undershirt to a party, or at all, for that matter. However, any guy who approaches two foxy women at a party like this is to be warmly applauded and encouraged, although as he's a bit on the dorkey side, not too enthusiastically obviously. Meanwhile, friends of Jasmin arrive and the sofa area is soon buzzing. Well, not quite buzzing. More like humming. Someone gets me a drink. The journalist is being attentive and must be rewarded with interesting conversation. I spy a couple of sexy men floating about and decide that I will target them once I have had another drink and feel a bit braver.

Just as I am about to start enjoying myself, Nick appears from nowhere. I haven't seen him for ages (as I have been off the scene due to having a boyfriend). I don't need to tell you, I am sure, that he is the last person in the world I want to bump into. He expresses surprise at seeing me at such a party and I brazen it out, but we both understand the tragedy of the situation. Nick – living on Planet Nick as he does, with other human beings satelliting around him and his needs – is oblivious to the fact that I am being extremely hostile to him and he wedges himself next to me on the sofa. In fact, he makes himself so comfortable, the journalist clearly feels somewhat ousted and excuses himself to get a drink. Nick is clearly unaware of the possibility that he may be interrupting my chance of happiness with someone else (he's not, as we know, but that's not the point; it simply has not occurred to him).

He starts by saying how sorry he is that things worked out as they did and that we are no longer able to be friends. He says he misses me. Before I have a chance to tell him how pleased I am that things did not work out between us on account of his lousy bedroom skills, he launches into *further* reasons why it would not have worked out. I cannot quite believe his arrogance and, more importantly, the fact that he has *more* reasons! Obviously, I am intrigued and let him ramble through a few before politely interrupting him to ask him to please just fuck off once and for all. For the sake of completeness, I ought to tell you the three further reasons:

16. Having had no sisters and going to an all-boys school, he

sees women as essentially mysterious creatures and I should have realized this and been more reserved and generally more enigmatic.

17. I had told him that I liked him and this had put too much pressure on him. He tells me I should have used my womanly wiles to seduce him in a more casual way, rather than coming straight out with a declaration of my feelings. In one way he is right; I will never again unilaterally declare feelings of love for a man. On the other hand, in his case, I do not believe it would have made a blind bit of difference.

18. One of his ex-girlfriends does not like me and a relationship with me would have jeopardized their continued friendship. For the record, I don't like this woman either. She hung around Nick waiting for romance and commitment even longer than I did and will do anything (and I mean *anything*) for him. She's not what I would call a "sister." When Matt and Nick were laughing at a picture of a "fat" celebrity on holiday in the *Sun*, I pointed out that she was not actually "fat," just an average size twelve and that was in fact how most women looked without their clothes on. This ex-girlfriend then piped up and defended the boys, saying, "Come off it. She even has cellulite." I looked at her in disbelief as I listened to her betrayal of women. Then I comforted myself that when she and Nick split up he showed me and Matt a pair of her panties (enormous) which he then put on over his trousers and deduced, quite correctly, that he could have played football in them.

As Nick walks away, I start wilting and shriveling up. It isn't him. I couldn't give a toss about Nick. I just feel like a complete fuck-up, who will never meet a decent guy; firstly, because there are none, and secondly, because I am not seductive, mysterious and enigmatic enough to attract and then keep one. I know my face is contorting with bitterness and anger, and not wanting anyone to see me looking anything other than radiant, I decide to retire to the toilet to grimace in private. Thank God for the Ladies' loos.

En route, I meet a friend of a friend (a guy) who tells me that I look like I need some good sex, not that he is offering he adds, but he thinks I need the advice. I thank him for his kind concern but patiently explain that it is due to assholes like him that I have been put off sex for good. He smiles blandly back at me and then continues without pause, to patronize the very young girl who had previously been receiving his wisdom.

I slink off to the loo and whimper quietly to myself about the horror of my existence. It isn't just men, by the way. My new high-powered job as a media lawyer at a scriptwriting agency crammed full of overachievers is not working out and on the Friday afternoon before the Jew Do, my new boss confirmed to me that I was a disappointment.

The whimpering in the loo helps and as I reapply my lipstick, I think that what I really need most now is for someone to put his arms around me, hold me tight, murmur sympathetically and tell me that I am a wonderful person just as I am and that everything is going to work out fine.

I return to the sofa feeling tragic but proud. A guy is sitting opposite me also looking rather tragic. He has large dark circles under his eyes and they are filled with existential sadness. As we obviously have something in common, I decide to approach him and offer him what I wish someone would offer me. Basically, I decide to give in the absence of there being anything to receive. I go up to him and introduce myself. Then I put my arms around his shoulders and hug him. I whisper in his ear, "You are a wonderful person and everything is going to be all right." He looks at me with gratitude and, somewhat bewildered, asks how I know that that was exactly what he needed. I tell him that I know because it is exactly what I need too. So we hug again. Then we stand up so that we can have a full-length body hug. I am standing in the middle of a Jew Do, hugging a complete stranger and suddenly, strangely, everything feels an awful lot better. I have made a human connection that cuts through all the shit of polite, social, casual conversational encounters. I have offered warmth and compassion and I feel great. You should try it some time.

Having exhausted our hugging and merged our energy fields, we return to the sofa to continue our acquaintance and bemoan our existence. Now, before you get excited and think I've gone and found myself a new boyfriend, I had better tell you that I don't fancy him. And it's in an I-will-never-fancy-you-and-I-know-that-for-a-fact kind of way, despite the fact that I soon realize that he is extremely wealthy and I want to give up work and become a poet. As we reveal our careers and lifestyles, it turns out that he is great friends with my dream man, Dominic.

Now I know I haven't mentioned Dominic before, reason being that he is a kind of dream. I'd better explain.

About a year-and-a-half earlier, Claudia had won a freebie vacation from work for two to stay at a five-star hotel in Madrid for a long weekend. Although Claudia is constantly dating, she is still somehow almost constantly officially single, and her Plus One, therefore, is usually me. The only time we could both go to Madrid was in August, when Madrid is deserted. I happen to love deserted cities – the roads are empty, there is no jostling or queuing, just a chilled out, relaxed atmosphere where anything goes as no one is around to tell. So, August it was and we robustly set off to enjoy our freebie.

We turned up at this beautiful, sophisticated hotel and once we had settled ourselves into our lovely air-conditioned room and discovered that there was no free porn on the satellite TV, we decided that we might as well go and explore Madrid. We wandered around the Modern Art Museum, chilled out in a bar, ate tapas and discussed how we were both going to improve our lives when we returned to London. There was practically no one else in town and we were served immediately wherever we went, which was heaven for an impatient person like me.

I'll tell you how impatient I am. I am too impatient to go to restaurants. I can't bear all the waiting, over which I have little or no control. You have to wait to be seated, wait to be served, wait three times over for the courses to be cooked and brought to your table, wait until your dinner companion has stopped eating so you can have a cigarette, wait for the waiter to appear so that you can ask for the bill, then you have to wait for the waiter to bring the bill and then you have to wait until your card is brought back (the waiter has normally forgotten about you by this point, so this is a particularly excruciating long wait). Then you have to wait to go home before ripping your clothes off after all the wine you've drunk which has made you feel horny as hell. Or, alternatively, you have to wait to go home before ripping your clothes off because you have completely overeaten and you feel sick and bloated and your stomach is busting out of your trousers and the waistband is cutting deep grooves into the skin of your tummy.

The thing is that when I am hungry, I want to eat. I don't want to wait. At home, if I am hungry, I open up the fridge and make myself something to eat, end of story. And it's no use talking to me about the beauty of delayed gratification because I don't even particularly like food. Most people can't understand this, but I would be just as happy to take a food supplement in the form of a pill and dispense with the real thing altogether. I can't really be bothered with it: buying it, preparing it and, worse, clearing away after it. I do enjoy some food, like my mum's cooking and chocolate desserts, but the rest I can take or leave. I am also not too keen on sitting upright at a table for too long, my favorite position being horizontal.

While on the more recent vacation in southern Spain, Claudia was astounded at the speed at which I managed to maneuver the whole eating-out experience. In the lazy hills of Spain where we were staying, I think the locals were both intrigued and appalled by my fast-food attitude. I would enter a restaurant and, instead of waiting to be seated, I would march up to the bar and ask to see the menu (saves about half an hour of sitting at the table feeling hungry and thinking bitter thoughts about the lazy waiter who refuses to acknowledge my presence). Once I'd got the menu in my hands, I ordered all three courses immediately, pressuring Claudia to do the same. I then seated myself and waited for the food. Once I had eaten, and often before the plates had been cleared away, I went back to the bar and asked for the bill, which I settled immediately.

Am I weird?

Anyway, back to deserted Madrid. Claudia and I set out from the hotel very late in the evening for the night-time activities. We were both in a relaxed but jaunty mood (staying at very expensive, luxurious hotels for free is even more enjoyable than staying at very expensive, luxurious hotels and paying for them) and we decided to hit some recommended bars. There was no one about and it was not that our expectations for meeting men were low, it was more a case of not having even considered meeting men that night (for once). It was a very warm, sultry evening, we were in Madrid and we were going out for a nice, quiet drink.

We eventually found a bar that was open and sat at a table outside, drinking double measures and empowering each other with laughter, compassion and encouragement in our respective life endeavors. We were bonding so deeply and so exclusively that we failed to notice the two very attractive men sitting at the table next to ours. When we finally took note of their presence, we realized that they were speaking English. They had obviously been waiting to introduce themselves to us and they were soon sitting around our table ordering us more drinks. The really, really good-looking one decided to focus his charm on Claudia. This left me with the just plain good-looking one, who turned out to be stimulating and delightful company. We talked at length about literature. Now, if a man can talk to me intelligently and interestingly about books, then he has unwittingly found the way to my heart. He was so well-read, sophisticated, informed and stimulating. He was gentle, but strong. Self-assured, but unassuming. Interested and interesting. And guess what, you're not going to believe this.

He was Jewish.

I drag myself around parties in London searching for a sexy Jewish man and there in Madrid at one o'clock in the morning, I met a sexy Jewish banker from Hampstead. We laughed about the fact that we were both Jewish and from the same part of town, but London and religion all seemed so irrelevant and so far away from the wonderful, warm, stimulating evening that we were currently enjoying and, for once, the future was just that. The present was all I wanted and all

I needed and I was living completely in the moment. And loving it.

Now, to be honest, one of the reasons that I did not contemplate a future with this dude was that he was on a six-month work secondment in Madrid and, having just arrived, he would understandably want to keep his options open. And the other reason, is that the guy was out of my league. He was just too gorgeous. Blonde, well-toned, independently wealthy, non-Jewish babes hooked guys as cute as this. This did not depress me as much you think (I've got work to do on my self-esteem and deservability beliefs, I know, I know) as everyone was having such a fabulous evening and no one was having depressing, miserable thoughts, even – for once – me.

Claudia's new friend was a real jerk, but the kind of good looking jerk that you couldn't help liking, such was his vivacity and complete indifference to people thinking that he was a jerk. We bar hopped all over town with the guys, making friends wherever we went. You see, *that's* why I like deserted towns, there's a resistance party going on for all the people left behind. Barriers are dropped and everyone talks to everyone. A Spanish couple offered to take us to another bar where we could dance. The four of us jumped into the back of their car, legs and arms draped over legs and arms. I was squeezed into a genuinely unintentionally intimate position with Dominic. Although we had talked for four hours, this was the first physical contact we had had. I was on his lap and I could feel the heat from his groin burning into my leg. Suddenly all the passion that had been mounting during our intense encounter became conscious and I longed to kiss him. Based on previous life experience, however, I didn't like to count my chickens before they hatched and I quickly put all lusty

thoughts out of my mind. I had to remind myself: no expec-
tation, no disappointment.

When we arrived at the bar, Claudia's man grabbed me
after she refused to dance with him. Having been to two
Lambada lessons (and having been drinking fairly consistently over a five-hour period), I considered myself something of an expert and was only too happy to pair up and
show off. Eventually Dominic came to reclaim me and then
he told me that he was tired and thinking of going home. My
heart sank, I gulped and said, "Fine, it's been lovely meeting
you."

Then he said, "Can I kiss you?" and before waiting for me
to answer, he moved towards me, took me in his arms and his
lips melted on to mine.

He was the most incredible kisser. His repertoire encom-
passed both tender, warm, soft and loving, and hard, hungry,
passionate deep-thrust kissing. We couldn't get enough of
each other; it was five o'clock in the morning, we were drunk,
we were at a crazy Spanish bar in Madrid, miles from home,
it was still very warm outside and we were MAD FOR IT.
After about an hour of kissing, I suddenly realized that the
world did not consist only of my tongue and that of Dominic. I also had a body, a mind and a friend called Claudia
who I could not see anywhere. I thought I'd go to the loo
before organizing a search party. And who should I find in
the loo shacked up against the automatic hand dryer but
Claudia Plus One. Things were clearly getting out of hand
and we decided to decamp to our hotel, raid the mini-bar
and party all night. The three of us trooped out of the Ladies
to find Dominic who was warmly enthusiastic about our
hotel plan.

We arrived back at the hotel and before I could stop
Claudia, I witnessed her making a seriously bad move. She

actually asked the uptight guy at reception whether we could invite visitors to our room. As we watched the guy shaking his head in an international gesture that everyone understood, Dominic decided to brazen it out and walked straight to the elevator, all nonchalant, and headed up to our room. The good-looking jerk, being a jerk, decided to be all adventurous and find the tradesman's entrance (which, amazingly, he did) and we were all soon in the bedroom, continuing the party. Actually, it all got rather immature, with me and Dominic on one bed under the sheets exploring each other's bodies in a frenzy of delight, and Claudia making out with her guy on the adjacent twin bed. Who knows what would have happened had the manager not knocked on the door. I like to think that we would all have behaved ourselves (actually, I am pretending to be prudish, I think the whole thing could have been quite horny and would have proved to be a new bonding experience for me and Claudia to laugh about when we are grandmothers). But the manager did knock on the door and was quite insistent that the gentlemen left. They could only stay if they gave him their passports and paid for the night. We felt like naughty kids at a summer camp, rather than adults staying at a five-star hotel. After a long kiss goodbye, I watched Dominic disappear through the hotel door and out of my life.

Of course, he could have rung me at the hotel the next day, but he didn't. I prayed that he would, but I knew deep down that he wouldn't. I reasoned out my disappointment; he was only twenty-six (to my thirty) and I was still partying my head off at his age. He had only recently arrived in Spain. Early in the conversation he had mentioned a girl he had met just before leaving for Spain. But the sad truth was, although he was my dream lover, I knew that I was not his. So there I left him, my dream man, in Madrid, in my mind and as part of a wonderful evening, full of adventure, surprise and laughter.

And now it turns out that this rather tragic guy (name, Simon) knows him and, get this, Dominic is single. I tell him: "Bring me the head of Dominic. In return, I promise that I will offer you a hug once a fortnight and thereafter weekly calls to tell you that you are a wonderful person and that everything will be okay." He agrees and we draw up a contract on a scrap of paper. I ask someone nearby to witness our signatures and the guy comments that he knows business deals are made at these events, but he's never heard of one quite like this. Simon and I don't care. We have a mutually rewarding agreement.

Actually, I am rather scared. I have seen Dominic a couple of times in London over the last six months, but from afar, and in London he seems even more out of my reach. The first time I saw him I was returning from a lunch party where the only attention I received was from a sadistic (anti-Semitic? Probably) Pole. I was disappointed, especially as I had looked so nice that afternoon. It seemed such a waste. It was a warm summer's day and I should have been lazing on the Heath with some champagne, a joint and a boyfriend with an erection. As I sat in my car at the traffic lights, a little red convertible whizzed past. Dominic was in the passenger seat, looking cool in his shades. I don't know what came over me, but before I knew it I had jumped the lights and was giving serious car chase. As I hurtled down the street, there was a group of people crossing the road. I had to make a quick choice between mowing down the elderly pedestrians who had not been able to sprint to the curb in time or keeping up with the convertible. Naturally, I slowed down, smiling weakly at the grateful pedestrians who waved at me with thanks. And then I wended my way home. Empty-handed.

I have also seen him jogging on the Heath. I was not looking my best. In fact I looked like a teenage boy with jeans, sneakers, bomber jacket, short hair and no make-up. Not the ideal gear, I am sure you agree, in which to renew an acquaintance with your dream man.

And now, an arrangement has been made; dinner for Simon, Jasmin, Dominic and myself in a week's time.

Wow!

More All-night Madness

During the week, some rather unfortunate events occur which mean that by the time the dinner date with Dominic, Simon and Jasmin arrives, I am in a murderous mood. In fact, as bad weeks go, I would easily put it in my Top Ten. And believe me, there is some pretty strong competition for a place in the Top Ten.

The Number Three position goes to a week which took place about five years ago. Ironically, the week in question began extremely well. On the Monday, I smugly told a friend that I had finally simultaneously achieved the three main objectives in life: hot job, hot lover and hot apartment. During the remainder of the week, I not only lost my job (told I was completely unsuitable for a responsible professional position, should consider alternative career options and then fired) and split up with my boyfriend (first time I have actually been *physically* rejected – I spotted him at our local subway station; he thought I hadn't seen him and he actually ran down the platform away from me), I was also evicted from my flat (ejected by psycho landlord – an ex-boyfriend – who threw all my stuff out of the window). To complete the week, while sitting in a park late on the Friday having a puff with friends, still reeling from the change in my circumstances resulting from the events of the week, I was arrested for possession of cannabis.

As I sat in the detention room in the police station (which I had previously imagined would be a little like a doctor's waiting room, with saggy but comfy old armchairs and back copies of *Bella* and *Woman's Own*, but which in fact turned out to be your basic cell, with a mattress, toilet, bars and gray paint), I suddenly remembered my self-congratulatory words to my friend on the Monday and thought how funny life can turn out. And I didn't mean funny ha ha.

I'll tell you how bad the Number One and Two positions in the Top Ten Bad Week list are; not only can I *not* tell you about them, I can't even *think* about them. They are so bad, I am actually ashamed of having had them.

Anyway, the week before I met Dominic was a bad week. Remember I said that my new boss at the script-writing agency had told me that I was a disappointment (and apparently all the other directors at work thought so too). Well, I found his comments rather demotivating, and I found rising to the challenge of proving him wrong unenticing due to the fact that I hated work anyway and the idea of putting in even more hours was too revolting to contemplate. It was also difficult to be enthusiastic due to the fact that I now hated his and the other directors' guts with illness-inducing intensity. Instead of concentrating on work, I had non-stop evil thoughts about them. The situation had obviously become untenable and rather than wait for the inevitable firing, I decided to take matters into my own hands this time and quit. It was not quite as liberating as it should have been as the boss was so relieved, I felt as if I had been fired. Once I had handed in my notice, the boss's secretary told me that she had heard him making comments about stingy

Jews, so I had obviously done the right thing. But nonetheless, it was all rather depressing.

It was clearly time to retrain in a new profession and I had set my heart on doing a course in a journalism, something which excited and motivated me. Roger, a mega, and I mean *mega*) rich friend, has consistently promised (unasked) to lend me some money to pay the fees for the part-time studies for my new career so, currently jobless and in a state of some turmoil, I telephone him early in the evening on the night of the Dominic dinner, desperate for a new direction and positive outlook to take with me on my date. Roger has made the promises in front of my other friends on numerous occasions, proclaiming his belief in me and wanting, as he put it, "to invest in me." Another male friend queried whether "investing in me" meant he wanted to make a sperm deposit. When I put this suggestion to Roger, he reassured me that he just wanted to help me with no strings attached.

I am confident that Roger will be pleased that I have finally swallowed my pride to ask for his help. Well, I did tell you that it was a bad week, so you can probably guess that during the conversation Roger denies ever having promised me a penny. He is lying and he knows that I know that he is lying. And he doesn't care. That's when you know a friendship is over. If he had told me that he had changed his mind, I would have been sorely disappointed but the friendship could have been saved after a week or so of major sulking on my part. But the audacious lying is completely unacceptable. And I don't appreciate feeling like a beggar either.

So by the time eight o'clock arrives, I am in a truly *terrible* mood. I should have canceled; I am in too bad a mood to (a) meet the man of my dreams and pretend to be a happy-go-lucky, carefree, together catch and (b) go out at all. But I hold this crazy notion (which you may have seen examples of before) that if things are going badly in my life, I deserve to have one good experience that will make up for the shit. OK I have just lost my job, a friend and the funding for my new career, but I am meeting my dream lover tonight and he could fall in love with me and we could live happily ever after and I could laugh at the events of the week, none of which will matter anymore.

Jasmin's an angel. She offers to lend me one of her new designer outfits and spends time making me look gorgeous on the outside while giving me one of her existential theories about choosing to rise above life's shit, to enjoy being young and vibrant while we can. I ask her bad temperedly why, if it is that fucking easy, she doesn't give it a go.

"Actually," Jasmin admits, "it's not that easy at all. I am fed up with always compromising and being nice to people all the time. You say you have all this conflict in your life with jobs and men. All my conflict is kept inside. Each time someone upsets me, instead of being like you and saying how I feel, I swallow my annoyance so that everyone carries on liking me and thinking what a nice young lady I am. It is a real strain keeping jobs when you hate the boss, as I do with my boss, but he will never know. Instead, I get to keep my job and I rage inside."

We agree that a composite of her and me would make an acceptable human model – a mix of honesty, assertiveness, tact and diplomacy.

Jasmin and I turn up at Simon's place in Kensington. I am still frothing at the mouth with hatred for Roger, while all residual hate capacities are fermenting with loathing for my Jew-hating boss. I am unaware that I am actually overheating and should really be tied to a chair and gagged. Dominic looks very cute, but I am too shy to talk to him as I know that he knows all about the deal with Simon. I have lost vast quantities of self-confidence over the week and while we are all sitting in Simon's huge interior-designed house on one of the finest streets in London, I become the poor church mouse. Quietly sipping my drink and trying to blink back the tears after my conversation with Roger, I feel so bewildered and lost. I am preoccupied in my own nightmare world of unhappy endings, whilst the other three chat happily about how much more their properties are worth now than when they bought them.

Next hurdle is dinner at a chic restaurant in Holland Park where, obviously, I eat nothing. I would have taken a beta blocker, but you remember the fate of the last beta blocker (in a plastic bag covered in vomit). In order not to look weird, I make out that due to a big business lunch and after-work drink and nibbles, I am not hungry. The other three tuck into a three-course cordon-bleu dinner, which they all seem to enjoy very much. The seating at the dinner table has gone horribly wrong and instead of sitting opposite Dominic, I am sitting next to him, which means that he is sitting opposite Jasmin, to whom he is listening very attentively (just as he had to me in Madrid).

I think that a glass of wine might help, despite the fact that I have a totally empty stomach and can't hold my booze at the best of times. Unfortunately the wine loosens not only my tongue but my hatred too. I soon start ranting and telling a surprised audience that I have not quite decided on which revenge route to go down with Roger. At the moment, I explain to my quietly stunned dinner companions, it's a choice between cutting off his balls or sending him a letter so venomous and cruel that it will make him never want to leave his house again. I am now receiving discreet warning signals diagonally across the table from Jasmin, who is aghast at my socially inappropriate disclosures. I now project my self-hate on to her and feel resentment at her "we must be nice girls in front of the men" attitude. But mostly I feel resentment that Dominic is paying her loads more attention than he is paying me. Not her fault, I know, but still a justifiable reason for hating her too.

I do manage to make something of a comeback when the conversation turns to blowjobs, and I cheer up considerably when Dominic consequently turns his charm on to me.

"It's been well over a year since we last saw each other. I had a wonderful evening that night in Madrid," he says.

"Well, actually, I have seen you several times in London since you came back from Spain."

"Why didn't you come up to me?"

"Because I wasn't wearing any lipstick."

I think he understands the dilemma as he laughs. He now starts to flirt with me, thank God, and I drink more and more wine to deal with the stomach-churning possibility of a happy ending. Please remember that I have still eaten nothing at this stage and the wine is sloshing around my empty insides.

I remember some leg touching under the dinner table at the restaurant, but I don't remember the cab back to Simon's place. I remember kissing Dominic on Simon's sofa when he and Jasmin went to the kitchen. I vaguely remember knocking over a glass of red wine and I definitely remember Simon's pained expression when he saw the red puddle in the middle of his new cream carpet. I remember Dominic asking me to come back to his place for the night and I remember agreeing. The next thing I remember is Jasmin driving me home to stay at her place and my cell phone ringing and Dominic asking why I had gone home with Jasmin when I said that I was going back to his place. I told him I didn't remember why. Dominic then showed up at Jasmin's place to take me back to his place. I remember sitting on his sofa and being too freaked out at finally sitting on my dream man's sofa to have a conversation, and lunging at him instead. I don't remember going to bed and I certainly don't remember what actually happened in bed, although you will be pleased to hear that my panties stayed on (I think). I remember having a joint and I am afraid everything after that is completely crystal clear.

Whereas before, sitting on his sofa, I had had a mild freak out, once I had smoked this joint, I was totally fucking crazy. Weird, fucked-up, self-destructive thoughts spinning around my head, lying next to him, eyes open in the dark, pretending to sleep, wanting to puke, frightened and lonely.

Suddenly, all the events of the week and their implications hit me. And I fully and completely took the blame for the events, and for the implications; it had been conclusively proven that I was unemployable, unlikeable (social outcast at the Dominic dinner), unlovable (Tom, Nick, Mark, *et al*) and that I had crappy judgement (choosing Roger, *inter alia*, as a mate). I surmised from the sum total of my life's experiences and achievements that I was crap at life and I no longer wanted to play anymore. I had basically had one bad week too many.

Now, you will be (rightly) concluding to yourself that these were rather negative and damaging thoughts. You may be thinking that I was being self-pitying and ungrateful. After all, I have two arms, two legs, plenty of food to eat (even if I choose not to eat it), a loving family and a wide circle of (mostly) wonderful friends. But somehow this made it worse rather than better. How could I get it so consistently and totally wrong with all of the above advantages and blessings?

And then I despised myself even more for being self-pitying and ungrateful and such a general fuck-up. These thoughts and beliefs should ideally be discussed with a competent and compassionate therapist (hard to find), a sister whose love and kindness is unconditional, a very good (female) friend who also suffers periods of self-doubt and will therefore be empathetic rather than disapproving and impatient. They should not, however, *under any circumstances*, be disclosed to:

1. A man;
2. One's dream man;
3. A man trying to sleep;
4. A drunk man;
5. A stoned man;
6. A very successful, self-assured, confident man who seems to effortlessly and consistently land on his feet; or
7. A virtual stranger.

As Dominic fulfilled all of the above criteria, I did not feel I should share my suicidal thoughts with him. Apart from which, I also concluded that Dominic would probably have quite gladly taken Jasmin back with him that night; it was just that by making the deal with Simon, I had made it so abundantly clear that I was his for the asking. I am sure he didn't mind taking me back, after all, he did come and pick me up from Jasmin's, it was just that I knew he would not have minded taking her home either. Having since mentioned this to Jasmin, she unconvincingly denied that Dominic would have taken her home but we both knew she was being "nice" again. Basically, therefore, there was very little warmth and connection between Dominic and me (all very different to the night in Spain) and lying in bed next to someone I didn't know but who I was still pathetically trying to impress intensified my feelings of isolation.

In the immediate absence of therapist, sister or girlfriend, I just wanted to be on my own, but it was four o'clock in the morning and I didn't want to wake Dominic. I did actually manage to wake him fifteen minutes later whilst retching in the loo (which, I cursed inwardly, was right next to his bedroom). Most times, after I've been sick, I feel better. On that occasion, however, I felt worse. I tried to get back into bed and act normal, but I was hyperventilating and generally freaking out so this was difficult. He was also awake by this stage and obviously wondering what kind of weirdo was in his bed. I wish I could have just stayed in his bed and fallen asleep, but the voices in my head berating me were becoming louder and more menacing, and my heart was beating furiously. The irony was that although I needed to be held, being held by Dominic would only have made things worse; it would simply have increased my anxiety and triggered undeservability beliefs. Not that he was offering, mind you. I could sense his impatience with me for failing to fade out quietly. He didn't ask me if I was OK (clearly I was not), he just turned over and fell asleep. It was at that point that he ceased to be my dream man.

Continuing to lie in bed became intolerable and I retired to the living room for a cigarette and a major rethink designed to calm me down. After about five cigarettes and an unsuccessful rethink, I decided it was time to give up, give in and get out. I called a taxi. I slipped into Dominic's bedroom to retrieve the rest of my clothing and, without saying a word, disappeared. By this stage, Dominic was the least of my problems. My first priority was not killing myself. Reclaiming my sanity came a close second.

It was half past five in the morning and there was only one place to go. I haven't said much about my sister up till now. You should, however, know that apart from being kind, generous, sensitive, funny, highly successful and valued at work, glamorous, hard-working, uncomplaining, loyal, a witty and compelling raconteur, warm, loving and affectionate, she is also the most wonderful sister you could hope for. And it was her address that I gave the cab driver. It was not relevant that it was half past five; we have a deal that we are on call to each other twenty-four hours a day, seven days a week, three hundred and sixty-five days a year. When we were little, if one of us were ill in the middle of night, the other would uncomplainingly look after the sick sister until she fell back to sleep. At that moment I was sick and I needed looking after.

She opened her front door to find me, shivering and shaking, trying to cry but too choked to let out any tears.

I spent the next two weeks in bed.

You will be pleased to hear that, finally, I managed to cry.

Setbacks Pave the Way for Comebacks

The first time I saw this motto I was fifteen years old and on the bus coming home from school. I always looked out for the large, reassuring messages printed on the fluorescent placard outside the church on the bus route. I was flirting with converting to Christianity at the time on the basis of the message "JESUS LOVES YOU" that had been pinned up on the placard the month before. How nice, I thought, at least *someone* loves me. I even persuaded my (Jewish) friends at school to attend Icthus, the Christian Union weekly lunchtime meeting, making fifty per cent of attending members Jewish. I hit it off with the religious zealots and before I knew what was happening there was talk of me being baptized. Clearly, things had got out of hand and it was with some pretty dogged resistance on my part that I managed to avoid being ceremonially dunked.

But there were always the most inspiring messages (to an anguished adolescent) outside this church, none of which I remember, apart from "JESUS LOVES YOU" and "SETBACKS PAVE THE WAY FOR COMEBACKS." I often quote the latter to friends when their lives hit a particularly sticky patch (I have found the former fails to offer any reassurance whatsoever). Matt cheerfully quoted it back to me a couple of years ago when he had been fired (or "discouraged from staying" as he preferred to put it), from a high-pressured, high-profile job, along with "WHEN THE GOING GETS TOUGH, THE TOUGH GET GOING" and "POTATO PEELINGS REALLY AREN'T THAT BAD WHEN YOU GET USED TO THEM."

A comeback of some sort is clearly required after my two-week crying fest. It is also quite clear that major changes need to be made in my life in order to make the comeback both successful and permanent. A life devoted to cock-hunting has not only been spectacularly unsuccessful, it has also proved totally demoralizing and seriously bad for my health.

Now I am aware that there are whole industries based on women's dissatisfaction with their lives, particularly the desire of single women to change their circumstances in order to make themselves more attractive to men. The diet industry is worth billions, the cosmetics industry is worth billions, the fashion industry is worth billions. The subliminal message is that we constantly need to change and improve. We should join a gym so that we can work hard to achieve the perfect body: pert pointy tits, flat stomach, long, slim, toned limbs and firm, tight buttocks. We should invest in the constant influx of new scientific skin care products (which have been scientifically proven to be total crap) so that we avoid the ageing process altogether. Don't forget to cover up the gray hair while you're at it – the ammonia is really bad for you by the way, but don't let that put you off. After a long relaxing bath, instead of flopping into bed with a good book/cock, we are obliged to laboriously rub body cream over our bodies so that they are soft to the touch (of a man). We buy books promising to tell us how to hook men (look at the success of

The Rules), how to understand men, how to keep the relationship on track; basically we take on the responsibility of
emotional housework. We join slimming clubs despite the
fact that apparently ninety-eight per cent of women put the
weight back on again.

No wonder I have so far devoted so much fucking energy
to cock-hunting. Finding a man is the ultimate female success
story. It is a woman's validation. A woman can be really successful professionally, but if she is single she will nevertheless
be pitied for being lonely and incomplete. If a woman finds
a wonderful man who loves, adores and cherishes her, she has
well and truly made it.

Don't get me wrong, I still want a man. I want to wake
up to a cuddle. I want to fall asleep spooning. I want a partner
with whom to share the ups and downs of life. I want children (I think). I want to have sex on a regular basis. I want to
be normal. But I now decide that finding a suitable cock
owner, a mission that has previously been the sole/main
occupation of my life, will be relegated to equal status with
making money, finding creative and enjoyable means of
making money, and appreciating and enjoying the love and
friendships I already have in my life.

It finally dawns on me that I am not suited to bosses or
full-time employment and I therefore decide to go freelance
and work on short-term contracts so I can leave before
anyone pisses me off too severely. Once the decision has been
made, I find that working as a locum is just about the most
liberating approach I could have taken to work and I am
delighted with my independence. I book into a journalism
course for the following autumn and I plan to work part-
time while I study.

I decide to make other changes in my life. For a start, I
realize how hypocritical I have been for bitching at Mark for

refusing to deal with his emotions by taking Prozac for two years when I have been numbing out on weed every time I start feeling difficult emotions such as fear, anger and hate. And I decide that while I'm about it, I might as well give up cigarettes as well. Every time I lit a cigarette, I hated myself for being a smoker. This meant I was hating myself twenty times a day, which is quite a lot of deeply negative thoughts if you think about it.

I decide to go for a massive binge session with Claudia before quitting cigarettes and pot. The idea is to reach and then surpass self-disgust levels. A week before the quit date, fixed as the date Claudia is due to attend a stop smoking clinic, I up my cigarette intake by fifty per cent until it actually hurts to take a deep breath. I then invest in fifty quids' worth of top quality skunk that a professional dope smoking friend at work recommended very highly. Now, you may be confused as to what I mean by a "professional dope smoker"; would it clarify matters if I told you that she regularly has a joint first thing in the morning (which I admit I have done, but only on very special occasions like being dumped by a boyfriend) although she tells me, with some pride, that she always gets up, gets dressed and brushes her teeth first. She and her boyfriend smoke between six and ten joints every night, and one Monday morning she told me that they had smoked ninety quids' worth of dope that weekend. Everyone else has to trudge around to their dealer. Her dealer arrives at her house within ten minutes of her call.

And the amazing thing is that she is the liveliest person at work, full of the joys of spring, always ready with a laugh and a joke, whereas everyone else walks around like zombies. It is quite remarkable. Now do you see what I mean by "professional"? So I reckoned she will be just the person to supply me with some top quality skunk for my week's blowout session. Being a lovely, kind, co-operative person, the next day she brings in my bag of weed, which is burning a hole in my handbag so we decide to dip into it and roll one during our coffee break. So as well as being stoned in the evenings, I am spending my work days in a stoned haze too.

I spend every evening for a week completely on my own, house-sitting for a friend who has fifty-four channels on her TV. I watch eye-blinking amounts of TV, live off McDonalds and cakes, chocolates and cookies and smoke as many ciga-rettes as I can (we're talking two packs a day). Not a lifestyle I would recommend as a permanent way of life, but I'll tell you what – I fucking enjoy it for a week. On the final night, I invite Claudia around and we smoke weed all night while intermittently hoovering up the contents of the fridge. At times, I start to drop off, but she prods me and pleads with me not to be a sap and light up again. Each breath I take is followed by a sharp pain in my chest, whilst Claudia's breath-ing has been replaced by a rather annoying whistle.

I get up the next morning feeling fine and dandy, unlike Claudia whose plan backfires. She is too mashed to make it to the stop smoking clinic.

Blind Dates

The whole thing about my new freelance career is that I get to meet loads of new people and as a result my social sphere is considerably widened. I am a familiar kind of person. Not an overfamiliar kind of person, I hope. Not the sort of person who asks you how much money you earn, what your father does for a living or where your mother buys her meat. No, not that type of person. By familiar, I mean friendly, open and confessional. This means that I make friends very easily and within days, sometimes hours, of arrival at a new company, I am contrasting and comparing makes of sanitary towel, discussing the effects of the morning after pill and commiserating with a permanent member of staff over the fact that her boyfriend prematurely ejaculated the night before.

So it is to be expected that I often receive inquiries about the existence of a boyfriend in my life. Most people are kind and act surprised on being told that I am single. Others cross the sensibility barrier and probe further: "Why not?" As I am also a bit on the touchy side, I interpret this question to mean: "What's wrong with you?"

I used to reply, "Because I am hideously ugly and have no personality," which would confound my inquisitor. Lately, however, I am mellowing due in part to a growing realization that my attached friends are not necessarily happier or more satisfied with their lives than my single friends, and due also in part to a new attitude that I am currently fostering that gives me the right to live, breathe and participate in daily life without the validation of a boyfriend. So instead of replying with barely concealed aggressive sarcasm, I reply with a straight answer, "Because I haven't found the right man yet." I often receive a pitying gaze in response and I do have to try my very hardest not to respond with a matching martyred downcast expression.

Sometimes though, such an admission of my single status can result in a set-up or blind date scenario, for which I am genuinely grateful. I have set up loads of people in the past and I do believe that anyone who indulges in a bit of match-making is to be very highly commended. I also happen to *adore* blind dates. I love meeting new people and I there-fore do not suffer pre-date nerves, in marked contrast to the stomach-churning hell that I endure before a date with someone I know and like. Blind dates are also a no-lose situ-ation. If the guy is a creep then the date can be terminated as soon as you like. I have no qualms about requesting to be taken home within an hour of being picked up. If all goes according to plan, it should not cost you anything either. There have to be some advantages to being a woman and the unwritten rule is that on blind dates, the guys pay. If they are a bit on the poor side, then they can just take you out for a drink so it needn't break their bank account. In fact, if any-thing, a drink is a much better idea. A meal is far too formal an affair to undergo with a complete stranger, unless you have hit it off extraordinarily well on the initial telephone recon-naissance. I always offer to pay my share, of course, although as I'm sure you realize, I am horrified if the offer is actually taken up. But please bear in mind my advice: Only Offer Once. It is not unusual for the offer to split the bill to be accepted on the second offer. Maybe the guys don't want to be thought old-fashioned and chauvinistic for denying you your right to contribute. Offering once looks good; offering twice is just plain stupid – chances are you'll end up forking out when your wallet was the last thing you expected to be groping at the end of the evening.

My first foray into the world of blind dates came when I returned from Italy (aged twenty-seven) and I was still technically within the acceptable age limits for singledom. A woman at work said she knew a nice Jewish boy, Ben, who was single and who would be delighted to make my acquaintance. I readily agreed. Meeting a nice Jewish boy without having to attend a Jew Do sounded like a very good deal. We met for a drink (he paid) and at the end of a fairly pleasant evening he invited me to a party he was hosting at his apartment in a couple of Saturday nights' time. I agreed to go because although I was not initially attracted to him, I thought he might have some nice friends. I arrived at the party on my own, quite a brave move when you know no one there and have only met the host once on a blind date, although our method of meeting turned out to be a good conversation booster once first name exchange had taken place.

Ben was friendly and attentive in a way that suggested to me that a second date would be imminent. Working on the assumption that he was going to ask to see me again, I thought I would pre-empt the question by informing him that although I had enjoyed his company very much, I did not think I was attracted to him and I thought I would just like to be friends with him instead. Before he had time to plead with me to change my mind, I excused myself and wandered off (in the direction of a guy to whom I *knew* I was attracted). I settled myself in the living room where the guy whose scent I had been following was sprawled on the sofa with a few of his cronies. He was my type: dark, muscular and socially confident. He made eye-contact with me and addressed me across the room:

"Who are you?" he asked.

I decided to act cute and give him my nickname: "Chips."

"Why are you called Chips?" Everyone in the room was listening by now.

"Because I love eating them," I replied. "What's your name?"

"Pussy," he said.

He'd won the repartee and I was speechless. He turned his attention from me and continued to chat with his friends. It was time to go home.

The following Tuesday, I received a telephone call from Ben who invited me to lunch (we worked in the same part of town). I was delighted that he had accepted the olive branch and harbored no bad feelings towards me. I accepted and when we met two things happened: (1) We got on brilliantly, i.e. it was riotously good fun rather than just plain pleasant, and (2) My non-attraction to him solidified and I knew for certain that we would never be lovers. This has actually turned out to be a terrible shame as he is now a wonderful husband to a very lucky woman, but you can't force yourself can you?

At the end of lunch, he told me that he had a confession to make. He was so incensed by my rejection speech at his party that he had wanted to take me out to lunch to berate me and give me a piece of his mind, and had been surprised to find that as we had got on so well, he could not bring himself to remain angry with me.

I wanted to know why he was so angry.

"When you gave me that speech about how you didn't think it would work out between us, were you aware that I had not actually even asked you out?" Before I could start spluttering, he went one stage further. "Not only had I not asked you out, but I did not even intend to ever ask you out. You're not my type." He then said that I was the only girl who had ever finished with him before he'd even asked her out.

Well, at the risk of sounding arrogant (which I don't mind doing) I quite simply did not believe him. And I told him. Of course, this enraged him, but not seriously as we were now laughing about the situation.

During the first few years of our friendship (which is still going strong, by the way; his wife is the non-possessive, together type who is sure of her husband's love and is not threatened by his friendships with women), I always told him, "Nothing you ever say or do will convince me that you did not fancy me and that you were not going to ask me out."

He laughed at what he called my "self-delusional fantasies," but I was convinced I was right and a year or so after he got married and before he emigrated to Israel, he finally confessed that he had intended to ask me out.

When Ben met his wonderful wife-to-be I was invited to the engagement party. By this stage, I believed that I was hovering over the acceptable age limit for singledom and this belief was confirmed when I attended the party and found to my horror that I was *the only single person there*. If I had known, I would not have bothered wearing such a short skirt and foundation. I got chatting to someone's fiancé and we got on really well, in a platonic way obviously. I am magically and thankfully imbued with a mechanism that automatically stops me flirting with an attached man. He told me that one of his

friends was single and a good-looking, fun, funky photogra-
pher. As he listed his friend's selling points, I was forced by
pride to decline and act all casual and nonchalant. Until the
friend mentioned that his friend, David, had a Yamaha 850cc,
which he had just bought and was crazy about. I interrupted:
"Give me his number."

Once I got home from the party I decided to take my
destiny into my own hands and I dialed David's number. He
sounded like I had woken him from a nap. It was early
Sunday evening and there he was in his apartment, minding
his own business, and with no warning he got a complete
stranger (albeit a woman) on the phone.

Undeterred, I introduced myself. "Hi, I've just been given
your number by a friend of yours who I met this afternoon
at an engagement party. He said you'd take me for a ride." He
was either desperate or the adventurous type (I wouldn't
know till I met him) and he said he would love to take me
for a ride and arranged to pick me up on Friday evening.

He sounded reasonably entertaining on the phone and I
therefore awaited the date with pleasurable anticipation. As it
was a blind date there was no need to starve myself through
nerves for three days beforehand. When I opened the door
and we caught sight of each other, we both smiled broadly. I
was smiling from relief. He was rather cool and good looking. He was smiling, I was later told, because he remembered
me from another engagement party when I had been
wearing a black rubber bathing suit and see-through chiffon
skirt and he had been dying to come and talk to me but
hadn't quite dared.

The relationship lasted about three months. Why so short?
Because we had nothing in common apart from his Yamaha
850. Why so long? The sex was phenomenal (I'll tell you

about it sometime), especially after long rides on his Yamaha 850.

You can see that so far, although the blind dates did not fulfil their objective, i.e. marriage, they were nonetheless successful in terms of a friendship and a phenomenal lover. Only once have I felt the urge to close the door straight after opening it. Of course I couldn't, and I was forced to persuade the blind date in question to change the proposed venue of the evening, i.e. from a bar frequented by people who might know me to a pub in the middle of nowhere. I sat opposite the guy and with some mental agility listened politely to his conversation while privately wondering why the woman who fixed me up thought I would be well-suited to a big, blobby, socially incompetent moron. But then the big, blobby moron was her brother so she probably had not thought of it in those terms. However, it transpired that even big blobby morons have their charm, and despite the total lack of sexual attraction on my part, we had a nice evening and – please don't hate me for saying this – it's also nice to have your ego boosted by a kind and attentive man, even though he is big and blobby.

Following this date I seemed to be inundated with offers of introduction and I greedily accepted all help. The first offer I took up was not a success. I should have guessed that this would be the case from the message left on my answering machine. The guy's voice sounded so bleak and depressed that the only reason I called him back was to make sure he had not committed suicide straight after leaving the message. He was still alive; unfortunately, after the date with him, it was me that was seriously depressed. It was the sort of date that gives you the distinct impression that, at my age, the only men on offer are the leftovers.

The next date sounded a lot more promising. A film pro-
ducer, who also happened to be the right age, the right religion and *single*. I would have preferred a complete blind date
but the guy who was promoting the match obviously wanted
to watch the show and I was invited for dinner with him, his
wife and the spare man instead. These dinners can be a bit on
the cringe-cringe side; I prefer to flirt in private, not in front
of a happily married couple who will watch my self-
conscious attempts at a public flirt with pity, and possibly
even joke about it later that night when they are curled up in
bed together before sighing with gratitude that they have
found each other and then falling asleep contentedly in each
other's arms.

But beggars can't be choosers, so I applied the warpaint,
squeezed into the heels, poured myself into the dress and set
off for dinner. Despite attempts to be the last to arrive, I did
not have the heart to be rude and arrive too late, so I ended
up being the first instead. The introducer, Mike, expressed
surprise at my smart appearance, while I inwardly cursed the
fact that he and his wife obviously thought they no longer
needed to make an effort to look good and were wearing
jeans. I looked overdressed and as though I was trying too
hard, but I think I managed to cover it up by pretending that
I had come straight from work. On arrival, Jason immediately
lost about three points: he was officially rudely late, he was
empty-handed and he was also wearing jeans. However, during dinner, he earned six points for his consistent wit, lively
and stimulating conversation and attentive charm.

I decided to be a little bit cool and was the first to make
a move to go. Jason murmured that it was about time he left
too. We both thanked our hosts for a wonderful evening and
as we walked down the path I was practically scrabbling in
my handbag for a pen to give Jason my number. As we said

goodbye and how much we had enjoyed meeting each other and made our separate ways to our respective cars, I thought, Gosh, he's leaving it a bit late. As I watched him get into his car, while climbing into my own I thought, It is now official. He has not taken my number. Then I thought, He'll ring Mike for it tomorrow. I suppose I was basically refusing to admit defeat. I had put on a dazzling performance during the evening. I had laughed at all his jokes. Genuinely laughed, by the way. I can't fake laughter. In fact, I directly link my lack of corporate success to my inability to produce a corporate guffaw. I had made quite a few good jokes myself. I had not been too loud; in fact, quite quiet by my standards as I had previously decided that my game plan for the evening was to concentrate on quality rather than quantity of conversation. What I am trying to say is that I was what you might call "demure," though, I hasten to add, not in a sick, soppy "girlie" kind of way. I wasn't crude, I wasn't brash, I looked great, I was slim, I was Jewish. *He had to like me. What the fuck was wrong with the guy?* Was he blind, deaf and dumb?

A week went by and I heard nothing. I was disappointed, but my life was now so full of new friends, old friends, phone calls, invitations, fun evenings out and new possibilities, that I was able to move on and continue life without an answer to the mystery of why Jason had not called. Then, out of the blue, a couple of weeks later, I arrived home one night to hear the following message on my answering machine: "Hi, it's Jason. Sorry I haven't been in touch for so long. I'll give you a call back in the week."

I was obviously delighted to hear from him, despite the fact that by that time I only had a rather hazy recollection of what the guy was actually like. After all, I had only met him once for a few hours and that had been over two weeks ago. The answering machine message was saved and replayed every time I needed confirmation that I was a sexually attractive woman. The positive change, not just in mood, but in basic self-belief that resulted from a message from someone that I barely knew was, I fully understand, tragic. I can be in a mood of such unending misery and despair and futility one minute; one phone call or answering machine message later, I can be dancing around the apartment and joyfully returning the long list of calls that have been accumulating whilst I have been waiting for the depression to pass, so that now, when I return the calls, I can sound genuinely optimistic and, ironically, in control of my life.

Within minutes of playing the message from Jason, I was planning our happy future together. I made a mental list of our many shared interests and belief systems, and by the end of the evening I was convinced that we would make an ideal couple; I could accompany him to premieres and film festivals and I would let him have the film rights to my books. There would be a meeting of creative and artistic minds, resulting in some superb cult films which would bring us both lots of money and worldwide respect. What a team we would make! The wedding would be bohemian but high-profile, with a colorful mix of writers, producers, actresses and actors. I went to bed that night, quietly confident that I could charm the pants off him on our impending date, and as I understood from his friend that he was looking to "settle down," decided that he need look no further. I was so excited that I felt like ringing him up to reassure him that his search for a bride was now over; I would be perfect for the job. I didn't ring, of course. I was just so happy for us both that I wanted to share it with my future husband.

He did not call the next day. He was a very busy man, don't forget. The last number recall after the message revealed an out-of-town number and I suspected that he was attending a shoot in somewhere like, I don't know, Elstree, perhaps. However, the next evening, I received a call.

"Hi, this is Jason." My heart fluttered, I started to tingle, my armpits prickled and I stretched the phone to the sofa where I could lounge languidly while we flirted. "I don't know if you remember me," he said humbly. I reassured him that I did, but he felt compelled to continue: "We met in the Lake District on the walking tour a couple of months ago."

"NO! OH MY GOD! NOT YOU! OH NO! PLEASE. NOT YOU. OH FUCK, OH NO! I DON'T BELIEVE IT!" I shrieked.

Hang on, maybe all was not lost, maybe *both* Jasons called?

"Did you call earlier in the week?" I quickly demanded.

"Yes," he replied meekly, "I left a message on your answering machine." His voice was now barely a whimper.

I later discovered that ever since this Jason (now referred to as Nice Jason, as opposed to my ex-future-husband who is called something else) met me in the Lake District, he had been plucking up the courage to ring me. Apparently, he had driven his colleagues at work nuts by his dithering (I had returned from the vacation in the Lake District just over two months ago), but having finally received sufficient reassurance from friends, colleagues and family that they were sure that I would be delighted to hear from him, he finally took the plunge and called me. Apparently, my response went far beyond his wildest nightmares and put him off asking anyone else out for the next six months.

When I realized that Jason would not understand why I was wailing I quickly explained that I was not wailing because *he* had called but because he was not someone else. That did not sound too great either, so I further explained that his calling meant that I was not now getting married to a witty, high-profile member of the Jewish elite after all. This did not seem to mean much to him either. It basically took about five minutes to explain the situation (over-thirty, single, recent disappointing relationship history, blind date, message on machine, wedding plans, extensive wardrobe planning for the film festival in Cannes, wrong Jason, cancellation of wedding caterers).

I also had certainly blown the new, mysterious, enigmatic approach to potential boyfriends as well, although Nice Jason had not done too well either by admitting to such chronic pre-first call anxiety and then compounding matters by explaining his own situation (left by his long-term girlfriend for his friend over a year ago, beginning to get over it, readjusting to return to dating scene, walking tour in Lake District, met nice girl, finally had balls to call her).

Inadvertently, we had pretty much covered everything within the first twenty minutes of the phone conversation and we were consequently soon chatting like old friends. I did remember him and although he was adorable, he was not my type. Wrong-shaped nose. Only joking. But surely I am entitled to go out with someone that I fancy? Anyway, the good news is that we now have a warm and supportive friendship; the bad news is that the other Jason never called. However, there is more good news when I hear that the bad news is, in fact, good news after all. I have since heard from people that know him and have worked with him that what I mistook for considerable social authority was actually impenetrable arrogance and the bad manners that were exhibited at the dinner party were characteristic of a fundamental disdain for other members of the human race.

"I've only Slept with one Guy and it wasn't very Good"

After eight months of total celibacy, I am coming to the conclusion that being single really isn't all that bad. I am in control of my emotions (apart from the occasional loneliness at family weddings, when the dancing begins and everyone leaves the table with their partner to smooch on the dance floor and I'm left alone waiting for my seventy-year-old uncle to finish dancing with my aunt so that I, too, can participate fully in the festivities). As a single woman, my life is unpredictable. I can go out any night of the week and who knows what will happen to me by the end of the evening. It is not inconceivable that my life will change dramatically by the end of the day. With a boyfriend, however, especially with one of the steady varieties, you pretty much know exactly what will happen to you at the end of the evening, which hopefully will be lovely but will not hold too many surprises (unless you get home to find that he wants to wear your underwear, for example. That is not such a nice surprise. Well, not for me, anyway).

Single life has higher ups and lower downs, which suits a drama queen such as myself. I love hanging out with my friends and catching up with all the gossip and scandal;

friends in steady relationships, God bless them, are not half as much fun. Nothing seems to change much in their lives – all being well – and I am afraid that for me, tragedy is linked to the high art of comedy.

You can't beat the thrill of getting dressed up to go out to a party on a Saturday night (excluding Jew Dos), the magic of transforming your ordinary face with make-up into a face of extraordinary beauty, and the fun of getting into outrageous clothes that, quite frankly, you would have no business wearing were you ensconced in a happy relationship. And then, best of all, there are the as yet unknown men you will meet and maybe even fall in love with. With luck, there will be a new chest to discover. It could be hairy, muscular or silky smooth. There could be a new mouth to kiss. He could be the passionate, hungry type or the soft, gentle, sensual type. He could be an accomplished ear-licker. He could be a bottom kneader. He could be a loud groaner (with luck) or he could be the challenger to Rick's crown of best oral sex performer in the entire universe. He could have the biggest banana-shaped cock in London *and know what to do with it*. He could make me laugh. He could make me see life differently. He could be the first man who is as affectionate as me. I live in hope.

When I was seeing Rob, and even Mark, I really missed my Saturday nights out with my girlfriends. OK, there was sex at the end of the evening, but there was no thrill in dressing up, no outrageous laughs, no excitement. It was pleasant, sure, but the x factor was missing; x signifying new experiences. I am sure that my feelings on this subject have been influenced by the fact that I have not been going out with guys that I really click with on a conversational/emotional/mental level for some time, and if I met a guy who stimulated me in these departments I would no doubt feel very differently on the subject.

However, for the first time, I am beginning to realize the implications for me of "the grass is always greener" syndrome. When I am with someone, I yearn for the unpredictability, freedom and new experiences of single life. When I am single, I yearn to have someone special in my life who will always be on my side, who I can kiss and cuddle and laugh and banter with, and with whom I can intelligently discuss the meaning of life (a subject never far from my mind).

I am due to go around to some gay friends, Andrew and Gavin, for the afternoon to discuss, no doubt, all of the above and I am really looking forward to it. When I first met Andrew and Gavin, I did not realize that they were an item, and if there were any justice in the world they would not be together. They would, instead, uncomplainingly double up as my love slaves. Each is delectably good-looking and charming in his own right, although some say they are phoney as hell. Despite the fact that they have been together for quite a long time, I understand that they still occasionally experience tummy tickles on account of each other.

Jasmin and I have been invited over to their house for a session of no-holds-barred conversation. Their friends are all very open and, thankfully, mostly debauched. I am due to pick up Jasmin, also recently single and reveling in her freedom from feeling obliged to make a relationship work with someone whom her family adored but whose seduction technique consisted of boring her horizontal.

We arrive at Andrew and Gavin's to find a riotous discussion underway on what constitutes an unacceptable number of sexual partners. Opinions differ so dramatically on what constitutes a slut that I feel compelled to join in and provide the feminist viewpoint. I don't know if you realized, by the way, but as I am an intelligent human being, I am also a feminist. I do actually call myself a feminist despite the unfashionable regard in which this label is now held. I sometimes meet women who, in company, relate an injustice suffered by a woman because she is a woman, only to end the story with something like, "But I'm not a feminist."

"Why the fuck not?" I want to ask. Instead I temper the question somewhat and it is rephrased into, "Do you believe in equal rights and opportunities for women and men?"

The only intelligent answer is "Yes" and I then crow, "Well then, you are a feminist." The woman in question is normally horrified that she has been tricked in this way into appearing to be something other than a wholly adoring man lover. I get the feeling that feminism is not something a lot of women would admit to in front of men in the fear that it might scare them off. They may think that you want them to participate in the cooking and cleaning and then you might lose them.

Anyway, where was I? Oh yes. Forget fat being a feminist issue, the number of partners a woman has is definitely a feminist issue. And I am not talking about what men think of women who have had more than, say, five partners. I am talking about what the women think of themselves. I'm telling you, one minute you are desperately catching up for lost time (due to a late start or a long-term relationship) and the next thing you know, you are sitting in a darkened room adding up numbers and swearing to yourself that the next time anyone asks you that question, the only acceptable thing to do is halve the number and then divide by five.

The best response I have ever heard a woman give a soon-to-be boyfriend when asked the number of her previous partners (apart, obviously, from "Mind your own business") was, "I've only slept with one guy and it wasn't very good." And the beauty of the reply was that it was absolutely true and she therefore had a perfectly demure but inviting expression on her face when she gave her coy response. This has always struck me since as the best answer to give a man – it is *exactly* what he wants to hear. You are not a virgin and they don't have to break you in. You've only had one partner which means that you are Madonna rather than whore. One partner means that you are sufficiently pure and unsullied to qualify as a contender for the marriage jackpot. And, crucially, your one partner was "not very good." This means that (a) there is only very minimal competition, (b) you won't know any better ("honestly, it's only supposed to last ten seconds"), and (c) you have unwittingly issued an attractive (and rather easy) challenge. The only problem is that when you get to my time of life, men know you are bullshitting with a line like that.

Listen, boys. Am I right? Would someone please tell me if I am wrong? I would be delighted to stand corrected. Would you like the "I've only slept with one guy and it wasn't very good" line? Am I right to think that you would instantly adore the girl and want her to be your bride? I won't be angry if you tell me yes, I just want to know if I've understood you guys right. My male friends have been carefully selected on account of their open minds and liberated outlook so I am not sure how reliable their opinions are (most of them love the "I've only" line, by the way). What would you secretly but honestly think if a woman told you that she had slept with over, say, fifty guys?

Whenever I have told a guy my magic number in a moment of past-swapping (having obviously checked out his tally first) I have always regretted it. Although I do very much

believe in honesty in relationships, it's also not that nice to be
called a slut when you have an argument. Now, I am not
going to tell you how many men I've had sex with as (a) it's
none of your business, (b) I want to retain *some* mystery, and
(c) despite being a feminist and this being a feminist issue, we
live in a patriarchal society where men are still allowed by
common consensus to sow their wild oats while women are
subjected to the horrendous label of slut, and since I have
exceeded the acceptable limit for a woman of seven partners
(well, you could have inferred that for yourself by now), I will
say no more on the subject.

As the company at Gavin and Andrew's is comprised
solely of gay men and straight women (and a couple, who
don't count), the sexist psychology stated above is reversed
and the confessions at this little party begin to sound rather
like boasts. In the middle of this uproar, I notice a new friend
of Andrew and Gavin appear at the door, and as he kisses
them both hello I feel a tinge of regret that all their friends
are gay, especially this one. I haven't seen him before and
although he is not what you would describe as traditionally
good-looking, he has a certain manly charm. He has dark
hair, small intense eyes, a big Roman-style nose and full petu-
lant lips. My heart gives a little flutter, especially when I see
the large package of tackle tucked into his jeans, and I start
to long for some straight action. Jasmin and I are going out
to our friend Nikki's birthday party later in the evening and
I am looking forward to meeting men to whom I am not
sexually invisible, which is how you can feel if you hang out
with gay men for too long.

Johnny, the guy lounging next to me on the floor, confides that the visitor is one of their gym cronies, and he is
jealous as hell as his ex-boyfriend is always going on about
this guy's physique. He calls him Pectoral Paul. Putting such

grievances aside, he waves to him. Paul walks over in an exaggerated sashay, swinging his hips and blowing everyone kisses. He leans over me to kiss Johnny on both cheeks and then introduces himself to me. Once I have introduced myself back, I adopt my familiar approach. "How many lovers have you had?"

His response of "I'm a virgin" meets a cacophony of whistles, which I take to mean that either he's had hundreds of partners or he's one of those gay men who don't take it up the ass but put it up instead.

"How many lovers have you had, then?" he wants to know.

"Men or women?" I shoot back.

"Men," he replies.

Only a gay man would be interested in the man count rather than the lesbian experiences (pleeeease, can someone out there tell me if there is *any* straight man on this planet whose ultimate sexual fantasy does *not* involve lesbian action; I would like to give him a medal for originality). I tell him how many and he looks impressed.

"I'm impressed," he tells me. "How many of them were good?"

I then give him a rundown on the all-time best fucks of my life (one of my favorite pastimes) and he nods appreciatively in all the right places. His interruptions are witty rather than irreverent and I can tell that this guy takes his sex seriously too.

You see, that is the amazing thing about most gay men that I've met. You can talk to them completely openly about sex and all the disgusting things you get up to and they love it in a completely empathetic and non-judgemental way. Tell a straight guy the same information and it will be used either as masturbatory fodder or as an invite to fuck and dump you.

The more outrageous I become, the more encouragement I receive from Johnny, Paul, Andrew and Gavin to cleanse my soul through confession. We are all having a wicked laugh until Jasmin points at her watch and we reluctantly kiss the menfolk goodbye and leave for Nikki's party.

In the car to the party, we rave about how gorgeous Andrew and Gavin and their friends are. The same internal mechanism that stops me fancying married men also stops me from fancying gay men too. There is nothing sadder than hearing a woman bleating on about how much she is in love with a guy who is clearly gay but who this woman has the impudence to believe she can convert to heterosexuality. I lived with a gay guy for a year in Italy and he taught me more about homosexuality than a degree in Gay Awareness. When I asked him that old chestnut, "When did you first know you were gay?" he answered, "When did you first know you were straight?" Right. Now I understand. "Say no more," I said. So, I wasn't going to start getting sad and mournful about the wonderful rapport I had just enjoyed with Andrew and Gavin's friend, Paul, whose wit and speed of repartee had impressed me considerably.

Jasmin and I arrive at Nikki's party to flirt with guys that neither of us fancy, but who we nevertheless decide need a mercy flirt to keep their peckers up. One of them has recently split up with a long-term girlfriend without his consent and the other acts like I do when I haven't had sex for a long time (i.e. trying *far* too hard). Actually, it is definitely one of those evenings when you are dying for the joke to be over and to just go home to your wonderful partner who is lying in bed and keeping it warm for your return so that he can listen to you tell him about the weird and wonderful people you have met that day before cuddling up and going to sleep (without, would you believe, even having sex, *and* not minding).

I therefore don't want to feel alone in the world on my way home from the party so I ring Gavin and Andrew on the cell to tell them what a great afternoon I'd had. Gavin is pleased the afternoon was such a success and starts to tell me how much Paul liked me when I reach a hostile signal area and his voice becomes warbled and the line then goes dead. I quickly put the radio on instead. It is one of those nights when I don't want to listen to the thoughts in my head. I drive home praying that Gabriela will (a) still be up and (b) have some chocolate.

When I get home I find her burning the photograph of the elusive northern businessman leaning against his Ferrari that she has been pawing for the last month while she has been waiting for him to ring. She looks triumphantly gleeful when I see the shriveled photograph and then she looks sad when she tells me that she decided to take control of her life and ring him and he was too busy to speak to her, and then she felt like taking her life rather than simply taking control of it. Despite Gabriela's protestations that all she wants or expects from men is sex and money, I think she really fell for this one. Since arriving in London as an au pair, aged eighteen, she has had to do everything for herself. She came here to improve her English and decided that life in London was preferable to the corrupt and dreary struggle she watched her parents experiencing in her home town in Eastern Europe. Since then, with focus and determination, she has taken qualifying exams and now studies at university where she supports herself with part-time jobs. I think that this time, with the northern businessman, she not only thoroughly enjoyed his company (he was very charismatic), she also fell in love with the idea of having someone by her side to help and support her, at least some of the time. I had suspected that he was married but my suggestions to this effect were brushed aside, despite the all-time classic sign that he would only give her his cell phone number.

Gabriela looks melancholic. I climb on to her bed and hug her tightly whilst realizing gratefully that I have arrived just in time to receive spoonfuls of the jar of Nutella she has single-handedly almost demolished. We have another cuddle and indulge in a spot of mutual reflexology. We do our toilette together; she brushes her teeth whilst I sit on the loo, and she takes off her make-up while I brush my teeth. A kiss goodnight. I pinch her behind, she wobbles mine. And we go to bed.

Thank you, God, for friends.

Will You be my New Best Friend?

Friendships are very important, particularly when you are single. Sometimes I think that I wouldn't mind living in a large house with my friends, with various men coming to visit a couple of times a week to service us. It's not socially acceptable, I know, but sometimes I think it would be the ideal situation.

Friendships are also a lot more fluid when you are single. People come and go, in and out of your life. It's easy to make friends when you are single. Women in steady relationships have their boyfriends or husbands to listen to stories of their day; single people need the intimacy of close friends in whom to confide day-to-day trivia as well as the heavy emotional stuff. And everyone wants to be your friend when you are single.

Married or settled women look to you to entertain them with spicy details so that they can get their kicks vicariously, or, alternatively, to regale them with your disappointments so they can feel relieved that they are not missing out on anything.

Single straight men want to be your friend (a) because they fancy you, (b) because they fancy one of your friends,

(c) because if they had a girlfriend, they would not be allowed to be your friend, and (d) because you provide the intimacy and emotional support they miss from their male friendships.

Gay men, both single and attached, want to be your friend because (a) they love the drama of single life and/or (b) you also fit into the social outsider category and/or (c) they can talk openly about sex without censorious disapproval as you realize that sex is not a moral issue.

And, of course, single women want to be your friend because (a) you have so much in common, (b) you can go out manhunting together, and (c) you might know some cute men to introduce them to.

For all of the above reasons, when you do get together with someone, the phone stops ringing. But, having been single more often than not over the last few years, my phone has been pretty hot. Admittedly, it has got quieter in recent months, partly due to my new selective approach to friendships. This is something that Gabriela taught me. When we first started living together, she was initially impressed at the number of calls I was receiving. But after witnessing the time and energy that went into these calls, the respect turned into disrespect. She heard me repeating the story of the day/week/evening up to five times a night, often eliciting five different opinions and five different sets of advice (only requested from two sources, but people are dying to help). My record one night was twenty-two calls (although, admittedly, five were from Jasmin). It was not unknown for me to get in from work, make and receive a couple of calls, then make my way towards the kitchen to prepare some dinner only for the phone to ring again. Half an hour and three cigarettes later, my appetite would be gone and I would decide to forget about dinner for the time being. I would then settle myself down to watch a television drama that I had been following when the phone would ring again and, of course, I would be dying to speak to the person and would turn the TV off. Inevitably, that call would necessitate another call to tell someone else the contents of the previous call and before I knew it it would be bedtime and I wouldn't have eaten, bathed, read, written, done my paperwork or caught up with Gabriela's news.

Gabriela pointed out that all my energy was going on repeating my news over and over again, listening to friends and offering support and, where necessary, sympathy. So I cut down dramatically on people that I kept in touch with on a regular basis and the effect has been really rather liberating. A twice-yearly clean out of friends is highly recommended. The unreliable ones who reliably let you down at the last minute go. So do the ones who go on and on about their own shit, only to say, "Listen, I've really got to go," when you retaliate with your shit. And male friends who go on about how gorgeous your single friends are the whole time have also got to be eliminated from the call-back list. Who else? Oh yeah, the ones who only ring you when they are single. You get the picture. All that lot have to go. So you are just left with friends who love and support you, who laugh at your jokes and who you could ring up in the middle of the night in emergencies to say, "Can you pick me up from Peckham? My car's broken down, I've just been dumped and I've got no money on me," and they'll come. Not that I've ever had to resort to this, but with a good friend you know you could call and you know they would come.

At the same time, I love meeting new people and I adore the honeymoon stage of friendships when you meet someone you click with and go through the getting to know you stage. You both instinctively feel that this is the start of something beautiful and you are optimistic that the wonderful new friend will be promoted to the stage where their name is written in ink in the formal address section in your Rolodex. You haven't yet got to know the other person's faults which may or may not turn out to be acceptable and they don't know the full horror of my mood-swinging hysteria.

So when I hear that Paul has called for me one evening in the week after the afternoon's festivities at Andrew and Gavin's, I am delighted. He is definitely someone I would like in my life. He is funny and wonderfully irreverent. He is open-minded. He is quite handsome in a gay, butch way. He is sharp and perceptive. And there is a vacancy in my gay man friend department. I had recently had to eject a gay friend who was inadvertently infecting me with his incessant whining about the lack of decent men in the world and how he would be on his own until he died of loneliness. I am glad that Paul felt he wanted to be friends and that he felt a connection with me.

So, I am a little bit disappointed when I find, on returning his call, that he has only called me to get the number of one of my friends. It turns out that Paul is a property developer and needs a new lawyer and Andrew had mentioned that one of my friends specializes in conveyancing.

"Have there been any additions to your conquest total since last week?" he asks.

"Unfortunately not, but I am going out cock-hunting at the weekend and with my looks and charm it shouldn't be too hard to find someone willing to become a statistic," I reply.

"Has anyone ever accused you of being romantic?" he wants to know.

"Romance breaks the heart," I say.

"Romance heals the heart," he counters, then adds, "so I'm told."

"Are you seeing anyone at the moment? I noticed that you were a little reserved on the confession front at Andrew and Gavin's place."

"I'm in the process of removing myself from a "sticky situation."

"Oh really? I quite like sticky situations. If all goes well on my cock-hunting expedition, I should be getting myself involved in a sticky mess at the weekend."

He laughs and we banter for a while until I feel the need to come clean.

"The truth is that I am now totally opposed to meaningless sex with someone who I don't know, like or care for, and although I don't mind playing the brazen hussy act for feminist promotional purposes, I am fed up with cock-hunting and I am in fact looking to settle down with someone on a permanent basis."

"How romantic. You can't be bothered to go out cock-hunting anymore so you need to find a cock to wait at home for you so that he can be at your beck and call and service you when you feel like it."

"Yeah, well. What's wrong with that? Isn't that why people get married?"

"What happens when you get bored of having sex with the same person?"

"You join a swinging couples group, don't you?"

"I'm not fooled by your nonchalant attitude, by the way. I reckon we are all looking for love, you included, sweetheart. I don't want to be alone all my life. I want someone to go through all the ups and downs with. I think I could be quite romantic you know, once I've stopped screwing around. In fact, I think I'm nearly there. I think that my obsession with new experiences has also, finally at the age of thirty-four, passed. I am planning on celibating for some time before I consider what exactly I am looking for in someone."

"Johnny's ex will be disappointed," I reply.

"What are you talking about?" he asks quickly.

But before I can reply to his question, my cell phone goes and I have to rush off the phone from Paul to attend to more urgent business. It's Claudia; a dejected, rejected admirer has just thrown a bottle through her window. I tell Paul I'd love to see him again when we go out for drinks with Andrew and Gavin and it is only later that evening that I realize that we were chatting away so merrily that I hadn't even given him my lawyer friend's number. Oh well, I think, he'll ring me again and we can continue our chat and I can charm him into wanting to be my friend.

Meanwhile, one of Jasmin's friends has just signed a recording contract after ten years of yearning and never giving up hope, and on Saturday night he is having a party to celebrate at a new bar in Chalk Farm. I am hoping that the party will be full of new men and, therefore, new possibilities. Who knows? I could meet my future husband there and I must dress myself in the correct attire to attract him. What would my future husband like to see me in, I ponder, while dressing for the party. Something funky, something sophisticated, something sexy but not too desperate. It looks like it's the fake snakeskin trousers with slinky tit-hugging top again. I do decide that he wouldn't want me to be extremely uncomfortable and therefore put the Wonderbra back in the drawer. I have never actually scored in this outfit, but it's my favorite partywear and it takes the right kind of man to appreciate that level of style. Basically, my kind of man and I haven't met him yet.

Jasmin and I arrive at the party early so that we can get a seat somewhere and thus avoid appearing to prowl later. Imagine our horror when a couple comes up to us to ask if we mind if they share our table. "FUCK OFF!" I want to scream at them. "You've found someone. Don't screw up my chances of meeting someone by blocking my potential husband's view of me." Instead, I scowl and say, "OK." Their eye-gazing, hand-holding and non-conversation begins to irritate the hell out of me and as Jasmin and I gather our things together to escape, I tell them, "You win. You get the whole table."

They look at me with incomprehension and return to grazing on each other's necks. Yuck. Jasmin and I saunter up to the bar looking harassed. A long-haired fifty-year-old rocker with pointy cowboy boots and leather trousers, who ought to be tucked up in bed with a cup of cocoa and a copy of *Playboy*, fancies his chances with me and Jasmin and actually asks us if "we come here often." I point out that this particular bar has only been open for a couple of weeks so it would be hard for it to have become our regular in this short space of time. He looks rather crestfallen and I feel mean, so to Jasmin's horror I introduce us and offer him my hand.

He shakes my hand and introduces himself, "Hi, I'm Malcolm." Turns out Malcolm is actually an accountant, Jewish and his alter ego is allowed to come out and play at weekends. He's going through a messy divorce and sleeping in his office. He looks a bit bedraggled and my maternal instincts are activated. He turns out to be a hilarious raconteur and I adore his 1970s suburban wife-swapping stories. Jasmin, Malcolm and myself prop ourselves up on some bar stools and get acquainted. Malcolm comments on how much he loves my snakeskin trousers. Well, at least someone does, I think to myself.

The next two hours are a bit of a blur. Malcolm is generously buying cocktails and I am finding it difficult to keep my balance on the bar stool. I am really quite drunk, so when I think I see Paul across the room and my heart gives a flutter, I decide it's time to sober up. I must be seeing things. What would he be doing here? I decide to investigate and I make my way towards him. It *is* him. As he catches sight of me staggering across the room he strides purposely towards me.

"You look fantastic," he says. "I love your trousers."

"You look gorgeous too," I tell him, "and although it is strictly against policy to fancy gay men, I could make an exception in your case."

He pulls me close to him and I experience the weirdest thing. A tummy tickle. I must be getting really sad if the only tummy tickle I have experienced in a long long time is generated by a gay man.

Please then imagine my horror when a long-legged, raven-haired *female* beauty comes along, puts her arm around his shoulder and says, "Darling, can we go home now?" Paul looks extremely awkward and absorbs my embarrassment as well as radiating his own. I make a mental note to ring Andrew and Gavin the next day to reveal my scoop. Paul is obviously trying to go straight! Yikes. His girlfriend is so gorgeous I didn't blame him – she's enough to turn me gay. However, I am pretty doubtful that you can force your sexuality one way or t'other and I believe that Paul's experiment will end in tears.

I want to go home. I've had enough of partying. It is all too confusing. Nothing is what it seems. We are all just a disparate band of wandering alienated weirdos trying to find happiness, all of us as sad and fucked up as each other. Some of us realize this (me) and most of us don't (Harry, Mike, Paul, etc.). I find Jasmin, who is having one of her deep and meaningful conversations with a Brazilian woman and I tell her that I've had enough.

"I thought you were enjoying yourself," she says.

"When I say I've had enough," I say, "I mean it in a general sense. I don't want to go out ever again."

Malcolm scurries over, looking concerned that his babes are about to leave and takes our numbers. I give mine on the strict proviso that he will never ever try to have sex with me.

The following day I telephone Andrew and Gavin with my news about Paul and the mysterious raven-haired beauty. Their reaction is not quite what I had anticipated. My "You are never going to guess who I saw with a woman last night" is greeted with indifference.

"So what?" Andrew asks. "Paul's been seeing Lara on and off for about six months."

"But he's gay, isn't he?" I say with some shock.

Once Andrew has stopped guffawing, he tells me that quite the reverse is true. Not only is he one hundred per cent straight, he is an extremely successful seducer, known (and admired, of course, as he is a man) for his extremely high number of conquests. I am horrified that I had got it so completely wrong.

"How many is extremely high?" I want to know. I am intrigued.

"Well, after you left that Sunday he confessed to having slept with over eighty women."

"That is *disgusting*," I respond, but I am also impressed. I wonder how many of them were any good.

"You are such a hypocrite," says Andrew. "Last Sunday

you were waving the banner for the campaign for promiscuity and now you've gone all coy and virginal."

"Hardly," I reply. "But what sort of guy sleeps with eighty women by the time they are thirty-four years old? That's what troubles me. It's OK for gay men to have that number of partners, but not straight men! The whole point is that I thought he was gay otherwise I would never have been so indiscreet about who I've slept with and I would certainly never have revealed such graphic details to a straight man that I fancy."

"Now we're getting to the point," says Andrew. "You fancy him and you are worried that you've blown it with him because he knows what you are really like."

And he's right. But it's not just that I fancy him. I have fancied lots of people in my time. It was also a certain feeling, a little like an electrical charge, that I had when he walked through the door at Andrew and Gavin's tea party. We just kind of immediately gravitated towards each other, almost as if we already knew each other, and when we got on so well and became so intimate so quickly, it just confirmed that feeling. I felt like we were on the same wavelength. I thought that he would appreciate my stories and he did. He knew that he could tease me and that I would not be offended. He knew he could interrupt and I wouldn't mind the interruptions because they were spot on and witty. It was just that we clicked in a way that made me think there was something between us.

Why oh why have I got such a big mouth? Why couldn't I just sit there like Jasmin, listening and laughing but not revealing? Why did I have to expose myself to someone who I didn't know just because I thought he was gay and he would not judge me? Why did I do it? Why do I have to be so outrageous? What's so great about being the center of attention and making everyone gasp and laugh? Don't bother to answer that one unless you are a qualified psychotherapist.

"Anyway," says Andrew, "you are wrong about your revelations putting Paul off. He thought you were amazing and said he had never met anyone like you."

"Yeah, right. He would love to be my friend so that he can borrow my porn films and get top tips from me on how to please his beautiful girlfriend, but he'll never consider me as serious girlfriend material now he knows what I get up to."

"First of all, he's not like other guys. He hangs out with Gavin and me and all our friends at the gym and not many straight men do that so easily. You saw the way he kissed everyone hello with absolutely no self-consciousness. He is just a very open and affectionate guy. And secondly, from what I hear, he doesn't need any tips in the sex department."

"Well, after screwing so many women I'm not surprised. But then it's not quantity but quality that makes a good performer in bed. It's in the long-term relationships, when you lose your inhibitions, that you really get down to experimenting and exploring. That's what turns you into a well-seasoned lover. Am I right or am I right?"

"Look, you are probably right. Just don't shoot the messenger. Actually, I've heard from a few sources, including Lara, that he is pretty wild in bed and an extraordinarily good lover. Maybe it was just out of the goodness of his heart that he screwed so many women. Maybe he just wanted to spread a bit of magic. To be honest with you, I think it's a bit weird too. He just cannot settle with one person for very long. He always finds reasons as to why the woman in question is all wrong."

"So what does he find wrong with Lara?" I ask hopefully.

"She's very quiet and he's a big conversationalist and it

drives him mad. He's the type of guy who likes to stay up all night having deep conversations and she's the type of woman who likes to have deep sex and then deep sleep; she's not really up for the deep conversations. But she's very sweet and she adores him and she won't take no for an answer. She also happens to be Jewish and his parents adore her. It's just that he gets bored quite easily and he reckons he needs more in the mental stimulation department. But, as I told you, he always finds something wrong. Lara's crazy about him and he likes that. He likes being adored by his women."

I think I'm in love.

I'm scared.

Easy

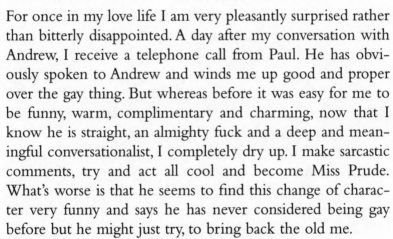

For once in my love life I am very pleasantly surprised rather than bitterly disappointed. A day after my conversation with Andrew, I receive a telephone call from Paul. He has obviously spoken to Andrew and winds me up good and proper over the gay thing. But whereas before it was easy for me to be funny, warm, complimentary and charming, now that I know he is straight, an almighty fuck and a deep and meaningful conversationalist, I completely dry up. I make sarcastic comments, try and act all cool and become Miss Prude. What's worse is that he seems to find this change of character very funny and says he has never considered being gay before but he might just try, to bring back the old me.

I ask him whether Lara would mind him turning gay. It is the first time that his girlfriend has been mentioned between us and my question is followed by silence. I am determined not to break the silence as I would normally feel obliged to do.

"I really care about Lara," he tells me. I tense up but say nothing so he continues, "But I just know deep down that she's not right for me. Everyone tells me that relationships are about compromise and that I am thirty-four years old and when am I going to settle down and Lara's intelligent and kind and laughs at my jokes and she's the right religion, the right age and she's beautiful. But I just can't do it. Am I a commitment-phobe? What do you reckon? My therapist reckoned that's my problem and she was always annoyingly right."

What I want to say is, "You haven't met the right girl yet," but what I end up saying is more judgemental and bitchy. "I think your therapist is right." I want to add the word "annoyingly," but I don't.

"I keep trying to break up with Lara but then she always rings me and I think I must be nuts to pass up on her, and I feel like some human contact, so I relent and see her again but something's missing. Maybe she's too straightforward for me. Maybe I need someone with a dark side. Someone a bit crazier perhaps?"

I am frothing at the mouth by now and I've practically got my hand in the air, silently screaming, "Me! Me!" Instead I say the complete opposite. "I thought she looked lovely and maybe it's not possible to find the perfect partner."

"Well, anyway, it's all a bit late for that now," he announces with a sigh. "I told her after the party on Saturday night that it was never going to work and that I was wasting her time and she ought to be free to meet someone who also likes *Friends* and *Four Weddings and a Funeral*."

This reply produces sweaty palms, a flushed face and somersaults in my stomach. I am so glad that videophones are not available yet. We end up talking for two hours about everything and nothing and eventually I say that I have to go. I don't want to but I think I should. He tells me that he will call me the next day.

The problem is that Paul already knows that I fancy him. He also knows that I want to settle down, and about my colorful past. Basically, he knows that I have slept with more than one man and that mostly it was very good. It is therefore time to go AWOL, and so when he calls me the following evening, I give strict instructions to Gabriela to say that I am out and am not expected home until much, much later. He calls again the following night. This time I take the call, but only stay on the phone for five minutes as I explain that I am about to go out. If videophones were readily available, he would see me sprawled on the sofa in my dressing gown with a video and a bar of chocolate, quite clearly going nowhere. The following night I am also out. But this time it is true.

Naturally, I have discussed the Paul situation ad nauseum with all my close friends and anyone else who will listen, so going out for an evening with some girlfriends who I have not seen for some time offers a brand new forum for discussion. Subjects on the agenda for the evening include what everyone thinks of a man who has slept with over eighty women and whether, knowing his track record, I should become number eighty-one, or number eighty-two or even number eighty-three. I doubt with the numbers in question that he is keeping an accurate count and if he is, well that is even more worrying. During the evening at the pub, it is mooted that he obviously loves women. It is then further mooted that a man who loves women on that grand scale could never love only one woman and, moreover, someone wants to know what kind of diseases he must have picked up en route. I start to feel a bit defensive on Paul's behalf. I point out that if you happen to be good at it and you haven't met the person with whom you want to spend the rest of your life, what is to stop you putting it about a bit?

"A bit?" yells Annette. "That is what I call an understatement. The guy is obviously a sex machine and with his track record, hardly the type to be faithful."

I feel a depression coming on and excuse myself. On the loo, I mull over what my friends have said. Apart from the fact that Paul has not actually made it clear that he sees me as anything other than a friend who he can talk to, I think about whether I am prepared to start seeing him, bearing in mind his history. The fact is, I tell myself, that I also have a history, with my fair share of lovers and nasty diseases. What would I think of a man who rejected me on the basis of my past? Not much, probably. It crosses my mind that maybe Paul has been sent into my life in order for me to confront my past and to learn not to judge myself negatively on this (high) score.

Please do not switch off and become cynical when I tell you that I believe that we are on this planet to learn about ourselves and develop and evolve from this knowledge. This belief extends to the people we meet, who I think appear in our lives not by coincidence but in order to teach us about ourselves. I choose to believe that people turn up in our lives as messengers, often mirroring our own foibles and hang-ups, so that we can learn to accept their limitations and thus our own. I try to learn a lesson from each of my relationships. For example, with Mark, I was very harsh on him about his use of anti-depressants to avoid dealing with matters, and it took a while for me to realize that he was just mirroring my own use of marijuana and cigarettes to numb out unpleasant emotions. My relationship with Mark helped me to realize what I was doing and largely eliminate these habits from my life. With the rich boyfriend who brought me breakfast in bed (yes, I did meet him but we don't talk about him), I learned from the subsequent disrespect that he showed me during the relationship (that's why we don't talk about him) the importance of growing up, taking responsibility and always remain-

ing financially independent from your partner. The only relationship I have failed to learn anything positive from, as hard
as I try, is my six years with Tom (other than the fact that men
appear to really love you and then inexplicably leave you and
break your heart. Not such a constructive lesson I know, but
it's all I can come up with at the moment).

I return from the loo in a pensive mood and it takes me
a while to realize that Ros is waving my cell phone in the air.

"You'll never guess who just called!" she shouts out. I am
totally miffed that she has had the nerve to delve into my
handbag and answer my phone although I do soften when I
hear that it was Paul who had called. "I told him that his ears
must have been burning as we were just talking about him,"
she says.

I am horrified and then furious. "You did what?! You
idiot! How on earth can you have reached the grand old age
of thirty-one and not realize that what you did was just about
the uncoolest thing in the whole world?"

She reddens with shame and starts blustering on about
how my phone kept ringing and everyone urged her to
answer it. I then feel guilty, especially when I realize that she
married her first boyfriend and has never had to play the high
stakes game of dating in the early twenty-first century. I apologize for my harsh manner and tell her that the matter will
be forgotten as long as she gives me a verbatim report of their
conversation. Apparently, there was a certain amount of
damage limitation when she thankfully refused to disclose
the details of our discussion. She told him that the five of us
were sitting in The Flask in Highgate having a drink and a
chat. He said that I was very difficult to get hold of and that
he was embarrassed at having to resort to calling my cell phone
during the evening. She said that he was charming until she
asked him what he was up to that night and he replied that

he was off to The Anvil. I happen to know about The Anvil, a gay fetish club, through a heavily pierced and tattooed, leather-clad Italian gay friend of mine called Luca who practically lives there on his jaunts to London. I had told Paul about Luca and The Anvil the other night in the context of a lively debate on the pros and cons of S&M, something I had been learning about in Luca's fascinating letters from various gay S&M hotspots around Europe.

I had already explained the initial confusion over Paul's sexual inclinations to my friends and we laughed at the irony of the enormity of my mistake. After further discussion of the phone call, the conversation then turns to Jan's news. I have had my turn and now it is somebody else's opportunity to have a problem dissected, analyzed and then solved. I am very slightly tipsy as we make our way out of the pub at the end of the evening and I am glad that I arranged not to bring the car (Ros has kindly offered to give me a lift home). I therefore imagine that once again I am hallucinating visions of Paul when I see him leaning up against a wall outside the pub, looking cheeky but gorgeous. But no, it is definitely him and he smiles at me.

"Oh my God!" I wail. "Paul's here! And I am not emotionally prepared."

I can hear Ros repeating the words, "Oh my God," followed by, "I know him!"

Then Annette scurries over to me and says, "Where? Where?"

Before she can do any further damage, I quickly kiss everyone goodbye and walk over to Paul. He says that after he spoke to Ros, he rang Gabriela to find out whether I had brought my car as it was starting to rain heavily and he thought I might appreciate a lift home. I cannot believe how gorgeous this is of him but I am too shaken by his presence and his gesture to express any gratitude, so I put on my non-chalant act and say, "Why not?" I immediately regret not having had more to drink in the pub and it takes all my resolve not to ask him to wait while I pop back into the pub to down a triple vodka in one. I am really tongue-tied in the car home. Thankfully, he starts chatting about how he reckons one of the properties he has just bought is haunted and he relates a load of freaky happenings in the house that I would normally be intrigued to hear about but I am now finding hard to absorb. I feel really wobbly at the implications of what he has done to see me and I cannot wait to get out of the car so that I can wobble and shake in the privacy of my own home. He comments that I am quiet and I explain that I am tired from too many evenings out during the week. Some-times, not very often, I am a good liar.

As he pulls up outside my place, I know that it would be rude not to invite him in and I pray that Gabriela will still be up so that she can take over as entertainer and detract atten-tion from my nerves at seeing Paul again. It is pouring with rain by this time and we both run from the car to my house. As I scrabble about in my handbag for my keys, I can feel him standing very close behind me. Suddenly I feel his arms around my waist and he whispers in my ear, "Turn around." It sounds like an order rather than a request and before I know it, I have complied. With his arms still round me so that we are nuzzled together, he gently pushes me against the door and we start kissing. The tummy tickles make their way straight down into my panties where they fizz and then start to explode.

After twenty minutes of the most passionate and intense kissing, I suddenly realize that it is still pouring with rain and we are both drenched. I pull apart from him and he says, "What's next?" I know that if I let him in, he will definitely become another notch on my bedpost, and me on his, and I also know that if he doesn't then ring me the next day not only will I be totally devastated, I will not be able to trust a man or go out on a date ever again. I will just be too disillusioned. I hunt for my keys in my handbag once again while I decide what to do and what to say. I open the front door and ask him to wait in the hall while I run up the stairs to my apartment. I come down a few minutes later with a couple of towels for him to dry his hair, kiss him on the lips, thank him for taking me home and say I want to go to bed alone. Before he tries to argue with me, I run back up the stairs and shut the door to my apartment.

I try everything to relax that night: hot bath, camomile tea, hot chocolate and herbal tranquilizers, but I am too agitated and excited to unwind. I turn on the TV but cannot concentrate on a word anyone is saying. I try to read a book, but cannot focus on the blur of black and white letters on the page. There is nothing for it but to wake Gabriela who can be disturbed any time of day or night if you come bearing something containing sugar. We sit in bed together, drinking hot chocolate and eating toast. She says I have done the right thing not asking him in and as we cuddle up together in bed, laughing over the events of our day, munching on our toast and slurping our hot chocolate, we agree that sometimes not having fun is more fun than having fun.

I am not even going to begin to tell you the extent of my angst, misery and pain when I realize by the end of the next day that Paul is not going to ring. I torture myself over whether I made a fatal mistake in not inviting him in. Some friends, especially the male ones, berate me for not allowing him to come up to the apartment, even if it was just to allow him to dry off. I practically collapse on the carpet with remorse and regret. Other friends say I did absolutely the right thing and this has been proven by the fact that he has not called. He was obviously only interested in one more conquest, they say. Imagine how you would feel if he had come up and then you'd had sex with him and *then* he had not called. Imagining this depresses me even more and I sullenly reply that at least I would have had a screw out of him. Every time the phone rings, my heart misses ten beats. I don't even bother to sound pleased to hear from the caller. One of the calls is from Ros who tells me that she actually used to know Paul. This perks me up a bit until I hear what she has to say about him. It turns out that her brother and Paul hung out together in their twenties when they both took copious amounts of drugs and screwed as many women as they could. Now he is a heavy drug user as well as an easy lay. Great. What else am I going to find out? Then I morbidly remind myself not to be too concerned as he hasn't rung me and he will soon be someone else's problem. I'll just go down in history as the one girl he didn't bed.

I am not even going to begin to tell you the euphoria I experience the following evening on my return from work when I find a card from him on my doorstep. I see the handwritten envelope on the mat and absent-mindedly rip it open, my mind not on anything other than Paul and his not calling me. I pull out a thick cream piece of card which simply says: "Dinner?" and is signed only "Paul." I could faint from happiness, relief, excitement, surprise and love. I decide that I can also be unpredictable. I ring Andrew for Paul's address (miraculously keeping my big mouth shut and not giving anything away for once) and then go straight out to the shops to buy a postcard, on which I simply write "Yes," sign my name and post it.

Paul rings me the next day and actually suggests a Saturday night for our dinner date. It seems like years, and it probably has been, since I was last asked out on a Saturday night. Claudia very kindly doses me up on beta blockers for twenty-four hours beforehand so that I can eat and, more importantly, drink.

What can I tell you about the evening? The conversation was animated, stimulating and on his part, confessional. He told me a little about his wild days of drugs and women after the breakup with his first girlfriend, who he had dated for seven years between the ages of sixteen and twenty-three and who he believed was the love of his life. It was a classic tale of her leaving him for his best friend. He then discovered that everyone knew that she was sleeping with his friend and she had apparently been screwing around behind his back fairly indiscriminately for a year before she left. He said he knew he needed help when he found himself smoking heroin one night three and a half years ago and loving it. He went out and found a good therapist the following day. He was in therapy for three years and reckons he has since bounced back, determined not to return to his old debauched ways.

I did not want to talk about my love life for a change, despite his tempting questions to do so.

As it was a mild night, we decided to walk home from the West End. As we left the restaurant, we unconsciously put our arms around each other and began the long walk home, stopping every ten minutes to kiss. When we arrived at my front door and as I fumbled for my keys, he said, "I suppose you are not asking me up?"

"How did you know?" I asked, astonished that he had read my mind.

"You don't trust me yet. Andrew told me that he told you about my long list of women. I wish I hadn't opened my big mouth."

I know the feeling.

Paul searched my face for a reaction. For once, I didn't know what to say. I didn't want to tell him how many times I had been disappointed in the past and I didn't want to tell him that I liked him so much that in his case, I did not think I would recover from the disappointment. I thought I would keep it simple. "Thanks for a wonderful evening and thanks for dinner." And with that I disappeared into my apartment.

As I walked into the living room, the phone started ringing. It was Paul on his cell phone. "I forgot to thank you for a wonderful evening too."

Would you believe me if I told you that I didn't let him up to my apartment for another three months? You would be right not to. But I did last out for another three weeks. God knows how – discipline is not one of my virtues but he was right, I needed to trust him.

The word I would use to describe our relationship during the nine months preceding our engagement is *easy*. It was all so easy. All my happily married friends had always told me that you know you have met the right one when the court-ship is easy. There are no major arguments and temporary separations. There are no rules. There is no game playing. You both instinctively know that you want to be together, that there is nothing that can't be sorted out. He calls when he says he will. He doesn't forget that you have made arrangements. He comes around when you are ill and he sends you flowers on Valentine's Day, your birthday and your anniversary. And that is exactly how it was with Paul and me. Easy.

And fun and exciting and warm and loving and supportive and snug and interesting and stimulating and affectionate and sexy.

Everything I dreamed it would be.